# DON'T STOP thinking about TOMORROW

# SIOBHAN CURHAM

WALKER
BOOKS

This is a work of fiction. Names, characters, places and incidents are either the product of the author's imagination or, if real, used fictitiously. All statements, activities, stunts, descriptions, information and material of any other kind contained herein are included for entertainment purposes only and should not be relied on for accuracy or replicated as they may result in injury.

First published 2018 by Walker Books Ltd
87 Vauxhall Walk, London SE11 5HJ

2 4 6 8 10 9 7 5 3 1

Text © 2018 Siobhan Curham
Cover illustration © 2018 Nathan Burton

The right of Siobhan Curham to be identified as author of this work has been asserted by her in accordance with the Copyright, Designs and Patents Act 1988

This book has been typeset in Berolina

Printed and bound by CPI Group (UK) Ltd, Croydon CR0 4YY

British Library Cataloguing in Publication Data:
a catalogue record for this book is available from the British Library

ISBN 978-1-4063-7923-5 (UK)
ISBN 978-1-4063-8780-3 (Australia)

www.walker.co.uk

*For Jack Curham. It's been such an honour
and joy to watch you find your story. . .*

"My life is a lovely story, happy and full of incident."
Hans Christian Andersen

# Stevie

"Anne Frank. Malala. Stevie Nicks," I whisper as I lie in bed gazing at a crack in the ceiling, wishing I could get sucked up inside it, genie-style. "Anne Frank. Malala. Stevie Nicks."

I do this every time I'm feeling close to vomiting with dread – like before a science test or a sports day or a dental appointment when I know I need a filling. I say the name of my heroines to remind myself that even the very worst of challenges can be overcome. If Anne Frank could stay hopeful in spite of the Nazis and Malala could stand up to the Taliban and Stevie Nicks could overcome her cocaine addiction – and then write an awesome song about it – I can definitely face the first day of a new school year.

I hear Shriek-Beak begin his dawn chorus and I get up and go over to the window. Shriek-Beak is my name for the seagull who stands on the roof of the cottage opposite every morning and squawks like a maniac until he's woken the entire street. Or woken me, at least. Sure enough, Shriek-Beak is perched in his favourite spot, on top of the chimney stack, his bright yellow beak opening and closing like a trapdoor. I undo the rickety window latch and lean out. The air is humid, with the salty hint of sea. My mum and I live in an ancient cottage in an ancient town called Lewes, about ten kilometres from the coast. My bedroom is tucked away beneath the roof. When we first moved here, two years ago, I found the low ceiling and sloping walls claustrophobic. It's kind of like living in a cave. Now I like it.

I glance around the room, which has been my sanctuary for the long, rainy summer holiday. I wonder if this is how death-row prisoners feel when they're looking around their cell for the last time. I wonder if they feel the same inappropriate rush of love for their surroundings. I'm suddenly overwhelmed by affection for the wonky book-shelves and the saggy armchair and the damp patch on the wall that looks like Jesus ... if Jesus had a Mohican. And the thought of being separated from my beloved guitar, which is leaning against the armchair, literally makes my heart ache. I stroke the old oak dresser and gaze at my col-lection of 1980s-inspired accessories – bangles, large hoop earrings, leather-studded wristbands – and the remains of last night's dinner, a couple of crusts of toast. Toast was all I'd been able to stomach on Back to School Eve, which was just as well, as all there was in the kitchen cupboard was half a loaf of bread. Then I look at the vintage record player on the floor beside the old fireplace and instantly my mood lifts.

I go over to the tiny fireplace, take *Stevie's Little Book of Big Song Wisdom* down from the mantelpiece and flick through the well-worn pages, searching for just the right song. I need something uplifting. Something that will stop me from vomiting with dread. I stop on the page with *SONGS THAT MAKE YOU HAPPY TO BE ALIVE* written in capitals across the top. The first song listed is "The Whole of the Moon" by The Waterboys, 1985. I search through the stack of records in the alcove beside the chimney breast until I find it. I slip the record from its sleeve, inhaling the smell of vinyl, and place it on the turntable. Then I gently lift the arm of the record player and bring it to the beginning of the track. As the needle touches down and the crackles drift from the speakers I feel the tension inside me ease a little. Maybe this year won't be so bad. Maybe Priya will have had a personality transplant and the government will have decided to ban homework and teachers will have decided to make learning fun. And maybe pigs will fly – or however that freaky saying goes. I start changing into my school uniform and let the lyrics soak into me. I want to be the kind of person the singer's singing about; the kind of person who sees the whole moon instead of just a crescent. But it's so hard to see any of the moon when the sky's covered in thick black cloud.

*The*

    *cloud*

        *of*

*your*

*gloom*

*eclipses*

*the. . .*

The first random words of a song start dropping into my head and I fight the urge to pick up my guitar. I haven't got time for music now! I have to get ready for my execution. As I do up my school shirt I notice the buttons straining over my chest – you can actually see through the gap to my ever-expanding cleavage. *Please stop growing,* I silently beg. I literally can't afford for my chest to get any bigger. Mum didn't have enough money to buy me a new uniform this summer so I'm stuck with this lousy shirt from last year. I put on my school jumper and hope it doesn't get too warm today. Thankfully, my skirt fits fine. If anything it's too loose. Without a free school meal every day I've lost quite a bit of weight from my stomach and hips. Once I'm dressed I tie back my hair and sit down on my bed with my make-up bag. My fringe comes down halfway over my eyes, just the way I like it. I sweep it to one side and root through my make-up bag, in need of some warpaint. I take out my black eyeliner, worn down to a stub, and apply a thick cat-eye. I started doing my eyeliner like this last year, inspired by Siouxsie Sioux. Of course, modelling my look on an eighties pop icon caused Priya's tiny mind to go into meltdown. But anything that hasn't been deemed "cool" by her

12

airbrushed-to-so-called-perfection celebrity heroes causes her to go into meltdown.

"The Whole of the Moon" comes to an end and I go out onto the landing and listen for Mum. She's normally not up this early but as it's my first day back at school she might have set her alarm. The cottage is silent. I go downstairs to the kitchen. No matter how warm it is outside, the kitchen is always cold. The flagstones on the floor are freezing beneath my bare feet. I turn on the kettle and stare out of the grimy window into the backyard. When we first moved to Lewes, two years ago, after Dad died, Mum vowed to fill the yard with pots of flowers and a honeysuckle trellis and a herb garden. But then her depression swept in and the yard became just a place to dump things. My eyes scan the old mattress, the broken TV and the countless bin bags stacked against the wall. I'm not bothered though. If I want to go outside, there are loads of cool places to hang out in Lewes.

I take two mugs from the draining board and put a teabag in each. Then I pop a couple of slices of bread in the toaster. I'm too tense to have breakfast but I need to make some for Mum before I leave, to be sure she eats something while I'm gone.

I take the tea and toast back upstairs. I look at Mum's firmly closed bedroom door and instinctively my stomach clenches. I once saw an advert for a mental-health charity on YouTube where they called depression "the invisible illness". I guess they meant that it isn't physically noticeable in the way something like meningitis is, but to me my

13

mum's depression is all too visible. Placing my own cup on the landing, I knock on the door. There's no answer. I open the door and step inside. The room is steeped in darkness and smells of stale sweat and sleep.

"Morning, Mum, I've made you some breakfast!" I say cheerily, placing the cup and plate on her bedside table.

Mum mumbles something and rolls onto her side. I open the curtain a chink. A thin shaft of sunlight pours into the room, landing like a spotlight on a pile of old magazines next to the bed. Faded copies of the music magazine Dad used to write for. Now it's my heart that clenches. She's been looking at mementoes of life BDD (Before Dad's Death) again. I don't know why she does that; it only ever makes her feel worse.

"I made you some toast," I say to the Mum-shaped lump in the bed.

The lump grunts.

For a moment I feel the overwhelming urge to climb in beside her. To hide from the world beneath the faded floral duvet, like Mum has been doing for months. But if I do that who'll take care of us? I have to keep going. I have to stay strong. *Anne Frank. Malala. Stevie Nicks*, I remind myself in my head. "I'll get ready for school then," I say loudly.

"School?" Mum heaves herself upright, her tangled brown hair spilling over her shoulders.

"Yes, it's the first day back today, remember?"

"Oh, yes. Of course." A look of panic flickers across Mum's

face and I feel instant guilt at leaving her on her own.

"I'd better go then." I wait a moment, hoping she might ask me to stay. She is the parent, after all. If she asks me to stay, I'll have to.

But Mum just nods and slides back down in the bed. "OK, love."

I swallow the lump in my throat and return to my room. I look at the picture of "Real Mum" on the mantelpiece. It was taken when I was little, when she saw life as an adventure instead of a curse. She's sitting on a park swing, her bobbed hair dyed bright turquoise, her face an advert for happy. As I put on my frayed-at-the-edges blazer and scuffed-all-over shoes I feel my real self shrinking away to nothing.

On my way downstairs I open Mum's door and peer inside. The curtains are closed again. The plate of toast lies untouched on the bedside cabinet. I take a deep breath and force myself to stand taller. "See you later then."

"Yes. See you later," Mum mumbles. She rolls away from me and pulls the duvet up over her head.

# HAFIZ

One day, when I was about eight years old, my dad called me to join him on the roof terrace of our house in Syria.

"I have to tell you something," he said, gesturing for me to sit beside him on the warm terracotta tiles.

The sun was setting, the cicadas had begun whirring and the evening call to prayer was drifting over the rooftops from the local mosque.

"What I'm about to tell you will change your life for ever – if you choose to allow it to," Dad said mysteriously.

"Is it how to score the perfect penalty?" I asked. I'd already been badly bitten by the football bug and was desperate for any knowledge that would put me in the same league as my heroes Ronaldo and Beckham.

Dad laughed and shook his head. "No, my son. It is something even more important than the beautiful game."

I frowned. Surely nothing was more important than football. "What is it then?" I asked.

"There is a story to be found in everyone," he replied.

I waited. There had to be more to it than that, but no, Dad

16

just sat there with a knowing smile on his face. "Is that it?" I asked. This wasn't big news. This wasn't exciting. Dad was a writer by profession. One in a great line of Arabic story-tellers, as he liked to remind people at every opportunity. He didn't have one story inside him, he had thousands. He'd even named me after his favourite writer – the Persian poet Hafiz, who'd lived in the fourteenth century.

"There is a story to be found in everyone," Dad repeated, lighting his hookah.

"You mean everyone is able to tell a story?" I asked.

Dad shook his head. "Everyone is born with a story, here, inside of them." He placed his hand over his heart.

"I don't understand."

"There is a story inside of you, Hafiz – a story you were born with. One that will help you greatly in your life and carry you through its challenges."

"Will you tell it to me?" I asked. Even though I was dis-appointed that I still didn't know how to score the perfect penalty I loved my dad's stories, the colourful casts of char-acters, the way he could conjure magical new worlds out of thin air. But he shook his head.

"This is one story I am unable to tell," he said.

"Why?"

"Because it is your job to find out what your story is."

I frowned. "But how?"

"You need to pay close attention to the stories you hear in life. The moment you come across the story that's for you,

you will feel a recognition deep inside. It will feel like being reunited with a long-lost friend. It will touch you in here." Again, he put his hand to his heart. "And once you have found it you'll be able to use it for the rest of your days, to help guide you through your life."

I sighed. He was speaking in riddles.

I'd forgotten about that rooftop conversation until the night I left Syria, two years ago, when Dad was hugging me goodbye.

"This journey you are about to go on, my son, is a great opportunity," he said, his eyes glassy with tears. "It is your chance to find your story."

I looked at him blankly, too full of fear about what was to come to understand what he was saying.

"Pay close attention to the people you meet," he continued. "Listen to their stories. Wait for the one that touches you deep in here." He placed his hand on my heart. It was trembling.

These past two years, I've clung to the search for my story as if it were a life raft. Every stage of my journey from Syria has been made slightly easier by the thought that maybe, just maybe, that would be the place I'd find my story. During the long trek through the desert heat. Shivering in the icy waters the night the boat capsized. In the Greek camp nestled among the silvery olive trees. On the endless crowded buses and trains. Arriving in France. Every step of the way I've tried to distract myself from the fear gnawing away at me by searching for my story. And every time I've been disappointed. It isn't that I haven't found any stories. I've found hundreds among my fellow refugees. Stories of triumph and pain and hope and disaster. But none of them has felt like the story that will guide me through my life. None of them has reached into my heart and said, *It's me.*

And now, as I stand in front of a tall, red-brick high school in a town in England called Lewes, some five thousand kilometres from my parents and home, I ask myself the question once more: *Will I find my story here?* As a rowdy group of students barges past me, I really hope so. I feel in need of guidance like never before.

# Stevie

I take a seat at the front of the form room and pretend to look for something in my bag. Anything to distract myself from the fact that – despite having been back at school for only a few minutes – the other students are already merging into their friendship groups, leaving me alone yet again. Their laughter and excitement about summer holidays and parties and seaside trips tears at my eardrums. I don't want to be included in their conversations though – I'd have nothing to say. I've spent the entire summer holiday at home in Lewes, with only my mum for company and my weekend paper rounds to break the monotony. I used to like having friends. I had loads back when we lived in London. But things were different then. *Everything* was different then. Now, just the thought of having a friend makes me feel tired. I don't have the energy to explain why I never have any money or why my mum hardly ever gets out of bed. And I don't have the imagination to come up with excuses for why I can never have a sleepover or a birthday party or even just hang out.

The classroom door opens and our Head of Year, Ms Potts,

comes in with a student I've never seen before. He stuffs his hands in his trouser pockets and looks down at the floor. He has dark, wavy, shoulder-length hair and olive skin – apart from the tips of his cheeks, which have flushed bright pink. He's very good-looking, which instantly puts me off him. In my experience, very good-looking people always come with a huge side helping of ego.

"Check out the new boy," someone whispers and a couple of the girls giggle.

"Good morning, Miss Kepinski," Ms Potts says to my form tutor. "This is Hafiz Ali."

Miss Kepinski looks up from her laptop. "Ah yes. Hafiz," she says. "Welcome to 10K. I hope you'll be very happy here."

"Thank you," Hafiz mutters, but he continues staring at the floor. He has a foreign accent but I'm not sure where it's from.

Miss Kepinski scans the classroom and her eyes alight on the empty chair beside me. "Why don't you take a seat over there, Hafiz?" she says, gesturing to it. "Stevie, could you make Hafiz welcome, please?"

Oh great. I edge to the side. Better make room for his ego. Hafiz glances at me as he makes his way over and I catch sight of the brightest turquoise eyes I've ever seen, all the more striking against his pale brown skin. Yeah well, tropical sea-green eyes don't impress me, mister.

"Hi," I mumble as he sits down.

"Hi," he mutters back. He looks down at his lap and his

thick hair falls forwards like a curtain. I tilt my head forwards so my fringe falls right down over my eyes. Two can play that game.

"OK," Miss Kepinski says, getting to her feet. She's wearing one of her trademark floral dresses, this one covered in bright pink roses. "Welcome back, everyone. Did you all have a nice summer?"

As the rest of the class nod, Hafiz and I sit motionless.

"Why don't we do a fun icebreaker?" Miss Kepinski says with a grin. "To reintroduce ourselves to each other and to welcome our new student, Hafiz."

I groan inside. Miss Kepinski is one of those rare teachers who's relentlessly cheery. Even on Ofsted inspection days she manages to keep smiling while all around her the rest of the staff go into meltdown.

"Let's take it in turns to each say our name and one thing we were grateful for this summer," Miss Kepinski continues. "I'll start. My name's Miss Kepinski and one thing I was very grateful for was being proposed to by my boyfriend, James." Her cheeks flush as she holds out her hand. A square-shaped diamond flashes under the strip light. Some of the boys whoop and the girls cheer. I wonder how much the ring cost, how many meals it could have paid for.

I breathe a sigh of relief as Miss Kepinski turns to a student on the other side of the room. I need all the thinking time I can get. What was I grateful for this summer? My mind remains as blank as the whiteboard at the front of the class.

One by one, the other students introduce themselves and talk about what they're grateful for.

"My name's Priya and I'm really grateful that my parents took me to Florida on holiday," my nemesis says.

*And I'm really ungrateful that they didn't leave you there*, I mutter inside my head.

"My name's Jo and I'm grateful that I got to go horse riding over the summer."

"Hi, I'm Sam and I'm grateful that I didn't have any home-work for six weeks." Cue much laughter and yessing. Hafiz and I remain silent. As the other students share their grateful things I keep racking my brains.

Finally, it's my turn. Miss Kepinski looks at me and smiles.

I glance at Hafiz. His head's still bowed, his hair still hanging between us. "My name's Stevie and I'm grateful that I got to see the sun rise over the Priory ruins one day. It looked so beautiful. It was like being…" I run out of words.

"What a weirdo," Priya whispers. Priya never runs out of words, especially nasty ones. But I don't care what she says – seeing that sunrise and the way it painted the crumbling bricks of the Priory pink, orange and gold was one of the happiest moments of my holiday. For the briefest of times I was able to slip into a magical world where anything felt possible and the sun burnt all the darkness away.

"Thank you, Stevie," Miss Kepinski says. "I love the Priory ruins. It must have looked stunning at sunrise." She turns to Hafiz. "Would you like to say something?" she asks gently.

The class stare at him, eager for the first offering from the new boy so they can figure out where to place him in the pecking order. For a moment I forget that he's probably got a super-sized ego and I'm probably going to hate him, and I wish I could warn him how much rests on whatever he says.

"My name is Hafiz." He speaks in a soft voice. "And I am grateful that I am still alive."

# HAFIZ

As soon as the words leave my mouth I wish I could suck them back in, but what else can I say? This year Death has stuck to me like an annoying defender who clings to your shirt to stop you from scoring. Death was my reason for leaving Syria in the first place – to try and escape the bullets and the bombs. But no matter how many miles I travelled, it still followed me. It stowed away on the boat and in the buses and trains. It checked into the camps like an unwelcome guest. It even gatecrashed my dreams. The truth is, I don't even know that I do feel grateful for still being alive. I know I *should* feel grateful but how can I, when so many of the people I care about are still in danger? I think of Adnan, my companion on the refugee trail, and I feel a pain deep inside. I think of my mum and dad and my grandma, still trapped in Syria, and the pain increases.

"Thank you, Hafiz," the teacher says, her smile fading into a look of sadness. "I can imagine you must feel very grateful." She faces the rest of the class. "Hafiz is from Syria," she says solemnly. The pain inside me reaches the edges of my body, pressing at my skin. "Would you – uh – would you like to tell the others anything about where you're from and your journey to the UK?" the teacher asks. I shake my head. There was a time when saying I was from Syria would have filled me with pride, but now it chokes me with sorrow. The teacher nods and smiles and turns to another student.

I breathe a sigh of relief and look around the classroom. And I ask myself the question that always helps me return to the present: *Will I find my story here?* Of all the people I've seen in this school so far, I reckon that the girl sitting next to me has the most interesting story to tell – and not just because she has a boy's name and her hair is the colour of ebony. I noticed her the minute I walked into the classroom and saw the way she was sitting on her own with a frown on her face. If there'd been a thought bubble over her head like in a comic I bet it would have said: *I WISH I WAS SOMEWHERE ELSE.* I'm glad the teacher made me sit by her. We can share the same thought bubble. I lean back in my chair and glance at her. She's looking at the desk, her lips moving slightly, as if she's whispering something to herself. Yes, she definitely has the most interesting story to tell.

The rest of form period passes by in a blur. After we've heard what everyone is grateful for, the teacher talks to us about what to expect from the next academic year. I switch off midway through. Thanks to my writer dad, who's crazy about British authors, I'm fluent in English. According to Dad it's a crime against literacy for people not to be able to read the works of writers like Shakespeare and Dickens in the language they were written. But English isn't my mother tongue, so it's easy to drift away. I settle back in my chair and close my eyes. I try and have one of the daydreams I used to have back at school in Syria, where I'm Ronaldo scoring the winning goal for Real Madrid at the Bernabéu Stadium. I picture myself streaking down the wing, the ball glued to my feet. Defenders try to win it off me but they're left dazzled in my wake. And now I picture myself bearing down on the goal. There's just the goalkeeper standing between me and my dreams of glory. I draw my left leg back, preparing to strike. Then suddenly there's a loud bang and the goalie is blown to pieces. I jolt upright in my chair and my eyes flick open. My heart's pounding like I've just run a kilometre. I notice Stevie looking at me and I tip my head forward so that my hair falls over my face. A loud bleeping noise echoes outside along the corridor and everyone starts to reach for their bags.

"Stevie, could you stay with Hafiz today, make sure he gets to his lessons and lunch OK?" the teacher asks.

Stevie nods and gives me a small smile. I wonder if she resents having to look after me and that thought makes me feel sick. I don't want to be a charity case. I don't want to be here at all. I want to be back in Latakia, with my friends, where I don't need anyone to look after me.

"Come on then," Stevie says, getting to her feet. "Let the fun and games begin."

# *Stevie*

They say that sarcasm is the lowest form of humour but for me, sarcasm is a sanity-saver. If I wasn't able to make fun of my situation I think my heart would crack right in two from the tragedy of it all.

"The louder they shriek, the more insecure they are," I tell Hafiz as we make our way past a group of girls giggling in the corridor. "Seriously. It's practically a scientific law, like Einstein's theory of relativity or whatever."

Hafiz looks at me blankly and I feel a twinge of embarrassment. Does he think I'm an idiot? But I don't care what he thinks, I don't want him to like me, I remind myself as we jostle through the hordes of students. I don't care that Hafiz is from Syria and therefore potentially one of the most interesting people I'll ever meet in this school. I don't want to be friends with him. I don't want to be friends with anyone.

I glance over my shoulder to check Hafiz is still there. I have to make sure he gets to his lessons at least. He's still there, his bag slung over his shoulder, his wavy hair flopping down over his face. I feel the urge to say something but I stop myself and keep trudging down the corridor, towards the science block.

In science I do my usual trick of plastering an interested expression on my face, while inside my head I'm miles away – onstage at Carnegie Hall in New York City, if you must know. I guess I inherited my obsession with music from my dad but, unlike him, I don't want to write about musicians, I want to *be* a musician. A singer-songwriter and guitarist, to be precise. As Mr Patel makes a huge deal about combining some chemicals in a test tube over a Bunsen burner, I dream that I'm standing breathless in the wings, while the crowd yells for more. I take a sideways glance at Hafiz. I'm guessing he isn't a fan of science either. He isn't even pretending to look interested in the riveting secrets of the periodic table; instead he's gazing out of the window. There's the slightest hint of a smile on his lips, which, I have to admit, is nice to see, because before in form, he looked so sad.

Just as I'm about to take my encore in New York the bell sounds for morning break and a horrible thought occurs to me. Morning break is twenty minutes long. There'll be no teacher droning on about transition metals and compounds. It'll just be me and Hafiz and two hundred different kinds of awkward. I turn to him. "There now begins a twenty-minute exercise in how not to die of abject boredom."

Hafiz looks at me blankly.

"It's breaktime," I explain as the other students start hurrying from the room. "I normally go to the library but we can go outside if you like."

"OK then." Hafiz picks up his bag and slings it over his shoulder.

Great. Why did I suggest going outside? At least in the library we could have logged on to computers and avoided speaking to each other. I pick up my bag and say a quick prayer to the god of sarcasm – or quick-swallowing sink-holes, I'm not fussy – to save me from this hell. "OK then."

# HAFIZ

We stand in a corner of the playground in total silence. I watch as a seagull circles above us, like a vulture. I think back to breaktimes in Latakia. Me and Aahil and Pamir and the rest of the gang, kicking a ball around in the dust. I miss the dust and the sweltering heat. I miss the banter. I miss my friends so bad it hurts. It's funny because back before the war we treated life like it was one big contest in insulting each other in the worst ways imaginable. Donkeys were often involved … and each other's mothers. But now I see that it's only when you have the luxury of peace that you can afford to pretend to hate. I glance at Stevie. She's looking at a group of girls over on the other side of the playground. She doesn't look happy. Then I realize that they're probably her friends and she wants to go and join them.

"It's OK if you want to be with your friends." I nod towards the girls and Stevie laughs.

"No, it's fine," she says. "Unless you want me to leave?" I've never really got why girls wear make-up but I like the way she's done hers. I like the thick black line around the bright

31

green of her eyes. It goes with her jet-black hair. It makes her look like a cat.

"No," I say. The truth is, I don't want her to leave. I've seen the way some of the other students are looking at me, their eyes full of cold curiosity. I can picture the thought bubbles over their heads saying: YOU DON'T BELONG HERE.

"No, what?" Stevie says.

"No, I don't want for you to leave me." It sounds so weird saying this to someone I've only just met. It's the kind of thing I imagine a jilted lover saying … or a mother whose son is about to embark on the refugee trail.

"OK then, let's do this break thing," Stevie says in what I can't help feeling is a fake cheery voice. The kind that shop assistants use when you can tell that they really don't want to help you and they really don't care whether you have a nice day.

Stevie looks at me. "So, you're from Syria?"

I nod, hoping she doesn't ask me to talk about it like the teacher did.

"I'm sorry," she says quietly, all the fake cheeriness gone from her voice. And that's it. No questions, no prying, just she's sorry. The relief I feel brings a lump to my throat.

"Thank you." I hear the unmistakable *thwack* of a football being kicked and I turn and see some boys having a game on the field beside the playground. My feet start to twitch. Before I left Syria I'd been signed to the youth team for Hutteen, one of the local premiership clubs in Latakia.

There'd been talk about trials for the national youth team too but my parents didn't want me travelling to Damascus, it was way too dangerous. Then they decided that the entire country was way too dangerous and I had to leave. Apart from a few kickabouts with some of the little kids in France, I've barely touched a ball for the past two years. A couple of the girls come walking over. One of them, an Asian girl, smiles at Stevie. It's the kind of smile that stays frozen on the mouth, never making it to the eyes. "Hi, Stevie," she says. "How are you getting on with the new boy?"

"Fine," Stevie says.

"We were just wondering if you've ever, like, spoken to a boy before," the girl continues.

"Shut up!" Stevie snaps.

I look at her curiously. I like this new, mean Stevie. Now she feels real, not faking a thing.

"That's not very nice," the girl says. "You're supposed to be making him feel welcome."

"I wasn't talking to him, I was talking to you," Stevie mutters.

The girl turns her blank gaze on me. "So, are you, like, an asylum seeker?"

*Asylum seeker* is a term I've come to hate these past couple of years, along with the words *illegal* and *refugee* and *documents*.

*No, I'm a human, just like you,* I want to reply but I remain silent.

33

The girl turns back to Stevie. "What's up with him? Can't he speak English?"

"Of course he can," Stevie replies. "Didn't you hear him in form period?"

"Well, why isn't he answering me then?"

Stevie's cat-eyes narrow and she glares at her. "I don't know. Maybe he's allergic to dumb questions."

I swear I can see Stevie's eyes actually sparking. For the first time in what feels like for ever I start to grin.

# Stevie

Priya stares at me, her stupid pouty mouth opening and closing like a goldfish's. She really needs to stop trying to be some kind of Mean Girl wannabe – she's way too easy to tie in knots. I shoot Hafiz a sideways glance. He's grinning, properly grinning. Dimples have appeared either side of his mouth and his turquoise eyes are shining. It's making him look like a totally different person and it makes me want to grin too. And I do.

"Well, I can see why Miss Kepinski put you two together," Priya finally splutters. "What a pair of freaks."

"I'd rather be a freak than a fake any day of the week," I say, and the notes to an accompanying guitar riff echo through my mind. I scramble in my blazer pocket for my notebook and pen and scribble them down.

"Are you, like, taking notes?" Priya asks, her eyes saucer-wide.

"Uh-huh." I snap the notepad shut.

"What for?"

"For my project."

"What project?"

"My project titled, 'Fifty Ways to Spot an Idiot'. You've been very helpful. Thank you."

Hafiz makes a weird noise. At first I think he's choking but then I look at him and see he's laughing.

Priya purses her lips so tightly it looks as if they might burst. "Come on, Gemma," she snaps, before taking her by the arm and marching her back across the playground.

Hafiz watches them go, still grinning, then he turns to me. "So, I'm guessing you are not friends then?"

I laugh. "Excellent observational skills."

"Thank you." He picks up his bag. "Do you want to go for a walk?"

"Sure."

Hafiz looks wistfully towards the school gates.

"Wishful thinking," I say.

"Yeah."

"Why don't we walk around the field?" I suggest. "We can pretend we're not here. We can pray that a sinkhole will open up and swallow us whole ... or something..." I break off, wondering if the whole sinkhole thing might have been a bit much, but Hafiz doesn't seem put off. We walk over to the playing field. I try and think of something to say, some way of making conversation. "So, where do you live?"

"Right now?"

I nod, but already I wish I hadn't asked. He's from Syria. He's probably a refugee. Where he lives could be a really sensitive subject – one he doesn't want to be reminded of. *Nice one, Stevie.*

"At my uncle and aunt's house, in Lansdown Place," Hafiz replies.

"Cool." Lansdown Place is one of my favourite streets in Lewes. I love the way it twists through the town like a river. I love the tall, thin grey-brick houses and the quirky cafés – and obviously it goes without saying that I love the record shop. Encouraged by his answer, I decide to ask another question. "How long have you been there – here – in the UK – in Lewes?"

"Just over a month." He looks across to the other side of the field, where a group of boys are playing football.

I take this as a sign that I shouldn't ask any more questions.

"Do you like it here?" he asks suddenly, but without taking his eyes off the game.

"What, here in Lewes or here at this school?"

"Both."

"Yes … and no."

He looks at me curiously.

"I like Lewes. I lived in London before. Lewes is nicer. Greener. Cleaner. Near the sea – and who doesn't like living by the sea, right? But I don't really like this school."

"Why not?"

I try to find the right words to explain how Lewes High makes me feel. It's hard. I don't want to put Hafiz off on his very first day, but I don't want to lie to him either. "I just don't really fit in."

"Why not?"

Why's he asking me this? Is he trying to embarrass me? But his expression is gentle. Definitely not mocking. "I – uh – I just don't." My skin prickles. The sun is getting hot. Too hot. But I can't take my jumper off, owing to the bursting buttons situation going on with my shirt.

"My dad always told me that it's good to be different," Hafiz says. "He always said it is far better to be a rare bird than a common sheep."

I feel a burst of curiosity. "Your dad – is he – where is he?"

Hafiz's face clouds over. "In Syria." He looks back at the boys kicking the ball. "Do you like football?"

"Not really."

"Oh."

The air around us shifts. The particles bump up against each other. I feel hot and awkward and stupid. I wonder if I'll ever be able to make a friend again. *You don't want a friend*, I remind myself. But, now I've met Hafiz, I know this is no longer strictly true.

# HAFIZ

By the time I get home from school every muscle in my body is rigid with tension. The only time school ever made me feel like this back in Syria was when we had exams. But today has felt like one endless exam – with me as the subject. Will I pass and be accepted into my new school? Or will I fail and be an outsider for ever? Back home, whenever I felt like this I'd run down to the beach, fling myself into the sea and swim all of the tension away. But I don't have that option any more. The sea in Brighton isn't far but I can't… The thought of the waves, the salt, the sound … it makes me sick.

"Hafiz!" My aunt Maria appears in the kitchen doorway, her blonde hair glowing like a halo in the sunlight pouring through the window behind her. She's wearing an apron and holding a wooden mixing spoon. "How are you? How was it?" She looks at me anxiously.

"It was fine," I lie.

"Oh, that's great!" she exclaims. "Come and have some mint tea. Tell me all about it. Your uncle will be back from the university soon. We're going to the refugee centre for dinner.

I've been making some baklava to take down there."

I nod but I don't want to go to the refugee centre. I don't want to do anything really apart from kill the thoughts buzzing around my head. I follow her into the kitchen, my favourite room in the house. With its brightly coloured mosaic tiles it's the room that most reminds me of home. But as I look at the tray of freshly made baklava on the counter my throat tightens. For a second I see Mum, silhouetted against the bright sunlight, humming her favourite song. She slowly turns to greet me – and then she's gone. *What if she's really gone?*

"Is there any news?" I say as I sit down at the table.

Maria shakes her head. My parents didn't join me on the refugee trail because my grandma Amira – my mum's mum – was too frail to make the journey and there was no way they could leave her on her own. A few months ago, they left our home town to seek refuge in the mountain village where my mum grew up. They should be safe from the fighting up there but it's really hard to get phone reception or Internet access. Uncle Samir hasn't heard from my dad for weeks. I haven't heard from him for even longer, as I lost my phone on the journey across Europe. "No news is good news," Uncle Samir always says to me. But I can tell he's worried.

"Would you like some?" Aunt Maria says, offering me the tray of baklava. It glistens gold with honey and smells delicious but I shake my head. I don't feel hungry.

I hear the front door open, bringing with it the hum of traffic from the street outside.

"Hello?" Uncle Samir's voice booms from the hall.

"Hey, love, we're in the kitchen!" Aunt Maria calls.

Uncle Samir comes in and places his battered leather bag on the table. Although he and my dad might look alike on the surface – the same broad shoulders and long noses and chestnut-brown hair – their personalities couldn't be more different. Uncle Samir is quiet and calm and studious, like an owl, while my dad is wild and flamboyant and loud, like a parrot. Or "a tornado in a teacup", as my mum likes to call him. I feel another pang of homesickness.

"Hafiz, how was your first day at school?" Uncle Samir looks at me with the same concerned expression as Aunt Maria.

"It was OK."

"Isn't that great?" Aunt Maria says with a smile as she comes over to hug my uncle.

He nods. "Yes, yes it is." He sits down at the table and looks at me over the top of his glasses. "You know, if you ever want to invite any friends over after school that would be fine, wouldn't it, Maria?"

"Of course."

I try not to laugh. Somehow I can't see the students at my new school queuing up to be friends with me. Not that I'm bothered. But I don't tell them how it was today. I don't want to worry them. "Thanks," I say. Beneath the table my feet start to twitch. The urge to kick a ball has been growing stronger all day. But my aunt and uncle only have a tiny backyard and somehow I can't see the studious Samir owning a football. I decide to daydream about football instead and picture myself lining up a free kick outside the penalty area – my speciality. I spent hours practising after school every day. I'd got so that I could curve the ball into the top corner of the goal, sometimes from deep inside the midfield. My coach at Hutteen used to call me Hafiz Beckham. I bet I'd never be able to score like that now. My heart sinks as I think of all of that time and training gone to waste.

"I can't wait to see what they've been doing at the refugee centre," Uncle Samir says as Aunt Maria pours us each a cup of tea. "Apparently the library shelves are all built and ready to be filled."

I force my feet to stay still and drive all thoughts of free kicks from my mind. I'm no longer Hafiz Beckham. I'm a refugee. Rootless and stranded like an upended tree.

## *Stevie*

As I make my way up the steep hill home a daydream flickers into my mind, like the opening scene in one of those wholesome American family TV shows. It's of me arriving at the cottage to find Mum up and dressed and in the kitchen. Everything is sparkly clean and there's a plate of freshly baked cakes on the table. Freshly baked cakes with bright pink icing. And glitter. The room smells of strawberries and cream. Music is playing on the radio – something jaunty and summery by The Beach Boys – and the air dances with light. I try to push the dream from my mind, but I can't. It's too nice. And so comforting after all the stress of the first day back at school. Daydream-Mum looks at me and smiles. "How was your day, sweetheart? Would you like some coffee? I've baked something special for you!"

I put my key in the front door and take a deep breath. Maybe my going back to school has been a good thing. Maybe it's given Mum the incentive to get up and do something. The freshly baked cakes might be pushing it a bit but if I could just find her up and dressed… Mum's barely been out of bed all summer. When she first got depressed after Dad died, her depression came in waves of good days and bad days, and the good days were like rocks for me to cling to. But ever since the second anniversary of Dad's death back in February, the good days are fewer and farther between. She did go to the doctors and got some antidepressants but they've made zero difference. I open the door and step into the darkened hallway. The air is icy cold compared with outside – and it's very, very quiet.

"Hi, Mum, I'm home!" I call. There's no reply. Maybe she's gone out. I feel a spark of hope. What if she's gone food shopping? My appetite, which had completely disappeared during the heat and stress of school, is suddenly back with a vengeance. I go into the kitchen and check the cupboards. They're still bare – apart from the remains of the loaf of bread. I feel the kettle to see if Mum's made herself a drink recently. It's stone cold. I take off my blazer and tie and make my way upstairs. There's no answer when I knock on Mum's door so I open it and peer inside, hoping to see an empty bed. But she's in the same position she was in when I left, a clump of matted hair trailing across the pillow. I feel sick with disappointment – and cross at myself for even daring to dream that things might be different.

"Mum?"

The lump murmurs and anger rushes into me, red and hot. Why should she get to lie in bed all day while I have to do the hard thing of living? It isn't fair. I swallow my anger like a horrible-tasting medicine.

"Stevie. What time is it?" Mum heaves herself semi-upright and rubs her eyes.

"Just gone four."

"Four – but…" She blinks and stares at me. The side of her face is red from where she's been sleeping on it and her eyes are puffy.

"Have you been in bed all day?" My words come out much terser than I'd meant them to.

"No. I – I wasn't able to sleep this morning. I took a sleeping pill after lunch."

I look at the plate on her bedside table, at the cold, untouched toast. She hasn't even had breakfast, let alone lunch.

"I'm sorry." She looks at me, her eyes wide and pleading, like a little girl's. "How was school?"

"OK." I learned long ago not to tell her the truth about school. The one time I did tell her I'd had a tough day, after Priya had taunted me for being a "bag lady" because I had a hole in my jumper, Mum burst into tears. "I just can't deal with this right now," she told me.

"That's good," Mum says flatly.

"Do you have any cash for me to get something for dinner?" I ask – even though I know what the answer will be.

Mum shakes her head. "I'm sorry, love. My benefits don't come through till tomorrow."

"OK." *Anne Frank. Malala. Stevie Nicks. Hafiz,* I say in my head. Hafiz has fled a war-torn country. He's thousands of miles away from his family and friends. If he can deal with that, then I can deal with this.

"Can you use some of your guitar money to get whatever you want?" Mum says. "Don't worry about me, I'm not hungry. I can pay you back tomorrow."

I sigh. I've been trying to save up for a new guitar for ages now but it's so hard. The truth is, there's hardly any guitar money left. I always seem to need to dip into it.

"OK." *Anne Frank, Malala, Stevie Nicks, Hafiz.*

"Thanks, love." Mum slides back down in the bed.

I see tendrils of Mum's depression creeping out from under the duvet and snaking their way towards me. I have to get out of here.

I race to my room and close the door behind me. I go straight over to my *Little Book of Big Song Wisdom* and flick through until I get to the page *SONGS FOR WHEN PEOPLE LET YOU DOWN … AND YOU WANT TO WALLOW IN IT!* Beneath it is written, "Pale Shelter" by Tears for Fears, 1982. I pull the record from the stack and put it on. As the opening chords echo around the room something inside of me cracks and in through the crack slips my dad. I picture him as a teenager sitting on his bedroom floor listening to this exact same song. Who did he think of when he heard the words? I know he listened to it a lot – the cover is coming apart at the seams and the vinyl is covered in scratches. Did he think of his own parents? A girl? Who was it who gave him "pale shelter"? Why did he include it in his book for me?

"Why did you have to leave?" I whisper to the writing in the book. A tear rolls down my face and plops onto the page, instantly smudging the ink. I feel so alone. When Dad died I didn't just lose him, I lost my grandparents too. Or at least, I lost being able to tell them anything. Mum doesn't want Dad's parents knowing about her depression because she says they have enough to deal with after the death of their son. They live in a retirement villa in Portugal anyway, so it's not as if they can just pop round. They call from time to time but I almost wish that they wouldn't. It's so hard not telling them what's been going on. Mum has never been close to her own parents. She and Dad used to jokily call them "The Stiffs" because they're so uptight. The one time I suggested she call them and ask to borrow some money, she burst into tears. "I don't want them knowing I've failed," she sobbed. "I can't bear how smug and self-righteous they'd be."

I don't get why she sees her depression as a failure. Like, you wouldn't tell someone who'd got cancer they were the world's biggest loser, would you? But there was no point arguing with her. I didn't want to make her even more upset. So her depression has become our guilty secret. Even though there's no reason to feel guilty. It's so messed up but that's the way it is. I wipe the tears away. *Anne Frank, Malala, Stevie Nicks, Hafiz.* I can do this. I've got this. I can be who Mum needs me to be.

# HAFIZ

I first came to Brighton when I was six years old and my parents and I were visiting the UK for Uncle Samir and Aunt Maria's wedding. I have only two clear memories of that trip. The first is of Uncle Samir and Aunt Maria kissing at their wedding party – and me wishing they'd stop so we could start eating the awesome five-tiered chocolate cake. And the second is of me and Mum and Dad standing on Brighton Pier, the day after the wedding, eating hot salty chips from a paper bag. "One day I want to live here just like Uncle Samir," I told my parents as we stood at the edge of the pier looking down into the frothy waves. A year later the civil war broke out in Syria – and so began the chain of events that would eventually bring me here. I wish I had never said those words. It's like I uttered some kind of prophecy. Back then I'd assumed that work would bring me to the UK, just like it happened with Uncle Samir when he got a job teaching theology at the university here. I had no idea it would be war.

As Uncle Samir drives along the coastal road I keep my eyes fixed firmly inland. It's bad enough that I can smell and hear the sea through the open window. I don't want to look at it too. Finally, Uncle Samir takes a turning and we drive through a labyrinth of Brighton's narrow backstreets until we arrive at the refugee centre. Apparently it was once a carpet store. Now it's a drop-in centre where refugees can come and get food and help and advice. The hand-painted sign reads, SANCTUARY BY THE SEA. I know I should feel grateful that places like this exist; that there are people in Europe who care about what's happening in the war-torn parts of the world, but I wish places like this weren't needed. Uncle Samir parks in the small car park at the rear of the building. The back door is open and I can hear the hiss of something frying in the kitchen, mingled with women's voices chatting in a foreign language. I think it's Tigrinya.

"Something smells good," Aunt Maria says cheerily as she checks her lipstick in the car mirror.

"It certainly does." Samir turns to me and smiles. "How about you and I go and see how they're getting on in the library, Hafiz? While your aunt checks on the kitchen."

"OK."

I wonder how many times in the two years since I left Syria I've said "OK" when I haven't really meant it. That simple word may have helped me get across Europe relatively unscathed but now I'm sick of the sound of it. Now I long to utter "no". As Aunt Maria disappears into the kitchen with her tray of baklava I follow Uncle Samir to the front of the building. The window is covered with posters advertising the different services on offer to refugees here. Then I see one I haven't noticed before. It's for five-a-side football. I stop and look at it. Uncle Samir notices and stops too.

"You must miss playing football?"

I nod. "Yeah, a bit."

"Hmm." My uncle looks thoughtful for a moment, then heads through the door.

I follow him into the narrow corridor that runs through the middle of the building. There are doors either side leading to offices and meeting rooms where classes are held or refugees can get legal or medical advice. Most of the doors are closed but I can still hear the murmur of voices. We walk to the far end of the corridor, which leads into a huge, open-plan area. One side of the area is set up like a café, with tables and chairs dotted around in front of a counter. The other side is lined with empty shelves. This is going to be the library. The library was Uncle Samir's idea and he's *very* excited about it.

In between the café and the library there's a pool table. Two African guys wearing low-slung jeans and hoodies are stalking around the table holding cues, engrossed in their game.

"Samir! Hafiz!" a woman cries from behind the café counter.

"Hi, Rose!" Uncle Samir calls back.

Rose volunteers at the café. She has snowy-white skin and pale blue eyes and long blonde dreadlocks that reach down to her waist. Before I came to Brighton I'd never seen white people with dreadlocks. I'd never seen people with so many piercings or tattoos, either. Rose has a tiny tattoo of a ship's anchor on her wrist and silver rings in both nostrils.

"Are you hungry?" she asks as we walk over. "We have *chalau* on the menu this evening. It smells amazing."

Chalau is an Afghan stew made with lamb and spinach. As I breathe in the smell of the meat and the spices my stomach rumbles. "That sounds great. Thank you."

Rose places a mound of rice on a plate and dollops a huge serving of stew on top. "Enjoy," she says, handing it to me.

I take my dinner over to a table and wait for Uncle Samir to join me. One good thing about being a refugee is you get to learn about food from all over the world. Or from the world's danger zones at least. Maybe there should be a special name for refugee cooking, like the French Cordon Bleu. *Cordon War*, perhaps?

As Uncle Samir takes his seat the guys at the pool table put down their cues and stroll over.

"Hey, Samir," one of them says.

"Hello, Majeed," he replies, "hey, everyone." Uncle Samir knows most of the people here. He's taught a lot of them how to speak English. "This is my nephew Hafiz from Syria."

Majeed shakes my hand. "Good to meet you, brother."

"Hafiz was interested in the five-a-side football advertised in the window."

"Oh, yeah?" Majeed looks me up and down. "How old are you?"

"Fourteen," I say, taking a mouthful of stew.

"He was a star player back at home. Played for one of Syria's Premier League youth teams," Uncle Samir continues, making me squirm. "It would be good if he could get a game."

"Sure." Majeed nods. "Come along a week Saturday. We have some other Syrians playing. It will be like World Cup – Syria against Sudan." He laughs.

I nod and smile and take another mouthful of stew. As Uncle Samir and Majeed start talking about asylum applications my feet do a celebratory tap dance under the table.

# Stevie

This morning, when I get up, I go straight over to my record player. I'm determined that today is going to be better than yesterday. I don't want to feel that angry and helpless ever again. Last night I prepared an empowering play-stack (the vinyl equivalent of a playlist) to listen to as soon as I woke up. I put the first record on. "Two Tribes" by Frankie Goes to Hollywood – listed on the page titled SONGS TO MAKE YOU FEEL UNSTOPPABLE in my Little Book of Big Song Wisdom.

As I get dressed the rousing beat starts working its way inside of me. Today is going to be better. As the song builds I start dancing around my bedroom – the way Paul Rutherford from Frankie Goes to Hollywood dances in their old music videos on YouTube. It's all going to be OK. Mum's going to be OK. I'm going to be OK. Everything will—

I feel something ping by my chest. I look down. The button that was straining has literally popped, revealing my once-white bra. (I accidentally washed it with some black jeans and it's now a skanky shade of grey.) My heart sinks. The record skips and gets stuck. The word "war" booms out from the speakers over and over and over again. It's official: today is going to be even worse than yesterday. I turn the record player off and pull my jumper over my shirt. Fears start creeping into my mind. *What am I going to do? How am I going to get the money for a new shirt?* The fears start reproducing. *How am I going to get through another year of school? What if Mum never gets better?* And then, the worst fear of all – the one I'm always trying to escape: *What if I catch her depression?*

When I get to the form room most of the class are there but Stevie isn't. My heart sinks. I sit down at the empty table and remind myself that I can handle this. I've been through way worse. The Asian girl walks in with a couple of her friends. She sees me sitting on my own and smiles. Once again her smile doesn't reach her eyes.

"So, have you remembered how to speak English yet?" she asks.

"I never forgot," I reply. *One–nil to Hafiz*, a commentator-style voice remarks inside my head, just like it used to when me and my friends dissed each other. But back then was different. Our banter was like a friendly match. Whatever is going on with this girl definitely feels like a grudge game between deadly rivals.

"Are you trying to be clever?" the girl asks, her voice louder. The other students' chatter quietens.

I shake my head. "Some of us don't need to try." *Excellent strike!* the commentator inside my head cries. *Two–nil to Hafiz!*

"Wow." She shakes her head deliberately slowly, then

turns to her friends. "You'd think he'd be grateful, wouldn't you? You'd think he'd be polite, being given a place in our school. No wonder no one wants asylum seekers if that's how you act." One of the girls looks away, like she's embarrassed, but the other nods in agreement.

*Two–one,* the commentator in my head mutters. She might have scored but it's the kind of goal that involved a deliberate foul. There's something about her knowing look that makes me mad. Because she doesn't know anything at all. She doesn't know about what I went through to get here. She doesn't know about the millions of people stranded all over the world right now with nowhere to call home. She hasn't felt the pain of having to leave family and friends, not sure you'll ever see them again. I feel anger building. The kind of raw, hot-headed anger that could earn me a red card. *Walk away, Hafiz.* The commentator inside my head has now morphed into Khalid, my coach at Hutteen. I pick up my bag and get to my feet.

"Where are you going?" the girl asks, looking genuinely surprised.

"Away," is all I trust myself to say. It's a weak attempt on goal – it hits the crossbar and bounces off.

The bell for registration starts bleeping. I march out of the classroom and along the corridor against the tide of students now pouring in. For a moment I panic that I don't know which way to go. The endless corridors all look the same with their shiny floors and harsh strip lighting. I keep on walking against the tide.

I hate it here. Doesn't that Priya girl get that? *I DON'T EVEN WANT TO BE HERE!* I want to yell at the top of my voice to all the students staring at me. *This prized possession that you think I'm here to steal – this place in your school, your town, your country – I never wanted it.*

I reach the door at the end of the corridor, push it open and stride out into the sunlight.

## Stevie

"What are you doing?" I stare at Hafiz as he barges past me, out of the school gates. "Where are you going?"

He stops, stands frozen for a moment, before turning to look at me. His face is flushed, his eyes look angry. "Away from here," he finally replies.

"Oh. Why?" I feel sick in the pit of my stomach. "Has something happened?"

His eyes flit back and forth up and down the street. "I need to go."

"OK."

He turns and strides off. As I watch him the weirdest thing happens. It's like my mind has become disconnected from the rest of my body and while it's telling me I ought to go into school, my feet have taken on a life of their own and have started walking after him.

I follow Hafiz to the end of the road. Then, as he turns to cross, he spots me. "What are you doing?" he asks. He's frowning, but only slightly.

*Following you,* I want to reply. But that would definitely

make me seem like a stalker, and even though I probably am a stalker, I don't want him to know it. "I – uh – need to go too," I say.

"Oh." He tilts his head to one side, like he's not sure how to respond. "Where are you going?"

I shrug and try and think of a reply. Where *am* I going? But then he smiles. And the dimples appear either side of his mouth. And everything feels OK again and I can't help smiling too. "So – uh – this is slightly awkward."

"My dad told me a story once," he says, running his hand through his hair. "It was about a silk merchant who was on his way to sell his goods at a bazaar – a bazaar so big and so full of people it could make him a fortune – but halfway there he lost his map."

"What did he do?" I ask, not sure why he's telling me this but keen to steer the conversation away from the fact that I just blatantly followed him out of school.

"Well, at first he panicked and then he cursed, and then, when he was about to give up and go home, he saw an eagle high above him in the sky. He watched the way the eagle let the wind carry it and he decided to do the same."

"What? Fly?"

Hafiz laughs. "No. He decided to let his heart carry him. He set off on his journey again and every time he came to a crossroads he asked his heart which way he should go."

"Did he get to the bazaar in the end?"

Hafiz shakes his head. "No. But he ended up somewhere

even better. And he had a lot of really cool adventures along the way."

"I like that. It's kind of like saying we should use our hearts as a satnav – a heart nav."

"Exactly. So shall we give it a try?" Hafiz looks at the junction in the road. "Which way?"

I close my eyes and picture a satnav and a little red arrow appears in my mind. "Right," I reply.

Hafiz smiles. "Come on then, let's go."

We both turn right and cross the road.

# HAFIZ

We follow our hearts around the corner and down the road and into the station and over to the ticket machine and down to the platform and onto the train to Brighton. It's only when the train's pulling out of the station that reality hits me. It's my second day at school here in the UK and already I've walked out and not only that, I've walked out of school with a girl I barely know. When I first saw Stevie following me I was annoyed. I thought she was going to try and persuade me to go back. But as soon as she said she needed to leave too I felt so relieved. And she understood the story about the silk merchant. It was like she was saying, *I get you. I'm not going to judge you like all the others.* And now we're sitting here, on the faded, frayed seats of the train, and it's speeding up, out of the tunnel and into the countryside, and I have no idea what to say or do.

I glance at Stevie, sitting opposite me. She's gazing out of the window at the rolling hills of the Downs. Her thin fingers are tapping out a beat on her thin legs. The sun is shining in long rays of gold on the velvety grass and the sky is deep blue, with just the thinnest white wisps of cloud. Even though I miss Latakia I have to admit the scenery here is awesome. The hills are so round and smooth and I've never seen so much green.

Stevie sighs. "I've never done this before," she says in a quiet voice, like she's afraid of being overheard.

"What?" I say.

"Skived off school. I mean, I've dreamed about it *loads* of times. Like, every five minutes – every five seconds when it's PE." She smiles and her whole face softens. "But I've never actually done it. Have you?"

I shake my head. I've had no reason to before. I always enjoyed school back in Syria. Not that I'm all that studious, but I loved being with my friends.

"Did you…? Did something bad happen? This morning?"

I look out of the window, watching the outline of the hills go up and down and up again. "Not really. I just…"

"It's OK. You don't have to talk about it if you don't want to."

"Have you ever wished that life was like a movie and you could just press the – press the pause button and rewind back to the happy bits?" I ask, keeping my gaze fixed firmly on the window.

Stevie laughs. "Oh yes. I feel like that right now, actually."

"You do?" I look back at her. Her bright green eyes meet mine. Her black eyeliner is even thicker than yesterday's. She looks fierce and vulnerable all at once.

"Yes. That's why I'm here. With you. It's my way of pressing pause." Now it's her turn to look away.

A recorded announcement comes on over the speaker system on the train, telling us we're approaching a station. It's the stop for the university campus that Uncle Samir works at. I slump back in my seat and feel a flush of shame. What would my uncle think if he could see me now? After everything he's done to get me here – the torturous legal process that took almost a year, the endless court hearings and trips to France. How is this any way to repay him?

"That's where our local football team play," Stevie says, pointing to the huge stadium that's looming into view. "Brighton and Hove Albion. I thought you might be interested – if you – if you like football."

"I love football." I look at the majestic curves of the stadium and inside my head I hear the roar of a crowd. I look away and the roar fades. How can I think about fun things like football when I don't even know what's happening with my family and friends? When I don't even know if they're—

"Why do you love football?" Stevie asks.

I remember how she said she didn't like football yesterday but from the way she's looking at me she seems genuinely interested. "I love it because it is when..." I break off, trying to find the right words. "It is when I feel the most – alive. Does that make sense?"

Stevie nods.

"Especially when I play it. Then nothing else matters. All

I think about is the game." I study her face to see if she understands what I'm trying to say. She's nodding thoughtfully.

"We all need something like that," she says quietly, before looking back out of the window.

I wonder what her thing is – if she even has a thing – but I'm too shy to ask.

"So, where do you want to go then, when we get to Brighton?" Stevie says.

I look out of the window, at the rows and rows of pastel-painted houses snaking down the hillside. "Anywhere really ... apart from the sea."

# Stevie

As I follow Hafiz off the train and across the crowded platform to the ticket barrier I have two thoughts on my mind. One: *don't say anything mean about football even though you think it's completely pointless.* And two: *why doesn't Hafiz want to see the sea?* I mean, coming to Brighton and not seeing the sea is a bit like going to Florida and not seeing Disney World. Not that I've got any burning desire to see Disney World – in my opinion it's on a par with football in the pointlessness stakes. But I can tell from the way Hafiz's face clouded over that not wanting to see the sea is a conversational no-go zone – along with all things Syria and dissing the so-called "beautiful game". I rack my brains for somewhere else we can go. There's the Lanes, of course, but I'm not sure Hafiz would be into boutiques and jewellery stores.

We make our way through the crowded concourse and outside I'm hit by a wall of heat. Earlier I'd taken my school tie and blazer off, but I can't remove my jumper, owing to the expanding-cleavage-skanky-bra situation. It's not fair. It was rainy and cold for most of the holiday. Why does summer finally decide to show up now, when I have to dress for winter?

"So, which way should we go?" Hafiz asks as we make our way past the burger stand and the taxi rank.

"Left," I reply. The streets to the right are all residential and straight ahead leads down to the sea.

Hafiz nods and we take the narrow road to the left of the station, underneath the huge dark arch of the railway bridge. We walk down the hill in silence, although all around us there's noise. Traffic. Laughter. The *thud-thud* of a car stereo. The yell of a homeless man lying on sheets of cardboard.

"This must be really different for you," I say. "Compared to Syria, I mean." Crap! We've been here two minutes and already I've blundered.

But Hafiz nods. "It is. It reminds me a bit of Berlin. Especially the graffiti." He nods to a painting of two policemen kissing on the wall of the multi-storey car park.

"You've been to Berlin?"

He nods. "Briefly."

"What, on holiday?"

He laughs. "No, not exactly."

Once again, I feel stupid but this time I'm determined not to make it even worse. "I'm sorry."

"What for?"

"Not knowing anything about what you've been through."

He frowns. "Why should you?"

"It's such big news, the war in Syria. The refugee crisis.

But I – I haven't really read much about it. I've been a bit – distracted."

He looks at me as if he's trying to work out how to respond. I hope I haven't made him angry. "It's OK. You don't want to know about it, trust me." He stops as we reach a crossroads. "Which way?"

I close my eyes. It's hard letting your heart guide you when your head knows that one of the best guitar shops in the world is just a few metres away. "Straight on," my head replies.

## HAFIZ

I follow Stevie along the street, my skin crawling with embarrassment. What must she think of me, saying I didn't want to see the sea? I must have sounded so weird. I could see it in her shocked expression. She's probably trying to figure out how to ditch me as soon as possible. She's probably dying to get down to the pier and look at the waves crashing on the shore. She's probably—

"Oh! A guitar shop! Do you mind if we take a quick look inside?" Stevie has stopped walking and she's pointing to a store. The sign on the front says AMPLIFIED in bright red and yellow letters. The window is full of guitars.

"Of course," I reply. I don't know a thing about music but I'm glad to see Stevie look so happy. I follow her in.

"Hello, stranger," a thin man wearing an old T-shirt that says AC/DC on it calls out from behind the counter. His hair is jet black and there are silver rings on all his fingers. "Haven't seen you for a while."

"Hi. Yes, I – uh – had a few things going on at home," Stevie stammers.

So she's been here before.

"Have you come to see your friend?" the man asks. I scan the shop for someone who could possibly be Stevie's friend, but all I see are a couple of older guys strumming random chords on electric guitars.

Stevie's eyes light up. "Is she still here?"

"Sure is." The man comes out from behind the counter and walks to the back of the shop.

Stevie turns to me and grins. "Do you mind?"

"Of course not." I'm actually intrigued by this turn of events. It's like one of the plot twists in my dad's stories. I really didn't see it coming.

We follow the man to the very back of the shop, past guitars of all shapes, colours and sizes. He takes an acoustic guitar down from the wall. It's shiny and black, with a beautiful engraving of birds in flight.

"Here you go," the man says, handing the guitar to Stevie. "So, how's the fund going?"

Stevie's smile fades. "Not too well."

The man nods sympathetically. "Never mind. One day, eh?"

"Yes, one day." Stevie sits down on a stool and carefully positions the guitar on her lap.

"Can you play?" I ask.

"Can she play?" The shop man laughs. He turns to Stevie. "Go on, show him."

Stevie gently strums the guitar and tightens a couple of

strings. Then she starts playing – properly playing – and a beautiful melody fills the shop. Even the guys trying out the electric guitars stop and watch. I feel a burst of pride, like the pride I used to feel when I watched a teammate score a goal. Then Stevie starts to sing and I almost forget to breathe. Her voice is so unusual and unexpected, so husky and raw. I grin but she looks right through me. It's like she and the guitar have become one and she's totally lost in the music. After a while, she stops playing and we all burst into applause. The trance she was under is broken and her face flushes bright red.

"That was awesome, man," the shop guy says, high-fiving Stevie. "Really awesome."

Stevie shakes her head. "I'm so out of practice. I totally messed up the key change."

"But that vibrato you did at the end," the man says. "It was sweet."

"Thank you." Stevie hands the guitar back to him. "And thanks so much for letting me play her again."

"No worries. You were born to play her."

Stevie sighs. Then she stands up and looks at me. "Sorry about that. I just – I couldn't resist."

"Don't be sorry. You were – that was great!"

"Really?" Stevie smiles at me. Then she purses her lips thoughtfully. "Do you like coffee?"

"I love coffee."

Her face lights up. "Correct answer. You've just won the

special bonus prize." She picks up her bag and hoists it over her shoulder.

"What special bonus prize?"

"An invitation to the best coffee place in all of Brighton. Come on."

## Stevie

"Wait till you taste this coffee," I say to Hafiz as we come out of the guitar shop and onto the bustling street. I blink as my eyes adjust to the sudden brightness of the sun. "It's so good it will make your eyes roll – guaranteed."

"Make my eyes roll?" Hafiz looks at me blankly. "I do not understand."

"Like this." I stop and roll my eyes in fake pleasure.

Hafiz laughs. "Ah, I see. So it's almost as good as Syrian coffee then."

"Is Syrian coffee different to the coffee over here?" I ask as we carry on walking.

"Yes, very different."

"Really? How?" We start weaving our way along Sydney Street, past the vegan shoe shop and the Indian street food restaurant.

"We call it *kahwa* and we drink it really strong and thick, in tiny cups."

"Like espresso?" I breathe in the scent of incense as we walk past a New Age shop. The blackboard outside is advertising dolphin CDs and tarot readings with someone called Psychic Bob.

"Kind of – but not quite."

I glance at Hafiz, worried that talking about Syria might be upsetting him, but he's smiling.

"Sometimes we have it with cardamom – you know, the spice?"

I nod. "That sounds nice."

"It is. So where is it that we're going for this coffee?"

"Just here." I point to Has Bean on the other side of the road.

"Cool."

We cross over and enter. It's even hotter in here than outside and I feel a bead of sweat trickling down the side of my face. Damn this stupid school shirt. I think of school. I wonder if I should phone in pretending to be my mum but quickly decide against it. It will be a lot easier to forge a sick note than fake a call. I wonder if Hafiz is aware of the school attendance policy.

"So – uh – do you know what you have to do if you have a day off sick?" I ask as we join the queue at the counter. "From school, I mean."

"I am not sick." Hafiz's smile fades.

"No, I know, but I take it that's the excuse you're going to give for why you left this morning."

Hafiz looks puzzled. "But it is not why I left this morning."

"Oh. OK." I contemplate asking him again why he walked out of school but decide against it.

"Don't worry," Hafiz says, his expression deadly serious. "I don't even know if I shall be going back there again."

"Oh." I'm shocked at how disappointed this makes me feel. And then my obvious disappointment makes me feel embarrassed, which in turn makes me feel even hotter. I want to clamber into the fridge with all the juices to try and cool down. We don't say anything more until we've been served. Hafiz orders an espresso. I order a small black Americano – even though I could really do with a large. My guitar fund will be down to zero soon if I'm not careful. Once our drinks are ready we take them over to a table in the window.

"OK, so while I can totally understand you not wanting to come back to school, I'm sorry to hear it," I say as we sit down. "And I hope nothing really bad happened this morning to make you want to leave."

Hafiz shakes his head. "It's just … I don't like being where I am not welcome."

"But you are welcome," I blurt out, way too eagerly. I stir my coffee – even though there's nothing to stir. I never take it with milk or sugar. To me, anything that waters down the taste of the coffee is a crime, like the really poor cover version of an epic song.

"Thank you." Hafiz takes a sip from his tiny coffee cup. "So, how did you get to be so good at the guitar?"

"Oh, I don't know if I'm that good."

"You are. I mean, I do not really know much about music but I know that when you played it – it – made me feel something. Like, in here, you know." He puts his hand over his heart.

"Really?" Hafiz saying this makes me feel all kinds of happy.

"So, tell me."

"Practise, I guess. I've had a guitar ever since I was a little kid. My dad always bought them for me, before he… I need a new one though," I say, quickly steering the conversation onto safer ground. "The one I have at the moment is getting too small – or I'm getting too big. But it's taking a lot longer than I thought it would to save the money." I sigh and gaze out at the street. The words to a random song lyric start appearing on the window:

> *Strumming*
>     *broken*
>         *heartstrings*
>            *and*
>                 *hoping*
>                   *for*
>                     *a*
>                       *tune.*

# HAFIZ

I stare out of the café window at the people streaming by. This place is even better for people-watching than the Latakia souk. There are people with hair every colour of the rainbow and outfits that look more like costumes for a show – a really crazy show. I wonder why Stevie hasn't been able to get a new guitar – why her parents won't buy her one. I have a feeling maybe they can't afford it. I glance at her across the table as she scribbles something in her notebook. She looks as if she might be poor. The ends of her jumper sleeves are ragged and fraying. And the collar of her shirt is off-white, as if like she's had it a long time. I decide it's probably better not to ask and take another sip of my coffee. Despite adding two sachets of sugar it's not nearly as sweet and strong as Arabic coffee. I miss the silver coffee pots from back home. I miss the ceremony of pouring the coffee into shot glasses. I miss seeing the friendly faces as we all drink together. I miss it so much it makes me ache.

"So, when did you last play football?" Stevie asks as she stuffs her notebook back in her bag. I wonder what she writes in there.

"Not since I left Syria," I reply, glumly.

"How long is that?"

"Two years."

"What? How come?" Stevie's pale face flushes. "Sorry, is that a really dumb question?"

"No. It just took me a lot longer to get to the UK than I expected."

"But you have family here, right? Your uncle and aunt."

I nod. "But it still took ages getting to France, and then applying for asylum once I got to Calais took over a year."

"That's terrible." Stevie looks so genuinely horrified that I feel some slight comfort – it's always good to be reminded that not everyone in the UK hates us being here. The worst thing is, I'm one of the lucky ones. I met people in France who'd been there for years. People whose only hope of freedom was risking their lives trying to escape on the back of lorries and, when they failed, getting badly beaten up by the police.

"Can I ask you a question?" Stevie looks me straight in the eyes.

"Of course."

"Do you want to be here?"

I look around the coffee shop. "Here? Sure. It is nice."

"No, not *here* here. Here in the UK."

"Oh." I finish off my coffee. "No, not really."

"I thought so."

"Why?"

"You seem so sad."

I sigh. There was a time when I was known as the joker, in my class, my family, my football team, always the one who made everybody laugh. Nothing is the same any more – not even me. Then suddenly, randomly, I think of my dad's theory that we are all born with a story inside us that somehow relates to our life. What if mine has changed from a fun adventure to a heartbreaking tragedy?

"Sorry, I didn't mean to upset you," Stevie says, looking worried.

"You haven't. It's just weird."

"What is?"

"How much has changed. I never used to be sad." And then I feel a spark of my old self light up inside me. I don't want my story to be a tragedy. I look back at Stevie. "Where do you go when you want to have fun?"

"What, here in Brighton?"

I nod.

Stevie's face lights up – then clouds over again. "Oh – but – it's by the sea."

"That's OK. Come on." I take a deep breath and get to my feet. My story is not going to be a tragedy.

## Stevie

I follow Hafiz out of the café, feeling slightly confused. He'd given me the most definite impression that he hated the sea. But now he's striding off along Sydney Street and I'm having to run to keep up – which isn't much fun, given the whole school-jumper-sauna thing.

"Where is this place then?" he calls to me. "Where you go to have fun?"

"On the pier." I feel a sudden stab of doubt. I really hope Hafiz gets ironic humour, otherwise my idea of fun is going to flatline fast.

"The pier?" Hafiz frowns.

"Is that OK?" I say, half wanting him to say no so that I can avoid any potential awkwardness before it begins.

But he nods. "Yes, of course."

We walk down to the front and head towards the pier. The sea is sparkling like a sheet of blue glass in the sun. The second I see it I feel better. And there's something so soothing about the sighing sound of the waves. I want to slow down, drink it in, but Hafiz is walking even faster. I'm starting to feel uneasy.

I should have thought of something else to do. Something that isn't ironic and is far away from the sea. He seems so tense again. We cross the road and walk past the kiosks at the pier entrance. Music is pumping from speakers above the entrance – some stupid hip-hop song about gangsters. I swear I was born in the totally wrong era when it comes to music. I've got ninety-nine problems and misogynistic lyrics are definitely one. I breathe in the smell of sugary doughnuts and vinegary chips. Seagulls squawk overhead, making me think of my annoying feathery alarm clock, Shriek-Beak. If someone had told me when I woke up this morning that I'd end up on Brighton Pier with Hafiz, I'd have sworn I was still dreaming. A couple of older girls walk past and I see them looking Hafiz up and down, checking him out. This is all new territory for me. Not only being out with a boy, but with a boy as good-looking as Hafiz. *Yeah, well, looks aren't everything,* I want to tell the girls. Hafiz does get bonus points though, for being a boy of very little ego. Or at least, that's how he seems.

"Where on the pier is it?" he asks, still looking stressed.

"Down there, in the arcade." Oh please, please, let him get irony.

We walk together along the wooden slats, past kiosks selling candyfloss and sticks of rock and a really tacky selection of china horses, cats and dogs. Hafiz's face is getting grimmer by the second.

"We don't have to do this," I say, coming to a halt. "In fact, let's not. Let's just go back."

He stops and frowns at me. "Why? You said it would be fun."

"Yes, but I'm not sure you'll think it is…" I take a deep breath. "Do you know what irony means?"

"Irony?"

"Yes, as in, an ironic sense of humour."

He nods. "Yes. It is when you say something but you mean the opposite. Like sarcasm."

I breathe a sigh of relief. "Correct. And do you *like* irony?"

"No," he replies and my heart sinks. But then he starts to grin. "I was being ironic."

"Oh, ha ha," I say, before starting to laugh for real.

We carry on walking along the pier, past the glass case containing the waxwork dummy of "The Great Fortune-Telling Zoro" and into the arcade. The noise inside is deafening – a crazy mix of trumpet fanfares and jaunty tunes and machine-gun fire and racing cars. I lead Hafiz past the wall of fruit machines – and the grim-faced men playing them like their lives depend upon hitting the jackpot.

"*Ta-da!* This is where I come when I want to have fun." I gesture at the claw machine with a grand flourish. The assortment of cuddly toys piled up inside peer at us mournfully through the glass.

# HAFIZ

She likes the claw! I look at Stevie and grin.

She frowns. "We don't have to play if you don't want to. I know it's kind of lame."

"Lame?"

"Stupid — and before you say it, I know it's rigged. I know hardly anyone ever wins. Ever. But that's what makes me love it — it's the ultimate challenge."

"Me too!"

She looks shocked. "You know this game? You like it?"

"Yes! And do you want to know the really weird thing?" My heart is racing with excitement now. "The really weird thing is that the first time I ever played the claw it was here, on this pier."

Stevie's eyes widen. "Really? How come?"

"I came here with my parents when I was six, when we were in the UK for my uncle's wedding."

"No way!"

I reach into my trouser pocket and pull out some of the money Uncle Samir gave me for lunch. I hand Stevie a pound coin. "Go on, have a go."

She shakes her head. "Oh no, I can't take your money."

"Why not?"

"I have my own." She pulls a faded purse from her school bag and takes out a coin.

I wonder if I've offended her. But she's still smiling.

"Do you want to go first?" she asks.

I shake my head. "No, go on, you go."

As Stevie puts her money in the slot I feel relieved. It had been so horrible coming to the pier, being so close to the sea, but here in the arcade is like being protected inside a brightly coloured bubble. And it's so noisy I can't even hear the waves any more. I watch as Stevie moves the claw all the way over to the back corner of the glass box, where the head of a toy owl wearing a pair of huge round glasses is poking out from the middle of all the teddy bears. Her face is tense with concentration. Slowly, she lowers the claw. The silver fingers close around the owl's head. I hold my breath as Stevie moves the claw upwards. This game gets me every time. *Will she do it?* the commentator inside my head cries. *Will she win the elusive owl?* But then, just as Stevie moves the owl back across the box, it drops from the claw's grasp.

"No!" Stevie exclaims. I love how seriously she's taking it.

"It's a travesty!" I cry.

Her look of disappointment fades and she starts to laugh. "It *is* a travesty! That owl should have been mine – this claw is rigged!"

"Let me have a go," I say. Suddenly, I want nothing more

than to win that owl for Stevie. She stands aside and I rub my hands together and blow on them. "My lucky pre-claw ritual," I explain.

She laughs. "Crap! That's why I didn't win. I forgot to do my lucky dance."

"Aw, shame, I would love to have seen that." I insert the coin and raise the claw. I move it over to the owl, then lower it. The fingers close around the owl's back, but I can't get a proper grip. The claw lifts the owl a couple of inches, then drops it. "Damn!" I shake my head. "This machine is definitely rigged." I turn to Stevie. "Are you going to have another go?"

She looks in her purse and her smile fades. "Better not."

I offer her a coin. "Go on. Have one more."

She looks at the money, then looks at the owl. "Are you sure?"

"Of course."

"OK. Thank you." She takes the money and is about to put it in the slot when I stop her.

"Aren't you forgetting something?"

"What?"

"Your lucky dance."

"Are you serious?" Her eyes are sparkling.

"Do you want to win this owl or not?"

"Oh, I want to win it. I am *determined* to win it."

"Well, go on then." I stand back, fold my arms and wait.

Her face flushes pink and she grins. "OK, here it is." She starts skipping round in a circle, waving her hands in the air. She looks so funny I have to stop myself from joining in. "There!" she exclaims breathlessly, before looking back at the owl. "Right, now I need to focus. I have some serious winning to do."

I watch as she carefully manoeuvres the claw above the owl, then slowly lowers it around its head. I can tell immediately the grip's a lot firmer this time. Stevie lifts the claw and starts bringing it slowly back towards us. *My God, I think she might have done it!* my inner commentator exclaims. The claw opens – and the owl drops down – into the winner's tray.

"Yes!" I yell.

Stevie claps her hand to her mouth in shock. "I did it!"

I slap her on the back. "Well done!"

"Thank you." Stevie takes the owl from the tray and holds it aloft like a winner's trophy. "This truly is the happiest day of my life."

I frown. "Are you being ironic?"

She laughs. "Of course I am!" Then she holds the owl out to me. "Do you want it?"

"What? No! You won it."

"I know, but it was with your money."

I shake my head. "It was with your skill." I suddenly feel starving. "Do you want to get something to eat?"

Stevie stuffs the owl in her bag and smiles. "Sure."

## Stevie

As Hafiz and I walk back off the pier I feel so happy I could do my fictional lucky dance all over again. And I'm not just happy that finally – *finally!* – I've beaten the claw. I'm happy because what just happened in there – me laughing and joking with Hafiz – *me dancing in front of Hafiz* – felt so good. I'm so happy I don't even care about being swelteringly hot, or having spent nearly all of my remaining guitar fund on train fares and coffee and the claw. It was worth every penny to feel like this.

"What would you like to eat?" Hafiz asks as we reach the seafront road and wait for the signal to cross.

"Chips?" I suggest. Chips are probably the only thing I can afford.

He nods. "Sure."

The signal turns green.

Hafiz is walking fast. I follow him towards the Old Steine and away from the sea and I get a waft of potatoes frying. I spot a kebab shop across the street.

"How about there?" I say, nodding to the shop.

Hafiz nods.

We each buy a bag of chips. I don't have enough money to get a drink but Hafiz buys two cans of Sprite and hands one to me.

"Thank you." I open it and take a sip and shiver as the lemony fizz erupts on my tongue. We sit down on a bench in front of the Pavilion.

"Wow!" Hafiz exclaims, gazing up at the domes and minarets. "It is just like that place in India."

"The Taj Mahal? Yeah. Apparently it was built for one of our kings as a holiday home. It's the royal equivalent of a caravan."

Hafiz looks at me blankly. I'm guessing they don't do caravan holidays in Syria. I take a bite into a crispy, golden chip. The potato inside is creamy and soft. I'm so hungry it tastes like the most delicious food that ever existed. We eat in silence for a few moments, then Hafiz turns to me.

"What's the best story you've ever heard?"

I look at him in surprise. I really did not see this question coming. "Oh – I'm not sure. Why?"

Hafiz looks back at the Pavilion. "It doesn't matter." He seems embarrassed. I don't want him to be embarrassed. I don't want anything to change how easy things are between us.

"I just need a moment to think," I say. "Do you mean a fictional story or a real-life story?"

"Either."

I flick through my mental filing system. I think of the bedtime stories my parents used to tell me when I was young. Stories about dark forests and scary wolves and sappy princesses and magical kingdoms. I used to love being told stories but none of them stand out as the best I've ever heard. I try to think of some real-life stories I've heard. And then I remember one my dad told me about how, when he was first starting out as a music journalist at the age of eighteen, he managed to blag his way onto the Rolling Stones' tour bus. That was a great story – but it would involve talking and thinking about my dad and that definitely would not be great. Then I think of the stories that inspire me every single day.

"I really like Malala's story," I say. "You know, the girl who was shot by the Taliban."

Hafiz nods.

Then I realize that the last thing he probably wants to hear are stories about violence and war. "I don't mean that I like the fact that she was shot. I hate that fact – obviously. But I love that she didn't let fear stop her – that she kept doing what she believed in and campaigning for girls to have the right to an education. Anyway, why do you want to know?" I say, quickly shifting the focus back on to him.

Hafiz takes a sip from his drink. "I'm trying to find a story," he eventually replies.

"What for?"

"For me."

"How do you mean?"

Hafiz sighs. "It's because of something my dad once told me."

"What was it?" I stop eating. A sure sign that I'm truly gripped.

"He told me that we are all born with a story inside us." He places his hand on his chest. "A story that will help us get through all the challenges we face in life." He glances sideways at me.

I nod. "OK. And how do we find out what our story is?"

Hafiz sighs. "Apparently we'll know it when we find it."

"But what if we never find it?"

"That's what I'm worried about."

I take a moment to let this sink in. It's weird. I don't quite understand what he's saying, but I really like it. I really like the idea of being born with a story inside me. "So that's why you asked me?"

"Yes. It's something I've been asking a lot."

"But you still haven't found your story?"

He shakes his head. "I guess I should stop looking. It's probably just a myth anyway."

I frown. "Don't say that."

"Why?"

"I think it's a great idea."

"You do?" His face lights up.

"Yeah. Maybe I could…" I break off, feeling embarrassed.

"What?"

"Maybe I could help you find it."

"Seriously?" Hafiz smiles. Then his smile fades. "I'm not sure it works like that. My dad told me he wasn't able to help me. I think we each have to find our own."

"Oh, I see." I gaze up into the clear blue sky and picture a story out there somewhere, waiting for me to find it. The thought sends a shiver down my spine. "But how will we know when we do?"

Hafiz shrugs. "I'm not sure. My dad just said that I'd know; he said that when I heard the story that was mine it would affect me deeply. Do you think that sounds dumb?"

"No! I think it sounds seriously cool." I smile at him. "And I think your dad sounds seriously cool too."

I told Stevie about the story idea and she didn't think I was crazy, she thought it was "seriously cool". The day that started so badly is now turning into the best I've had in a long time. I'm about to say "thanks to God" like I always used to when good things happened, but I resist. I stopped saying it years ago, after the war started. When I first set out on my journey to the UK I got into the habit of saying "God willing", like so many others on the refugee trail. Now I don't talk about God at all.

"You must really miss him – your dad, I mean," Stevie says.

I nod.

"If it's any consolation I know how that feels."

"You do?"

"Yes." Stevie starts fiddling with the ring pull on her can of Sprite.

"How?" I stare at her curiously.

"I haven't seen my dad for a long time either."

"How long?"

"Two years, seven months and one day." She pulls the owl from her bag and smiles at it. "Thanks for helping me win this."

"That's OK."

"I love owls, don't you?"

I nod. I want to ask her why she hasn't seen her dad in so long but it's obvious that she wants to change the subject. My phone vibrates in my trouser pocket, but I ignore it.

"I'm sorry," I say before eating another chip. A taxi zooms past, cutting up a bus. The bus driver leans out of the window and yells a stream of curse words. That's another random thing I've gained since leaving Syria. I now know how to curse in seven different languages.

"Why are you sorry?" Stevie asks.

"That you haven't seen your dad in so long."

"Oh. That's OK. I'm kind of used to it now."

The chip I'm eating almost gets stuck in my throat. I don't ever want to get used to not seeing my family. My phone starts vibrating again. My throat tightens. The only people who have my new mobile number are Uncle Samir and Aunt Maria. Why would they be phoning me? I take my phone from my pocket and my heart sinks. It's Uncle Samir. "Sorry, I'd better take this," I say to Stevie before answering the call. "Hello."

"Hafiz! Where are you?" He sounds so serious. My stomach churns. Has he heard from Syria? Has he heard bad news?

"Uncle Samir, what's wrong?"

"That's what I should be asking you," my uncle replies. "Where are you? Why aren't you in school?"

"What? But how...?"

"Your teacher rang me. She was worried. Some students told her that you walked out of class before the day even began. What happened? Where are you?"

I sigh. "I – I wasn't feeling well."

"So why didn't you go home?"

"I needed some fresh air." A car pulls up in the queue of traffic beside us, a hip-hop beat pounding from the stereo.

"It sounds like you're in a pub!"

"I'm in Brighton."

Stevie starts shifting awkwardly on the bench next to me. "Have you been busted?" she whispers.

I shrug and give her a weak grin.

"Brighton! What are you doing in Brighton?" Uncle Samir exclaims.

"I'm getting some fresh air." I'm embarrassed by how lame this sounds.

"Go home immediately," Uncle Samir says. "Your aunt has been so worried."

"OK," I say, but inside I feel really fed up. *I can't go home immediately*, I want to yell. *Maybe I'll never be able to go home again.* Stevie shifts slightly closer to me and gives me a sympathetic smile, as if she can read my thoughts.

"Do you promise you'll go straight home?" Uncle Samir asks.

"Yes," I mutter, balling up the rest of my chips and throwing them in the bin.

"Good. We'll talk about it when I get back from work."

"OK." There it is again, that stupid, pathetic word that always pops out when all I really want to say is "no". *No, I don't want to go straight back to your home. No, I don't want to talk about it. No, I don't want to keep doing what everybody else tells me.*

"Bye," Uncle Samir says, and the line goes dead.

## *Stevie*

We spend most of the journey back to Lewes in silence. Ever since the phone call, Hafiz has shuttered himself off again, his head tipped forward, his hair tumbling down over his face. It must have been his uncle who called. I wonder how he found out Hafiz wasn't in school. Maybe he'd asked the school to keep a close eye on Hafiz, or maybe they have a new policy and ring your parents if you don't come in. What if they've rung Mum? She won't have been able to call me, as she has no credit left on her phone, but what if she knows I've bunked off? She probably won't even care. I stare out of the train window, thinking of what Hafiz said about trying to find his story. If only he didn't have to find it on his own – I'd love to help him find a story to make him happy.

The train pulls into Lewes. I wonder if Hafiz is going to say anything at all before we go home. I try to think of something to say to him but everything I come up with sounds stupid.

"Thank you," he says suddenly as we head through the station and out into the sunlight.

"You're welcome. Uh – what for?"

"For today. It was fun."

"Oh." I feel a surge of relief. "Yes. I had a really good time … and I'm not being ironic," I add.

He laughs. "Me neither."

"I hope you don't get into trouble – about, you know, school."

"Thank you. You too."

We reach the junction that leads to his road.

"So, I'll see you then?" I try to make it sound like a question, hoping that Hafiz will say yes and tell me when.

But he just nods. "See you."

I start heading home, my happiness fading with every step.

As soon as I open the door to the cottage I know that something is wrong – something has changed. The pile of post that had been accumulating on the hallway floor has gone and I hear a banging sound coming from the kitchen. I make my way down the darkened passageway. Mum's facing the sink, thumping a cup on the draining board over and over again. She knows. The school must have called her. My stomach lurches.

"Mum," is all I can manage to say.

She stops banging the cup and slowly turns to face me. Her hair is tangled and her face is streaked with tears.

"Mum, I'm so sorry I—"

"They're going to stop my benefits," she says. "I had a letter from them."

"Oh." Now I don't know what to feel. Relief and worry churn inside of me.

"Look." She takes a crumpled piece of paper from her dressing-gown pocket and shoves it in my hand.

I uncrumple it and read. It's from the Department for Work and Pensions. It doesn't seem to be as bad as Mum thinks. "They're not saying they're stopping your benefits; they're just saying there are some changes and inviting you to a medical."

"It's the same thing!" Mum goes over to the table and slumps down into one of the chairs. "I've seen this on the news. Since they've changed the system, loads of people are having their claims turned down. They reassess you so they have an excuse to stop paying you."

I sit opposite her and clear my throat, preparing my special calm-Mum-down voice. "I'm sure they won't, Mum. They just want to meet with you, and see if you're still ill."

"But how can I go to a meeting? I can't leave the house." Her voice is shrill.

"Do you want a cup of camomile tea?" I walk to the cupboard. The box of teabags is empty. The whole cupboard is empty. I take a deep breath, remind myself that it could be worse, the school could have rung her. I've had a great day in Brighton with Hafiz and I haven't been busted. "Why don't you give me your cash card and I'll go and get some food and some more tea?"

"What am I going to do, Stevie? How are we going to survive without that money?"

Her hands are shaking and I can feel her fear scuttling across the table towards me. "You're not going to lose your benefits." I look back at the letter and see a phone number at the top. "Why don't you ring them – explain that you find it really hard to leave the house because of your anxiety? Maybe they can come to you."

Mum stops shaking. "Do you think they would?"

"Yes. Of course." The truth is, I have no idea, but I'd say anything right now to calm Mum down.

She nods. "OK, I'll ring them tomorrow. Or maybe…" She looks at me.

"What?"

"Maybe you could ring them for me?"

"Oh, I don't know. I mean—"

"Please. You know how flustered I get dealing with things like this."

I sigh. "OK."

She smiles at me through her tears, the weakest of smiles. Then she fumbles in her purse and hands me her cash card. "Thank you. Go and get some food. But don't spend too much, just in case…"

Her unuttered words hang in the kitchen between us, in thick black letters: *just in case we can't get any more…*

I'm back at school. Despite having vowed to myself yesterday that I wasn't ever going to set foot in this place again, here I am. Uncle Samir and Aunt Maria are here too. We've been called in to an early-morning meeting with my form tutor, Miss Kepinski, and the Head of Year, Ms Potts. The adults are discussing what can be done to make me feel more "at home".

"Would it help if you joined some of our after-school clubs?" Miss Kepinski says. "What do you like doing in your spare time, Hafiz?"

I shrug. There's no way I want to spend any of my spare time here.

"He loves playing football," Aunt Maria says.

"Yes, back in Syria he was a star player," Uncle Samir joins in, his face lighting up, making me want to groan. Doesn't he get it? Those days are over.

"Really?" Ms Potts looks at me over the top of her glasses. Her glasses make me think of the toy owl and that makes me think of Stevie. My only friend in this place – well, kind of friend. I wonder if she got into trouble yesterday too. I hope not. Something tells me she has enough to deal with.

"I could have a word with Mr Kavanagh, the PE teacher," Miss Kepinski says. "He coaches the Year 10 football team."

"That would be wonderful!" Uncle Samir exclaims, like she just said she'd got me a trial for Man United. "Wouldn't it, Hafiz?"

"Yes," I mutter.

"Well, that's settled then." Miss Kepinski writes something in her notepad. "I'll try and catch him in the staffroom before registration. Find out when the first training session is."

"OK."

"Would that make you feel a bit better, Hafiz?" Ms Potts looks at me through her glasses, like she's making double sure I'm not going to walk out of school again.

"Yes. Thank you."

"And you're sure there was nothing that happened yesterday to make you walk out?"

I nod. One thing I don't and never will do is tell tales.

"OK then. We'll see if we can get you a place on the football team. And if you ever feel like leaving school again, you'll come and see me first, yes?"

I look at Ms Potts and try not to laugh. "Yes, Miss."

"Excellent!" Ms Potts adjusts the pile of files on her desk.

Miss Kepinski stands up. "I'll go and grab Mr Kavanagh." She holds out her hand to Samir. "Lovely to meet you, Mr Ali."

"Lovely to meet you too."

All the adults smile at one another and shake hands. I'm

surprised they don't slap each other on the back, they're so happy with themselves. Problem Hafiz solved, just like that.

I follow Uncle Samir and Aunt Maria out into the corridor.

"Are you OK?" Uncle Samir asks. He looks concerned and I feel a pang of guilt for being so cross with him. But what else am I going to do with all this anger inside me? I force myself to smile and nod.

Once they've gone I head down the corridor that leads to Miss Kepinski's form room. On the way I see a disabled toilet. I'll wait here until the bell goes, then slip in. That way I can avoid a repeat of what happened yesterday. Everything's lower down in here – the light cord, the sink, the hand dryer – so that people in wheelchairs can reach them. I picture my friend Aahil wheeling himself in here, grinning his crooked grin at me. I haven't WhatsApped Aahil since I got to the UK. I haven't been able to.

Aahil lost his legs from his knees down in a rocket attack. After his injury my mum and dad became determined that I should leave. Aahil lost his legs and can't leave Syria but because of his injury I have. How is that fair? How can I message him now I'm here? How would it make him feel? I stand up and lean on the low sink and look at my reflection in the mirror. I wonder if I'll ever like what I see.

## Stevie

*Hafiz isn't here.* As I take my seat in the form room the real-ization fills my mind like a giant neon sign. *Hafiz isn't here.* I tuck my bag under the table and sigh. It's official. Today is going to be terrible. Not only has Hafiz left school but I'm supposed to be sorting out my mum's benefits assessment *and* I've got PE. The only thing that could make this day even worse would be for the door to open and Ms Potts to walk in and tell us that we all have detention. The door opens – *oh, come on, you have got to be kidding* – and Hafiz walks in. I fight the urge to grin and end up making some kind of weird grimace instead.

"Are you OK?" Hafiz asks as he sits down beside me. "You look like you've got toothache."

"No, I'm fine. I'm just trying not to..."

"What?"

"Grin." I pretend to search for something in my bag.

"Why are you trying not to grin?" Hafiz asks, slinging his sports bag down on the floor.

"Long story," I lie. It really isn't long at all. In fact, it can be summed up in six words: Hafiz is here and I'm happy.

Priya walks in. She looks stressed and tired – until she sees us and smirks.

"So, are you going to run away again today?" she says as she walks past. My heart sinks. She must have seen me leaving school yesterday.

"I wasn't running away," Hafiz says.

"Oh, really?" Priya replies as she sits down behind us.

I look from Hafiz to Priya and back again. She looks triumphant, like she just won a prize. He looks like he might be about to kill her. I knew something must have happened yesterday to make him walk out of school. And I should have known it would involve Priya. But why? Why would she want to pick on him?

Before Hafiz can say anything else, the door opens and Miss Kepinski walks in. She's wearing a dress covered in a large daisy print and as usual she's smiling from ear to ear, like she didn't get the memo that school totally sucks.

"Great news," she says, coming over to Hafiz. "I've had a word with Mr Kavanagh and there's football training this afternoon, after school. He says you're very welcome to join them."

"Thank you," Hafiz mutters. He doesn't seem thankful though.

As Miss Kepinski takes the register I try and process these latest developments. Hafiz is back in school – that's good. But something clearly happened between him and Priya yesterday. The thing I really don't get about Priya and her mean-girl routine is that she gets picked on too. I saw her one day by the ticket machine at Brighton station and a gang of Neanderthal boys were calling her names because she's Indian. I bet it wasn't the first time she's been racially abused either. You'd think it would make her more compassionate and less likely to want to hurt anyone else. Then the bell rings for first period and I feel sick. It's time for PE.

I used to love sports. Well, I used to love playing games outside with my friends back in London. There was a green in front of our house where all the local kids would congregate and play rounders or cricket. I even invented a game once for us all to play, called Water-Pistol Polo. It became so popular and caused so much mayhem some parents tried to ban it. Not mine though – they thought it was great. Mum was our water supplier, always happy to refill our pistols, and Dad told me that in the music industry getting a song banned used to be a badge of honour. When "Relax" by Frankie Goes to Hollywood was banned by Radio One it turned them into major stars. He told me I should be proud for creating a neighbourhood controversy. If only I still enjoyed games the way I used to, but here at Lewes High, PE doesn't stand for Physical Education – it stands for Physical Excruciation.

As soon as I get to the girls' changing rooms I head straight for my usual spot in the corner at the back. Last night I practised getting changed so that no one would see my buttonless shirt. I mentally run through the drill, then

I get my PE top out of my bag, turn my back to the rest of the room and slip out of my school jumper and shirt like I'm trying to break the Guinness World Record for Speed-Changing. If there was such a thing as Speed-Changing. Maybe I should invent it just so I can finally have a sport I excel at. For a terrible moment the back of my greying bra is on full display but within seconds – two seconds to be precise – I've got my PE top on. I stand frozen for a moment, wondering if anyone saw my bra and if Priya's going to make some snide remark, but everyone keeps chattering away. I breathe a sigh of relief. Then, keeping my skirt on, I pull down my tights, removing my shoes last, so no one sees the holes in the toes, and then I wriggle into my shorts, under my skirt, so no one sees my knickers. I always wear my best pair of knickers on PE days – and, just to clarify, by "best" I mean the least faded. Once I'm changed I turn back to face the rest of the room and sit down on the bench.

As always, Lucy Giles is still getting changed. Lucy Giles always takes her time getting changed. She's like the exact opposite of me – in every way. Her hair is long and sleek and blonde and her body curves in and out in all the right places. She's really rich too. She lives in one of the cluster of huge houses on top of the cliff, looking down on the rest of us – in more ways than one. I watch as she slowly unbuttons her crisp, snowy-white school shirt, revealing a lacy white bra, made all the more white against her honey-coloured skin. I see Priya watching her too, her expression a mixture of envy and awe. Lucy Giles is the only girl in our year that Priya wouldn't dare try her mean-girl routine on. In fact, she goes out of her way to make Lucy like her. It's pitiful really.

I put on my crappy trainers and wince at how shabby they look. I don't want to care about this kind of stupid stuff. That's another reason why I hate this school – it *makes* you care about this kind of stupid stuff. I think of Hafiz, down the corridor in the boys' changing rooms. Hopefully he'll enjoy PE. *But what if he enjoys it too much?* a voice in my head says. *What if he bonds with the boys during a game of football or something and won't want to hang around with me any more?*

I push the thought from my head and get to my feet.

"Today, you're going to be doing a run," the PE teacher, Mr Kavanagh, tells us, once we're all changed. He's stocky, with a red face and ginger hair and the flattened nose of a man who's been in more than a few fights. Maybe he was once a boxer. Or maybe he's just a badass.

I'm glad we're doing a run. Running is good because it doesn't involve having to talk to anyone. Or having to put up with any prying stares. It's weird because while I was travelling across Europe I got used to being stared at by the locals in the different countries I passed through, but at least there was some feeling of camaraderie among my fellow travellers. Even if we didn't come from the same country, we were all in the same situation – all being stared at together. But not here. Here I'm the only refugee.

"OK, lads," Mr Kavanagh says, taking a stopwatch from his tracksuit pocket. "Follow me."

As we file out of the changing rooms Mr Kavanagh hangs back. "You must be Hafiz."

I nod.

"Welcome to Lewes High." He holds out his hand for me to shake. "I understand you like football."

"Thank you, sir. Yes, I do."

"What position do you play?"

"Left wing."

"Excellent. We're always in need of a good left-winger." He slaps me on the back. "Make sure you come back here today, after school, for training."

"Yes, sir." As I follow Mr Kavanagh out of the building I hear high-pitched laughter and see the girls making their way onto the playing field. I look for Stevie. She's trailing along on her own. I wonder why she doesn't have any friends. I wonder if Priya has anything to do with it. I bet she does and this makes me mad. Why do some people make it their hobby to hate? Isn't there enough hate in the world?

"Right, lads, I've marked out a course for you," Mr Kavanagh says, once we've all gathered around him outside. "Just follow the yellow arrows, out of the school and round the lanes at the back. It's a four-kilometre circuit. You should have plenty of time to get it done. So no stopping off for a chocolate break, Jonesy." Mr Kavanagh grins at the boy standing next to me.

The boy laughs. "You're such a spoilsport, sir."

"And no stopping off for a fag, Price," Mr Kavanagh says, turning to another boy. The boy's pointed face and beady eyes make him look like a rat. His thin lips curl into a frown.

"If you say so."

"And, Hafiz…" All eyes fall on me. "Just follow the others. Unless, of course, you find yourself out in front. In which case, follow the yellow arrows."

"Yes, sir."

We all start jogging down the side of the field. The girls are making their way over to the netball courts. I think of Stevie and how she said she was trying not to grin when I arrived in class. Why was she trying not to grin? Why was she *wanting* to grin? Could it have been she was happy to see me? Then my mind ambushes me with a vision of my mum – and the way she'd smile whenever I arrived home from school. "Hafiz!" she'd exclaim, as if it had been six months not six hours since I'd seen her. It used to annoy me when she'd want to give me a hug. I'd be so keen to get to my Xbox or to football training or back out with my friends. Now I'd give anything to feel her arms wrapped around me. *Please let her be safe,* I silently plead, even though I know nobody's listening.

We jog through a gate at the far end of the field and out onto a country lane, lined either side by thick green hedges. The white cliffs of Lewes loom beneath a clear blue sky. It's so beautiful, it's like running inside a painting. At first my legs feel tired and stiff but soon my body warms up and I find my rhythm. I don't push myself. I take my time. And as I run, I feel some of the tension I've been carrying for so long leaving me. The tightness in my shoulders, scalp and neck eases with every step. I'd forgotten how therapeutic running can be. Without even realizing it, my pace quickens. I reach the end of the lane and follow the arrow round to the right. I'm overtaking some of the others now and it feels good. I feel free. I think back to training sessions with Hutteen, running on the beach, Khalid shouting at me, "Run faster, Hafiz!" I overtake again and again. *"Run faster!"* I fix my gaze straight ahead on the bright blue sky at the end of the lane. I feel the breeze rippling through my hair and against my skin. I imagine myself running from my thoughts and my fears and my memories. I push my body to its limits so that the only thing I can think about is the burning in my lungs and my limbs. *"Run faster, Hafiz!"*

I reach the end of the lane – no one is in front of me. I follow the yellow arrow round to the right, up a narrow footpath, under a bridge. I don't want to stop running. I don't want to lose the feeling of freedom it's giving me. I follow another arrow round to the right, hear footsteps pounding behind me. I glance over my shoulder and see another student bearing down on me. My old competitive streak sparks into life. *The race is on!* the commentator inside my head cries. I hold my head up and push my legs to go faster. The other guy is now at my shoulder. I take a deep breath and activate the Hafiz Rocket. This is the name Khalid gave to the extra spurt I'm able to pull out of the bag at the very last minute. It's what won me the title of top goal scorer at Hutteen. I surge ahead, my heart pumping furiously. I follow an arrow out onto the road to the school. The final stretch. I run faster and faster, until I can't hear anyone behind me any more. I race in through the school gates and down the side of the building, back to the field. Mr Kavanagh is sitting on a bench, looking at his phone. I run over to him and bend over double to catch my breath.

"Hafiz!" Mr Kavanagh grabs the stopwatch around his neck. "Bloody hell, son, where's the fire?"

I look at him, confused. "What fire?"

"Never mind, it's just a figure of speech." He pats me on the shoulder, then looks at his stopwatch again. "That was brilliant. Seriously. You make sure you come to football training this afternoon, you hear?"

"OK," I say. And this time I mean it.

## Stevie

I've come up with a cunning plan. A plan that could solve my school shirt crisis once and for all. And bizarrely, it was Priya who gave me the idea, just now in English, when one of her friends told her that she'd lost her watch.

"You probably left it in the changing rooms after PE," Priya said. "We'll have to check there at break. And if it's not there we can try Lost Property."

Lost Property. It could be the answer to all of my problems. Well, the shirt problem, at least. As Mrs Parsons, my English teacher, drones on about *Coriolanus*, the Shakespeare play we'll be studying this term, I start finessing my plan. I could go to Lost Property and tell them that I lost a shirt at the end of last year but hadn't realized it until the summer holidays. Then, if there's a shirt there that's my size, I could take it. *But that would be stealing,* my inner voice annoyingly reminds me. *But is it though?* I argue back. *If something's lost and hasn't been claimed, it isn't stealing, it's more ... rehousing.* Like people do with abandoned cats and dogs. Yes, it would be a rescue shirt. I would be saving it from a lifetime of misery, stuffed inside a school cupboard with a load of smelly socks and abandoned ties.

Next to me Hafiz starts bouncing his leg up and down. He smells really nice – of deodorant but a good one – unlike most of the other boys straight after PE. The bell sounds for break. I wonder if he'll want to spend it with me, or if he's made friends with any of the boys.

"What are you doing for break?" he asks.

"Oh, I don't know – having a picnic on the roof, throwing a party on the field…"

Hafiz looks confused.

"I was being sarcastic. Nothing really."

He nods. "So, do you want to do nothing with me?"

"Yes, please."

It's only when we get outside that I remember the phone call. Mum told me it would be easier to get through to the Department for Work and Pensions before lunch. But then I think of having to call them in front of Hafiz.

"I'm really sorry," I say as we find a spot next to the wall of the school building. "I've just got to make a quick phone call."

"Sure," he replies with a smile.

"It's a bit personal," I tell him, cringing inside. "So I'll just go over there, by the bike rack, to, you know, make it." Anger mixes with my embarrassment. I shouldn't even have to make this call. Mum should. "I'm really sorry. I won't be long."

"It's fine." Hafiz takes his own phone from his bag. "I need to message someone too."

"OK, see you in a minute then." I hurry over to the bike rack and take my phone and Mum's letter from the bag. I dial the number and immediately get through to a recorded message listing a load of different options. I hope it won't take too long. I topped up the credit on my phone this morning with the last of my guitar money but what if it isn't enough? I press the number for the enquiry line and follow the options. Some lame on-hold music starts playing. Hafiz is leaning against the school wall. I wonder who he's messaging. His family maybe. Or a friend back home. I read about the war in Syria in the free paper last night and now I'm finding it even harder to imagine what it must be like for Hafiz to be here. He must be so worried about all the people he's left behind. The on-hold music stops and for a minute I think I've been put through but it's a false alarm. There's a click on the line and it starts playing again. I decide to make the most of the wait by running through what I'm going to say in my head. *"Good morning, I'm calling on behalf of Mrs Sadie Flynn…"* Is "good morning" too formal? Maybe I should just say hi. No, hi's too informal. How about hello? Or hello there? There's a click on the line again and this time I get a human voice.

"Hello, Benefits Assessment Helpline," it barks.

"Oh, hello there!" I say and instantly squirm. That sounded ridiculous. I clear my throat and try to compose myself. "I'm calling on behalf of Mrs Sadie Flynn. You wrote to her recently about her benefits. I'm her daughter."

"Yes," the voice on the other end says impatiently.

"Well, you – er – you've asked her to come in for a meeting to – er – reassess her benefit claim but the thing is – the thing is, my mum's not able to leave the house at the moment."

There's a pause and then, "Why not?"

"She has anxiety, as well as depression, and it's really bad right now."

"Right." Now the person on the other end sounds suspicious as well as cross.

I'm so nervous about messing things up that the palms of my hands start to sweat. "She was wondering if there's any way you could come to her."

"Really. Would it be possible to speak to your mum, please?"

"Oh – uh – well, I'm not actually with her at the moment. I'm at school. But I've got the letter you sent her. I have her number – the reference number."

"I'm afraid we really do need to speak to her directly."

My heart sinks. "Oh. OK. I'll ask her to call you when I get home this afternoon."

"Thank you. Goodbye."

The line goes dead.

## HAFIZ

When the bell for end of school goes I say goodbye to Stevie and make my way back to the changing rooms. It feels like a long time since my run this morning and I'm starting to have doubts about playing football again. It doesn't help that Aahil hasn't replied to the message I sent him at morning break. I'd kept it as brief and sensitive as possible:

> I finally made it to the UK – now at my uncle's.
> How you doing, brother?

I open the changing-room door and step inside. A group of boys are already there; some of them I recognize, some I don't. They all look me up and down when I walk in. Some of them give me a nod of recognition, most of them don't. The boy named Price just glares at me like I'm a piece of dirt he scraped off the bottom of his shoe. I look around for Mr Kavanagh but there's no sign of him. This was a mistake. I should have gone straight home. I think of the story we learned about in English this morning, the story of a Roman general named Coriolanus who had a tragic flaw which led to his downfall. Could Coriolanus be my story? Could my tragic flaw be coming to football training?

The door crashes open and Mr Kavanagh strides in. "Right then, you lot, let's get out there and get warmed up." He turns to me. "Come on, Speedy Gonzales, let's see what you're made of."

I have no idea who Speedy Gonzales is but I take it he's talking about my run.

Once we're warmed up, Mr Kavanagh splits us into two teams and hands out different coloured bibs. I'm on the red team, which I take as a lucky omen, as red is the colour of the Syrian national team. Mr Kavanagh tells me to play on the left wing. As soon as we kick off, all of my doubts disappear. I focus on the ball. At first my tackling is rusty and my passes are off target but then something happens that is better than any pep talk. Price clatters me and as I crash to the ground he sneers and says, "Don't think much of Syrian football."

Suddenly it's as if my red bib has morphed into the red shirt of my national team. Now I'm not just playing for my own pride, I'm playing for Syria's too. I'll show that sneering, pale-faced boy. I'll show him what we Syrians can do. I line the ball up for my free kick. It's several metres out of the penalty area, but I've scored from here before. Mr Kavanagh blows the whistle and one of my teammates calls for me to pass to him. But I ignore him. I run up to the ball, stretch my leg back and kick. Time seems to stand still as everyone watches the ball arc into the air, then come flying back down. The goalie crouches, ready to leap. The ball is coming in high – is it too high? My heart pounds as I will it to go into the net. *Please, please, please! Yes!* The ball slots into the top right-hand corner of the goal, just out of reach of the goalie.

"Whoa!" Mr Kavanagh yells from the sideline.

And suddenly my teammates are all around me, slapping me on the back and grinning.

"Nice one!" one of them says.

"Quality," says another.

"Are you sure you're from Syria?" Mr Kavanagh calls out. "You sure you haven't come from the Man United academy? That was a superb goal."

I nod and laugh. "Oh, yes, I am from Syria." I look Price straight in his beady eyes as I say it.

He glares and looks away.

# Stevie

I stop off at the newsagent's on the way home from school. In Cunning Plan Number Two, I've decided to ask Tony, the shop owner, if I can take on an extra paper round. I'm so worried about telling Mum she's got to call the helpline – and what might happen when she does – that I need to have some good news to share too. I have to find a way to make more money, just in case we end up losing the little we get.

"Good afternoon, Stevie!" Tony calls to me from behind the counter. As usual he's sitting on his stool doing a crossword. Whenever Tony isn't serving a customer he's doing a crossword. He says he's addicted to them and that when he dies he wants his epitaph to be in the form of a crossword clue: *No longer with us (4 letters)*.

"Hey, Tony." I go over to the counter. "I was just wondering if you had any other paper rounds available."

He puts down his crossword and looks at me from beneath his bushy white eyebrows. I love Tony's eyebrows. They're so expressive it's like they're creatures in their own right, who just happen to live on Tony's forehead.

"Your timing is exquisite, my dear!" he booms. Tony used to be a Shakespearean actor and he still projects like he's on a West End stage. "The young man who delivers to Malling during the week has just quit."

"Malling?" My heart sinks. Malling is an estate on the other side of town. I had been hoping to get something a little closer to home, but beggars can't be choosers and right now I'm practically the dictionary definition of beggar.

"Yes. Do you fancy it?"

"Please."

Tony's eyebrows fold down into a frown. "But what about your weekend round?"

"I still want to do that too."

"Seven days a week? Are you sure?"

I nod. "I need the money."

Tony's eyebrows return to their default position. "Well, I have to say I admire your work ethic. Shame more young-sters today don't take after you."

"Thank you." Something about the way he's smiling at me reminds me of Dad and the way he used to smile when he lis-tened to me play the guitar. I look away, at the rows of sweets lining the counter.

Tony picks up the big ledger containing all the details of the paper rounds. "So when can you start?"

"As soon as possible."

"How about tomorrow?"

"That would be great."

"Wonderful! Come in ten minutes early and I'll talk you through the route."

I try not to think about how early this is going to be. "Thanks, Tony."

"No problem." He picks up his crossword. "Now, I don't suppose you can help me with six across. I've been stuck on it for half an hour."

"Sure. What is it?"

"Female domestic servant. Six letters, beginning with *s*."

"Skivvy?" I reply. The irony isn't lost on me.

All the way home I focus on the extra money I'm going to be earning to stop myself from stressing about Mum and her benefits. At least now I know that we'll have regular money for food. And, if Mum's payments don't get cut, I might even be able to start saving for a guitar again.

I let myself into the cottage and see that the living-room door is open. Mum's sitting in the old armchair by the window. Although she's still in her dressing gown, her hair is freshly washed and brushed and she's reading a book. I breathe a small sigh of relief.

"Hey, Mum."

"Hi, Stevie." She puts her book down and looks at me anxiously. "Did you call them?"

"Yes." I perch on the edge of the sofa. "But they, uh, they said you had to call."

Mum's face falls. "What? Why?"

"I don't know. They said that they had to speak to you

personally. But don't worry, I'm sure it'll be fine." I take the letter from my pocket. "Why don't you call them now?"

"I don't have any credit on my phone."

"Use mine." I take my mobile from my bag and hand it to her. "And I have some good news," I say, desperate to halt the gloom that's rapidly filling the room. "I have a new paper round – for during the week as well as weekends. So that'll mean more money." I look at her hopefully but if anything this news only seems to make her more stressed.

"What do I do? Who do I call?" she says, frowning at the letter.

"Just call the number at the top. You need to press two when you get through – for the benefits office – and then you might be put on hold for a bit, but don't worry, someone will answer." I really hope she gets somebody less blunt than I did this morning. "Shall I make you a cup of tea?"

"What?" She looks at me blankly, like I'm speaking in a foreign language. I hate it when she gets this stressed.

"A cup of tea? Do you want me to make you one?"

"No!" she snaps.

"Right." I feel tears prickling at the corners of my eyes. *No! You mustn't cry!* I hurry from the room and upstairs. I fling myself on my bed. *Don't break. Don't break. Don't break,* I tell myself. *You can't break. You have to be the unbroken one.* I shut my eyes tight to stop the tears from coming. *Anne Frank, Malala, Stevie Nicks, Hafiz.*

After football training I'm starving and tired. But for once it's a good tired because it's my body that's exhausted, not my mind. As I let myself in the front door I hear the low murmur of Uncle Samir and Aunt Maria chatting in the kitchen.

"Hello," Uncle Samir says, looking up from his laptop as I join them. "How did school go?"

I dump my bag on the floor and sit down beside him at the table. "It was OK."

Aunt Maria pours me a cup of fresh mint tea.

"And how was football training?" Uncle Samir asks.

"Good."

"Did you play OK?"

"I think so. I've been picked for the team."

"You have?" Uncle Samir's face lights up.

"That's great," Aunt Maria says with a smile. "Well done!"

"Thank you." Even though I know I shouldn't, even though I know I don't deserve it, this makes me feel good.

"I was wondering if you'd like to come to the mosque with

me this evening," Uncle Samir says. I notice him and Aunt Maria exchanging glances.

I shake my head. "No, thanks."

"Are you sure?" Uncle Samir stares at me intently. "It might help you."

"Help me what?" My shoulders tense. Why is he asking me this now? He knows I'm not interested. He hardly ever goes to mosque anyway.

"Get closer to God."

I have to bite my lip to stop myself from laughing. Closer to the God who allows so much hatred and violence? Closer to the God who tears families apart? No, thank you. "I'm sorry. I'm really tired after football."

Uncle Samir nods. "OK. No problem. In that case you can help me with something."

"What?"

"We need to come up with ways to raise money for the library at the refugee centre, so that we can buy some books."

"Couldn't we ask people to donate books?" I ask, adding a spoonful of sugar to my tea and taking a sip.

"We could – and we are – for English books. But it would be good to get some books from the refugees' countries, by their favourite writers. To help them feel more at home."

Again, I have to stop myself from laughing. It takes a lot more than books to make a person feel at home. Then I have a flashback to the night on the boat, and the leather-bound collection of poetry by my namesake – the Persian poet

Hafiz – being swept from my grasp into the raging sea. My dad gave me the book the day I left. It was his most treasured possession. And it was taken from me. That was the moment I gave up on God – when I realized he'd given up on me.

I look at Uncle Samir – at his broad shoulders and thick brown hair. He and my dad look so alike it hurts. It's a constant walking, talking reminder of what I'm missing. If my dad were here now he'd be full of ideas. The thought of raising money to buy books would make him so excited. I can see him now, pacing up and down the kitchen, scratching his head as he thinks, telling us a fable to demonstrate the importance of books, about a king who saved his people by telling them stories, or something. And now I can see my mum, too, standing to one side, shaking her head as if to say, *What is my husband like?* but gazing at him so lovingly.

I get to my feet – horrified I might be about to cry. "C–can I help you later?" I stammer. "I need to take a shower."

"Of course." Uncle Samir nods and looks back to his laptop.

"Dinner will be ready in about an hour," Aunt Maria says.

"Great," I reply. But I've completely lost my appetite.

Up in my uncle and aunt's guest room I take my phone from my bag and lie down on the bed. I still don't have a reply from Aahil. I click on to my Google account and start writing my daily email to Dad. I've done this since I arrived in the UK and got my new phone. I don't bother WhatsApping or texting him. He doesn't have a smartphone and I don't even know if his old phone is still working. So I send emails in the hope that at some point he'll be able to log on to his account and see them.

Hey Dad – and Mum!
I hope you are OK. All is good here. I got into the school football team today. I showed them how we Syrians play!

I stop typing. Unlike my message to Aahil, I tell my parents the good stuff. I don't want them to worry about me. I don't want them knowing that they shouldn't have bothered sending me here – that it was all a massive mistake. I want to make them happy.

I return to my email.

I know it must be hard to get reception where you are but if you do get the chance please send me or Uncle Samir a message, just to let us know you're OK. And tell Mum I'm really missing her. I miss you too, Dad.
Your loving son,
Hafiz

## Stevie

I can't sleep. I went to bed super early to try and compensate for the fact that I have to get up even earlier than Shriek-Beak but I ... just ... can't ... sleep. Mum went straight back up to bed after her phone call to the helpline They've told her that she has to go to her meeting with them this week; that they can't come to see her. I've offered to go with her, even though it would mean missing another day of school on my first week back, but she doesn't want to talk about it. She's burying her head in the sand – or under the duvet – again.

I sit up in bed and stare out of the window. It's just gone eight. The sky is turning inky blue. What if Mum doesn't go to her reassessment? What if they stop her payments? What will we do? We could end up being kicked out of the cottage. I think of the homeless people who sleep in the shop doorways in Lewes and I feel sick. I picture Priya and her friends walking past me and Mum huddled together outside Boots, next to an old hat of loose change. I imagine Priya kicking the hat away and laughing. I get up and go over to the window. I need to do something to snap me out of this mood. I look at my *Little Book of Big Song Wisdom*, flicking through it for a song that might help me. But I draw a blank. Surprisingly, SONGS FOR THE SOON-TO-BE-HOMELESS weren't all that popular back when my dad was a teen. *You have your extra paper round,* I remind myself. *You'll be earning more money.* But my paper-round money will never pay all the bills.

I start pacing my bedroom, but that only makes me feel worse, like I'm more trapped. I sit on my bed and look at the Punk Jesus stain on the wall, hoping I might get inspiration for a song. But nothing. Then, when I can't take any more, I pull on a pair of jeans and a sweatshirt and quietly creep downstairs.

Outside in the twilight, the birds are singing their final song of the day. I head downhill, to the end of our street, then into the garden of the Grange. The Grange is an old stately home that was built back in 1500 or something. It has the most beautiful walled gardens, which are open to the public. I often come here when I want to write a new song. It's a great place to come and think. I walk slowly around the flower beds, drinking in the colours. During the day the gardens can get packed, but now I'm the only one here. I imagine it's my own private garden. What must it be like to be rich enough to own a garden this size? How is it fair that some people have so much – and other people, like me and Mum, have virtually nothing?

I follow the footpath through the gardens and out of the gate on the other side. Now what? I head away towards the junction just before the station. Lansdown Place – the road where Hafiz lives – is right in front of me. Men in work suits with undone shirt collars and loosened ties are spilling out of the pub on the corner, talking loudly. I cross over and start walking down the road. I wonder which house Hafiz lives in. Part of me wishes he'd appear from one of them right now. Another, bigger, part of me doesn't. It would definitely look like I'm stalking him. And twice would be pushing my luck.

I follow the road down and around, until the tall thin houses turn into a row of shops. I walk past the art gallery and the printers and the barber's shop. And then I hear the loud strum of a guitar coming from the record shop at the end of the parade. But it doesn't sound like a recording. As I quicken my pace I hear a woman start to sing. It's live! There's some kind of gig going on.

The record shop is packed with people. I ease the door open and slip inside. Nobody notices me. Everyone's watching the woman who's singing at the front of the shop, next to the counter. She has long, flame-red hair and she's wearing a tight denim shirt and jeans, with a red bandana and cowboy boots. I don't usually like country music but her voice is so smooth and velvety and the way she's playing slide guitar is mesmerizing. As I study the way she moves the slide up and down the strings my fingers twitch like they want to join in.

*"Why do you hurt me like you do?"* the woman croons into

the microphone. *"You make me feel all smoky blue."* Her full lips are painted dark red.

I stand at the back of the shop, watching her sing song after song. She's called Lauren LaPorte and she's from Nashville in America, which makes her seem even more exotic. As I watch I imagine that I *am* her; that I have left school and Lewes and I travel the world with my guitar, playing one-woman gigs in all kinds of random places. My skin tingles at how amazing this would be – how free I would feel. Finally, Lauren stops playing and Simon, the owner of the record store, asks us to give her a round of applause. I clap so hard my hands burn – and not just because of Lauren LaPorte's awesome singing but because she's given me a spark of hope for the future. She's made me see how bright it could be. She's made me see that there's life beyond school and the cottage and Lewes. She's made me see that my music isn't just a hobby – maybe, just maybe, it could be my ticket out of here.

I'm about to slip out of the shop when Simon notices me.

"Stevie, come here!" he calls.

Suddenly I feel guilty. Was I supposed to buy a ticket? Will he ask me to pay? I slink over, feeling really self-conscious. "Hi, Simon, I was – er – just passing and I heard the music so I thought I'd pop in."

"That's great." Simon turns to Lauren, who's signing one of her CDs. "Lauren, I'd like you to meet Stevie. She's one of my regular customers and an awesome guitarist too."

"Oh, I – I don't know about that," I stammer. Simon

sometimes sells guitars in his shop and one time he let me try one. I played "Hurt" by Johnny Cash, which turned out to be one of his all-time favourite songs … which is probably why I made such a lasting impression.

"Hey there." Lauren treats me to one of her beautiful smiles. Her teeth are bright white against the dark red of her lips. "Always good to meet a fellow muso."

"Oh, I – I'm not really a muso. I don't really…" I'm so in awe of her it's like I'm standing in front of Stevie Nicks. She's making me stammer like a fool. "I – I loved your songs."

"Thank you!" Lauren offers me the CD. "Would you like one?"

"Oh – er – no, I – I don't have any money on me, sorry. I was just passing and I didn't realize you'd be here and…"

Simon grins. "Stevie's more of a vinyl kind of girl, anyway."

Lauren smiles. "No way! That's awesome. And your name's awesome too."

OK, what is going on?! I seem to have been teleported into some kind of mind-bending parallel universe where one of the coolest singers I've ever seen is telling me that *I* am awesome!

"Thank you. I was named after my mum's hero, Stevie Nicks."

"Seriously?" Lauren's eyes light up. "She's my hero too. Here …" – she presses the CD into my hand – "take it. It's a gift."

"But…"

"'Rooms on Fire' is one of my all-time favourite songs," Lauren continues.

"Mine too!" I squeak like a total fangirl. "I loved your slide guitar," I add.

"Thank you. You ever play slide before?"

I shake my head. "I'd love to though."

She reaches into her guitar case and pulls out a slide. It's shiny and rose-gold and looks brand new. "Here, why don't you have my spare?"

"What? Oh no. I couldn't. I mean, won't you need it?"

She laughs. "Don't worry, I have loads."

I take the slide from her, hold it in the palm of my hand. "Thank you. Thank you so much."

"If you want a real mellow tone the trick is in the muting," she says, picking up her guitar and slide. "Like this, see." I watch as she places a finger behind the slide, muting the string.

"Cool. Thank you."

"Uh-huh." Lauren puts her guitar down and gives me a hug. She smells of a rich, musky perfume. "It was lovely meeting you, Stevie. You keep hold of that music dream, ya hear?"

"Don't worry. I will!"

Lauren turns to greet the queue of people waiting to have their CDs signed.

Somehow I manage to stammer goodbye to Simon and make my way through the crowded shop and out into the street.

I stand beneath the glow of a street light and look at the CD and the slide in disbelief. I feel like a musical version of Cinderella … who just met her country-and-western fairy godmother.

# HAFIZ

Ever since dinner I've been lying on my bed, slowly driving myself mad, checking and rechecking my phone for a message from Aahil or my dad. Finally, when I feel as if my head is going to explode from frustration, I get up and look out of the window and there is Stevie. There she *is*, standing in the orange glow of the street light, staring at something in her hand. And she's really smiling. More than I've ever seen her smile before. But why? What is she doing? I pull a hoodie on over my T-shirt and tracksuit bottoms and quietly make my way downstairs. Uncle Samir and Aunt Maria have just started watching a comedy movie. I can hear the rapid-fire of Jim Carrey's voice followed by their laughter. I open the front door without making a sound and slip outside. Stevie is still there but she's putting whatever she was looking at into her pocket and looks as if she might be about to leave.

I cross the narrow street. "Hey," I say softly.

"Hafiz!"

It's the first time I've seen her without her black eye make-up. She looks younger, softer, and her eyes are even greener.

"What are you doing?" I ask.

"Oh, I – I've just been to a gig," she replies. "In the record shop." She points to the store at the end of the row opposite my aunt and uncle's house. "It was amazing!" Her face is lit up. "The woman who was singing gave me one of her CDs and this." She pulls a pinky-gold metal tube from her pocket. "It's a slide – for the guitar. You put in on your finger to change the pitch of the strings. It makes an amazing sound."

"That's so cool." But all I can think is, *Stevie* is so cool. The way she plays the guitar and goes to gigs. It's so weird that she doesn't seem to have any friends at school. Maybe she hangs around with other people outside of school. Maybe that's who she went to the gig with. I look up and down the road but, apart from a couple of adults coming out of the record shop, there's no one about.

"Where are you off to?" Stevie asks, putting the slide back in her pocket.

"Nowhere. I was just – I was looking out of my bedroom window and I saw you standing there. I thought I would come and say hello." I cringe. Does that sound really lame? Does it make me sound like a weirdo?

"Oh. Right." She smiles. "I think I might be living in a parallel universe."

"A what?"

"Nothing." She looks embarrassed. "It's nice to see you."

"Yes, you too." This is starting to feel really awkward and

I'm beginning to wish I'd never come out. At the far end of the street a drunken guy is stumbling from the pub. He clatters into a rubbish bin and veers off into the kerb—

"Hafiz!"

I jump at the sound of Uncle Samir's voice. He's standing, silhouetted, in the doorway of his house.

"It's my uncle," I mutter to Stevie. "Hi, Uncle Samir!" I call back to him, like it's the most normal thing in the world for me to be standing outside in the dark, talking to a girl.

"What are you doing?" he calls.

"Just chatting to a friend," I say. Now I really wish I hadn't come out. Could this get any more embarrassing? Yes, clearly it could, as Aunt Maria joins Uncle Samir in the doorway.

"Hafiz! Thank goodness you're all right," she cries.

"You should have told us you were leaving the house," Uncle Samir says. "We're just going to make some popcorn. We wanted to know if you'd like some."

My entire body is now crawling with shame. "I'd better go," I say to Stevie.

"Why don't you invite your friend in?" Maria calls. "Would she like some popcorn?"

"Oh. I – uh – I don't know." I turn to face Stevie, trying to block their view. "It's OK, you really don't have to," I whisper.

"Oh." She looks disappointed.

"Unless you want to?"

Stevie grins. "OK."

I turn back to Uncle Samir and Aunt Maria. "OK!" I say,

gesturing awkwardly in the direction of the door. In my head I see my dad throwing up his hands in horror at the fact that my knowledge of the English language seems to have become limited to a single word. I take a deep breath and follow Stevie into the house.

# Stevie

It's official. I *have* entered a mind-bending parallel universe where things actually go right for me. Not only have I just met the coolest singer ever but it turns out I'm also now somebody's friend! Hafiz said so and so did his uncle and aunt – although they were just copying what he said, so obviously that doesn't count – but anyway, Hafiz said that I was his friend. And now I'm in his kitchen. And his aunt's making popcorn and his uncle's talking about Jim Carrey and I have to keep pinching myself to make sure I'm not dreaming.

Hafiz pulls one of the chairs out from under the table and offers it to me. "Would you like to sit down?"

"Sure."

I sit down and glance at the clock on the wall. It's almost nine thirty. Not that it matters. It's not as if Mum ever comes to check on me. I feel a sting of resentment as I think of how worried Hafiz's uncle and aunt looked when he'd gone missing from his room. And how relieved they were to find him on the street, talking to me. But then, after what he's been through to get here, I guess it must have made them extra protective.

"Would you like an apple juice?" Hafiz's Aunt Maria asks me. She looks really nice and smiley. And she's wearing fleecy pyjamas covered in cartoon dogs, which I'm hoping is an ironic thing, as she has to be about forty.

"Yes, please." The smell of the freshly popping corn is delicious and triggers a rumbling deep in my stomach. I only had beans on toast for dinner and I'm suddenly starving.

"So, you two are in the same class at school?" Hafiz's uncle says. He has the same accent as Hafiz but not as strong.

"Yes." Hafiz sits down next to me and runs his hand through his hair. He seems pretty stressed for some reason. I hope that reason isn't me.

"We sit next to each other in class," I say.

"I see." Samir looks at me. His eyes are big and dark brown. He looks really kind and wise.

There's an awkward moment of silence, thankfully broken by Maria placing a large bowl of popcorn on the table.

"Here you are," she says. "And here are your drinks." She puts two glasses of apple juice down in front of us. "OK, Samir, shall we leave them to it and get back to our film?"

Samir thinks for a moment, then nods. "But no more disappearing acts," he says to Hafiz.

"OK," Hafiz mutters. "Sorry about that," he says to me as soon as his uncle and aunt have gone.

"Why? They're really nice." I take a handful of popcorn. It's still warm and it tastes delicious.

"So, do you go to many gigs?" Hafiz asks.

I nearly choke on my popcorn. If only! "No, not really. Tonight was – well, it was a bit of an accident, actually."

"How do you mean?"

"I hadn't planned to go there. I just went out for a walk and thought I'd try doing that thing we did in Brighton the other day, you know, the following-your-heart thing? And I ended up coming down this road and I heard the music, so I thought I'd investigate."

"That is very cool." Thankfully Hafiz is smiling – and not in a mocking way. "My dad's story was right. Great things happen when you follow your heart."

"Yes, yes, they do—" But before I can say anything more, Hafiz's uncle bursts through the door.

"Hafiz!" he cries, holding out his phone. "It's Tariq. I've heard from Tariq!"

# HAFIZ

My fingers tremble as I take the phone. Can it really be true? I'm expecting to see a text message but the screen shows that it's a call. A call! I bring the phone to my ear.

"Dad?" The word comes out more like a gasp.

"Hafiz! My son! Oh, thanks be to God!"

"Dad." I crumple forwards, like a balloon deflating. "Where are you? How are you?"

"My son!" he says again. And even though the line is faint, I can hear that he's crying.

"Are you OK? And Mum? Is Mum OK?"

"Yes, my son, my Hafiz. We are OK."

Aunt Maria comes into the room, stands behind Uncle Samir and puts her arms around his waist. I take a deep breath. "Where are you, Dad?"

"We are in Athens."

My heart nearly stops beating. "What? Where?"

"Athens."

"But Athens is in – it's in Greece!" I look around the room just to make sure that I'm not mistaken and that Athens isn't actually in Syria. But Uncle Samir and Aunt Maria are nodding.

"Yes. We are on the same continent. Thanks to God."

"But how – how did you get there? What about Grandma? Can I speak to Mum?"

"I will explain all soon, Hafiz. I can't talk for long. We are in a refugee camp. I've had to borrow someone's phone. I just needed to hear your voice. Find out how you are doing."

"I'm good, Dad. I love you, Dad." I don't care that the others are here. Mum and Dad are alive – they're no longer in Syria. My eyes fill with tears.

"I love you too, son. Can I speak with Samir again? I promise I will call again soon."

"Of course. Oh, Dad?"

"Yes?"

"I've been doing what you told me. I've been searching for my story."

There's a moment's silence, then: "And have you found it?"

"No. Not yet. But I will keep looking."

"Oh, Hafiz…" I'm not sure if it's the line breaking up or Dad's voice. "You make me so proud."

"Thanks, Dad. Speak to you soon."

"Bye, my son."

I hand the phone to Uncle Samir. He starts talking to Dad and leaves the room. Aunt Maria follows him. I wipe the tears from my face but they just keep on coming. For so long

I've been so worried, thinking of Mum and Dad trapped in Syria, trying not to think the worst. And now they're free. They're free!

Stevie is looking at me, confused, and I realize she wouldn't have understood a word of my conversation with Dad.

"My parents – they're in Greece," I say, tears still sliding down my face. I know I should feel embarrassed, crying like this, but I don't. My relief outweighs everything. They're alive! Mum and Dad are alive. And they're in Europe.

"That's amazing." Stevie smiles. "And you didn't know they'd left Syria?"

"No. I hadn't heard from them for weeks. None of us had. They'd been hiding in the mountains, where there's no phone reception. I had no idea that they'd left."

Stevie's eyes widen. "It must have been so scary."

"Yes. Syria is a very scary place now. They must have been through hell."

"No, I meant for you. It must have been so scary not knowing how or where they were."

"It was." I blink away my tears. It feels so nice to have someone who understands how I've been feeling. It makes me want to cry even more, but I can't, I have to pull myself together. I go over to the fridge and take out the juice. "I bet you didn't expect all of this to happen when you followed your heart tonight."

Stevie laughs. "I didn't really expect anything that's happened tonight." She stands up. "I should go."

"Oh. Why?"

"You probably want to be with your family – talk about what's happened."

"No. I like it, you being here. And anyway, I need you to celebrate with me." I top up her glass of juice. Now she'll have to stay a bit longer.

"OK then, if you're sure." She sits back down and raises her glass. "To refound parents."

I clink my glass against hers. "Yes! To refound parents." I notice that her smile has faded slightly. I wonder if she's thinking about her dad. I wonder what's happened to her dad; why she doesn't see him.

"So, will your parents be coming to the UK too?" Stevie asks.

"Yes. I guess so. I hope so." My heart sinks as I think of how hard it was for me to get here – all of the legal hoops Uncle Samir had to jump through. But I got here in the end. And my parents will too. They have to. Tonight is not a night for doubt. Tonight is a night for celebration. They're alive!

Uncle Samir returns to the kitchen. "So, what do you know, Tariq is in Greece," he says with a grin.

I smile back at him – and I have to stop myself from saying, "thanks to God".

## Stevie

I lie in bed and gaze up at the ceiling, slowly going over everything that happened this evening like I'm revising for a test – a test in the subject of miracles. I've left the curtain wide open and an almost-full moon is casting its silvery glow across my bed. It's the perfect end to a perfect night. I ended up staying at Hafiz's until ten thirty, then he and Samir walked me home. They insisted on walking me right to my door, which was a little bit stressful, as I suddenly panicked that Mum might have needed something in the night and discovered I was missing. But when we arrived the cottage was silent and dark, as usual. I crept up to bed and I've been lying here ever since, reliving every magical moment. I have to get up in five hours for my paper round but I don't care.

I don't feel quite so excited when my alarm goes off at six. And I feel even less excited when I arrive at the Malling estate, laden down with an extra-heavy bag of papers. The strap is cutting into my shoulder like a blade. I wonder if Lauren LaPorte ever had to do a paper round. I picture her riding around an American neighbourhood on a bike, humming

145

country-and-western tunes and slinging rolled-up papers onto vast manicured lawns. I wish I was delivering papers in America right now instead of Lewes. It turns out the Malling estate is full of flats. And it turns out that just about everyone living on the top floors wants their papers delivered. I made the mistake of wearing my school uniform to save time, but, after an hour of running up and down stairs and searching for the right numbers, I'm hot and sweaty and desperate for a shower. But I barely have time to return the bag to Tony's shop and race home to get my school stuff.

I arrive at school late and hot and flustered. My stupid buttonless shirt is stuck to my back with sweat. I need to get to Lost Property as soon as possible to get another one to change into so I don't have to wear a jumper all day. I hurry into the form room and take my seat next to Hafiz. As soon as he grins at me I remember last night and instantly feel better.

"What are you doing this evening?" Hafiz whispers as Miss Kepinski searches her desk drawers for some information about a school outing.

"This evening?" I echo back, too surprised to be able to come up with an answer.

"Yes. After school."

"Oh. I – uh – nothing. Why?"

"My uncle and aunt wanted to know if you would like to come to Brighton with us – for dinner."

"Oh." My heart lifts and immediately sinks. Dinner equals money – money I don't have. "I don't know."

Hafiz looks at his lap and down falls his curtain of hair. "That's OK. Don't worry about it."

"No, it's not that I don't want to… It's just that … I don't have much money at the moment."

Hafiz sweeps his hair back from his face and frowns at me. "Why would you need money?"

"For dinner."

He smiles. "Oh no, my aunt and uncle have invited you. You are to be their guest. You won't have to pay. And anyway, we're only going to Sanctuary by the Sea."

"What's that?"

"A centre – for refugees. They have a café there." He suddenly looks embarrassed. "Seriously you do not have to come if you don't want to."

"I do want to."

"Really?" He studies my face as if to make sure I'm not lying.

"Yes. Thank you for inviting me."

"That is OK."

I lean back in my chair feeling hot and stressed but also excited. Hafiz has asked me to come out with him after school. I actually have something to look forward to – or I will do, as soon as I get my sweaty shirt sorted.

The bell rings for first period.

"I'll meet you in the classroom," I say to Hafiz. "I just have to go to the – uh – toilet."

"Sure."

I pick up my bag and hurry out.

Lost Property is kept in a store cupboard down by the school office. The door of the office is open when I get there but I knock on it anyway.

"Yes!" one of the administrative assistants, Mrs Barber, barks, while still staring at her computer screen.

*You can do this, just play it cool, and remember your lines*, I tell myself. "Oh, hello, I was just wondering if I could take a look in Lost Property."

"What for?" she snaps, still frowning at her computer.

In all the time I've been at this school I've never once seen Mrs Barber smile. I take a step into the room. "Oh, yes, sorry. I didn't mean I just fancied a look in Lost Property, like I'm some kind of Lost Property tourist, like I just..." *Get a grip!* I tell myself. "I – I lost a school shirt. At the end of last year," I mutter. "After PE."

Mrs Barber sighs and gets to her feet. Has she seen through my lies? Has she realized that I'm about to commit Lost Property theft? Is she about to march me off to the head teacher's office? But she takes a set of keys from a hook on the wall. "Follow me," she mutters.

I follow her across the corridor to the Lost Property cupboard and wait while she unlocks the door. "Shirts are in the box on the bottom shelf," she says, before turning and heading back to the office.

I breathe a sigh of relief that she won't be watching me, then I start rifling through the tangled mess of shirts. Some of them are torn and some are stained and look even worse than the one I'm wearing. But then I find one at the bottom. It's snowy white and crisp and all the buttons are intact. They have a really pretty pearl effect too. I hold the shirt up to check its size. It looks as if it would fit me perfectly. I quickly check the label. There's no sign of any student's name. The label is from a shop I've never heard of before – called Amelie. Excitement and relief start doing a celebratory jig inside me.

"Any luck?" Mrs Barber calls from the office.

"Yes." I take the shirt over, hugging it to me. "I can't believe it's here. I never thought I'd see it again."

Mrs Barber looks at me weirdly.

"Sorry. It – it's just that I was very attached to this shirt," I stammer.

She purses her thin lips together. "Clearly."

"So, do I need to do anything?" My heart starts pounding. Surely it can't be this easy?

Mrs Barber is looking back at her screen again. "Like what?"

"I don't know, like sign anything?"

She looks at me with disdain. "No." She glances at her watch. "Haven't you got a class to go to?"

"Yes." I start backing out of the room. "Thank you. Bless you." *Bless you?!* my inner voice screams. *Bless you?!* "Sorry, I didn't mean to say 'bless you'. I meant… I'm just very happy to have my shirt back."

Mrs Barber shakes her head and sighs, then starts tapping away on her computer again. I race from the room before she puts me in detention for Lost Property lunacy.

Stevie and I are sitting in the back of Uncle Samir's car. I'm trying not to look at her because every time I do I want to smile and I'm worried that I'll seem like some kind of crazy person. Ever since I found out that Mum and Dad are safe it's like someone's opened the door on the darkened room the world had become and light is pouring in. Everything makes me smile. The sunshine, the birds, the Arabic music playing on the car stereo. And looking at Stevie. I'm not sure why looking at Stevie is making me feel happy. It could be the funny things she says. Or the way she doesn't fit in – or even try to. I glance at the outfit she's wearing – a black and white T-shirt advertising a music band called Tears for Fears, tight black jeans, torn at the knee, and black boots with a row of silver buckles on the sides. I look at her long black hair falling loose over her shoulders and her matching black fingernails. I feel my mouth curling into a smile and quickly look away.

We pull up at the refugee centre and Aunt Maria turns to Stevie from the front passenger seat. "I hope you're hungry," she says. "I was down here earlier and the Ethiopian and

Eritrean women were planning a feast."

Stevie nods. "Yes. I'm starving. Thank you. Thank you for inviting me." She looks really shy all of a sudden, which makes me like her even more.

We get out of the car and head over to the open back door. The smell of food cooking drifts over to greet us and my stomach rumbles.

"Have you ever had Ethiopian food before?" I ask Stevie.

She shakes her head.

"It's really good."

"Yes," Uncle Samir says, rubbing his stomach appreciatively. "You're in for a treat."

The kitchen is a hive of activity, with women bustling about, attending to the steaming pots and sizzling pans on the stove. African music is playing loudly from a portable CD player in the corner.

"Hello. Good evening! Hello, Miss Maria," an Eritrean woman called Adiam greets us, her hips swaying in time with the beat. She's wearing a bright orange and red dress, with a matching scarf twisted around her head.

"Hi, Adiam!" Aunt Maria calls back. "It smells delicious in here."

"Yes." Uncle Samir nods in agreement. "Any chance of a taste?" He pretends to dip his finger in one of the pots.

Adiam flicks him with her tea towel and laughs one of her deep laughs. "Get away! You are just like Goldilocks and the porridge!"

Uncle Samir has been teaching Adiam English, using kids' books. Her favourite story is *Goldilocks and the Three Bears*. It inspired her to learn how to make porridge, which she now serves every morning in the café for breakfast, with a sprinkle of brown sugar and cinnamon on top. It's delicious.

Stevie is looking round the kitchen, her black-rimmed eyes wide. I wonder what she thinks of this place. I hope she likes it.

"Shall we go through to the café?" I suggest.

"Yes, before Adiam throttles Samir with that tea towel," Aunt Maria says, laughing.

"Hurry up!" Uncle Samir calls over his shoulder as we leave. "You have four very hungry bears to feed here."

We go through the kitchen and out of the door leading into the café.

"Oh, wow!" Stevie exclaims as she looks around at the brightly painted murals on the walls.

The murals were Uncle Samir's idea, with a different section for each of the different homelands of the refugees who come here. By the time I got to the UK the mural was already complete, but I helped to add a picture of a footballer beneath the Syrian flag.

"What's that?" Stevie says, pointing to the other side of the large room, to the empty shelves.

"That's going to be the library," I reply.

"Yes. And we need you two to help us come up with

some money-raising ideas so we can buy some books," Uncle Samir says.

"Cool." Stevie says. She looks genuinely enthusiastic.

We all sit down at a table near the back of the café.

"Do you think there's anything you could do at your school?" Aunt Maria asks. "To try and raise some money?"

My heart sinks. Although I want to help I really don't want to draw attention to the fact that I'm a refugee – especially not at school. "I don't know."

Stevie looks thoughtful. "We could try. But it might be best to speak to one of the teachers about it. I'm not sure how much Hafiz and I would be able to do on our own."

Uncle Samir nods. "OK. Yes, I'll email your teacher tomorrow."

I lean back in my chair and look away. I suddenly feel queasy, like there's a family of snakes writhing around in my stomach. I don't want him to email my teacher. I don't want a big fuss being made. But what can I say? I can hardly stop him from trying to help refugees – trying to help people like me.

## Stevie

I watch as the African lady, Adiam, comes out from the kitchen holding a huge tray laden with food. She places the tray on our table. It's full of steaming dishes of different kinds of stews, plus a bowl of green, leafy vegetables and a plate piled high with what look like pancakes.

Samir helps place the dishes on the table.

"OK, Daddy Bear," Adiam says to him with a chuckle. "Now you may eat."

Samir laughs and nods. "Thank you – it looks wonderful."

Adiam's face goes serious for a moment. "No, thank *you*, Samir, for all you have done." She turns and smiles at the rest of us. "Thank you. Thank you."

I feel slightly embarrassed as I haven't done anything. But as she's so nice it makes me doubly determined to help raise money for this place. I wonder what we could do at school to help. Maybe we could arrange some kind of sponsored event. Maybe we could sponsor Priya to be silent for a week. I'd give all of my paper-round money to make that happen. I can't help grinning at the thought.

"What's funny?" Hafiz says.

"Nothing. I was just thinking of ways we could raise money at school."

"Oh." I could be wrong but Hafiz doesn't look all that interested.

"OK, guys, tuck in," Maria says.

I look around the table for some cutlery but there isn't any. "Shall I go and get some knives and forks?" I ask.

Hafiz shakes his head. "No, we're eating Ethiopian-style, with our fingers."

"With our fingers?" I look at the bowls of stew, and picture dipping my hands into them, trying to fish out some food. Somehow I don't see this ending well.

"Yes, with the *injera*," Samir explains, taking one of the pancake things from the pile and tearing off a bit. "*Injera* is Ethiopian bread." He dips the bread into one of the bowls, scoops out some stew and pops it into his mouth. "Mmm! You have to try the *doro wat*, it's delicious."

"*Doro wat* is like a chicken stew," Hafiz says to me. "It is really good."

"Great." I tear off some of the bread, then look back at the dishes. There only seems to be one of the chicken stew. Are we all supposed to share it? "Do we … is it OK to take some from here too?" I ask, gesturing at the same bowl Samir is eating from.

"Of course." Samir moves the bowl closer to me.

"It's an Ethiopian tradition for everyone to eat from the

same dish," Hafiz explains. "They believe that if people share food now, they won't betray each other later."

"Cool." I dunk my piece of bread into the stew and fish out a piece of chicken. It tastes amazing, really spicy and gingery. "Are the women who cooked this – are they all refugees?"

Maria nods. "Yes. We have women from all over the world working in the kitchen. It's a lovely thing for them to do together. When they first came here none of them could speak English – or each other's languages – but since they've started cooking together it's like they've bonded for life."

"The universal language of food," Samir says with a grin, scooping what looks like a hard-boiled egg from the stew.

"You wouldn't believe what some of them have been through to get here," Maria says. "Adiam, the lady who served us, had to travel through the desert for weeks to escape the war in her country. Her father gave up all of his life savings to pay the people smugglers to help her escape."

"And when the authorities found out she had gone they killed him," Samir says, his face suddenly grave.

"What?" I put down the piece of bread I'd been holding. "Why? Why would they kill him?"

"As a punishment and a deterrent," Samir says. "To try and stop other people from sending their loved ones to safety."

"But that's..." I can't even find the words to describe how horrible this is. I think of Adiam and how cheerfully she greeted us, while all the time masking this huge tragedy.

"Maybe we should talk about something happier," Hafiz says to Samir and Maria.

I think of what he must have been through to get here and what he's going through, so far from his family and home. It feels as if my heart is splintering apart. Why is there so much pain in the world?

"Yes, sorry," Samir says, offering me the dish of vegetables. "We didn't mean to depress you. It's just so important that British people know what's going on in the rest of the world." He gestures around the café, which is now filling up. "The struggles these people have been through."

"You didn't depress me," I say. "You've made me feel determined – determined to do something to help."

Samir looks at me and smiles. "Thank you, Stevie."

Next to me Hafiz shifts in his seat and smiles at me, his turquoise eyes shiny.

I think something's up. No, scrap that. I *know* something's up. Tonight, after we dropped Stevie at her house and came back home, I overheard Uncle Samir and Aunt Maria talking in the kitchen. "We can't tell him," I heard Aunt Maria say. "Not yet."

They must have been talking about me. What other "him" could it be? I wasn't able to hear any more because Uncle Samir opened the door and saw me standing there. He immediately said, "Yes, that's a good idea. I'll go and get the book," which didn't make any sense. He was obviously making something up to change the subject. But why? What don't they want to tell me?

I go over to my bedroom window and stare out at the night sky. The stars shine so brightly here in Lewes. They're blinking away at me, like diamonds. *Did I ever tell you the story about the king who was so greedy he once sent his bravest warrior on a mission to catch some stars?* I hear my dad say. I open the window and inhale a deep breath of the cool night air. At least I know that Dad isn't dead now. At least I know that when I hear his voice in my head it's from my memories and not the spirit world. But still… What is it that Uncle Samir and Aunt Maria don't want to tell me? Maybe they're worried that Mum and Dad won't be able to get asylum here. It took so long for me to get asylum – and I was classed as an unaccompanied child. But that's OK. I can go and join Mum and Dad, wherever they end up. All that matters is that we're together and we're safe from the war. But when I think about leaving the UK I feel a twinge of sorrow. After so long roaming the globe with nowhere to call home it will hurt to have to leave and start all over again. I look across the road, to the street light that Stevie magically appeared beneath last night. And it will hurt to have to lose my new friend.

## Stevie

When I get home I head upstairs and, instead of going straight to my room, I knock on Mum's door. What I saw tonight moved me so much I need to talk to someone about it.

"Yes?" Mum calls out faintly.

I go in. She's sitting up in bed, reading.

"Hey, Mum."

"Hi. Did you have a nice time?" She puts her book down.

"Yes. Well, I'm not sure if *nice* is the right word exactly."

"Where was it you went again?"

I'd told Mum exactly where I was going and with who but her depression clouds her brain in more ways than one. It makes her so forgetful – especially when it comes to me.

"To a centre for refugees in Brighton. It was amazing. There are people there from all over the world. And they so badly need our help, Mum. They've been through some terrible things."

Mum sighs. "Haven't we all."

I feel anger building in me as I think of what Adiam and Hafiz have experienced.

"But, Mum, these people have had to flee violence and war. There was one woman there whose dad had been killed for paying to send her to safety. Her dad was *killed*, Mum."

Mum sighs again. "I'm sorry, Stevie, but I can't really think about anything else right now. I'm too worried about my assessment tomorrow." She picks up a pack of tablets from her bedside cabinet. Her sleeping pills. She pops one in her mouth and takes a sip of water from the glass beside her bed. So that's it. Conversation over. I feel like grabbing her by her thin shoulders and shaking her. Telling her that she doesn't know how lucky she is. But instead I keep my anger tight inside me. I walk back out of the door and into my room. I take my photo of "Real Mum" down from the mantelpiece. I throw it in the bin. Then I shut my bedroom door, bury my head under a pillow and silently scream.

"OK, lads, listen up," Mr Kavanagh says as we all gather around him on the benches in the boys' changing room.

The other school's team have just arrived – I can hear the clatter of their football boots on the concrete outside. It sparks a fire in my belly – the old familiar desire to win.

"I've decided to make a couple of changes to the starting line-up," Mr Kavanagh says, "give our new Syrian signing a go." He looks at me and grins.

The fire in my belly grows. I've got a game!

"I'm going to play you on the left wing, Hafiz," Mr Kavanagh says.

"What?" Price glares at me. "That's where I play."

"Don't worry, Price," Mr Kavanagh says, "I'll put you on at half-time. I just want to get a look at Hafiz."

"Half-time?" Price's beady eyes shrink even smaller as he turns his glare on Mr Kavanagh. "Are you putting me on the bench?"

"Just till half-time." Mr Kavanagh claps his hands together. "Right then, let's get out there and show them what we're made of. First game back after summer's always a tough one – especially if the closest you've got to a game all holiday is playing FIFA on your PlayStation." A couple of the guys snigger. "But push yourself through the pain and let's try and get three points in the bag." He turns and heads for the door. We all stand up and file out after him. I feel someone grabbing the back of my shirt. I turn and see Price, his pointy face right in mine.

"Do yourself a favour, towel-head, and get yourself subbed or sent off ASAP."

I pull away from his grasp. "What do you mean?"

"What's up? Don't you understand English?" He's so close now I can smell his sour breath. "I don't sit on the bench for no one, do you understand? And especially not an asylum seeker." He shoves me on the shoulder and marches off.

I stand there motionless. For a moment I actually think about doing what Price says – faking an injury so he can come on and play. But then something else takes over. For months and months I've had to deal with people like Price – total strangers who hate me just because I wasn't born on the same patch of earth as them. And for months and months I've had to take it. Ignore the stares and the insults, tolerate being spat at and pushed and shoved around. But not any more. I don't have to take it any more. He has no right to tell me what to do, no right to speak to me in that way. And I'm going to show him what I think of him and his hate in the best way I can – through my feet. I take a deep breath and head outside.

# Stevie

I stand by the edge of the playing field and watch as the two teams file onto the pitch. At first I can't see Hafiz but then he appears, slightly behind the others, his hair tied back in a ponytail. It's weird because normally I'd rather watch beige paint dry than watch football, but the fact that Hafiz is playing has put a whole new slant on things. As he walks past I feel something dangerously close to excitement. I really hope he plays well.

The two teams gather in huddles around their coaches. I imagine Mr Kavanagh giving some kind of cheesy pep talk about playing for the pride of the school and country – or whatever it is football coaches say. Then the players get in their positions, Mr Kavanagh blows his whistle and the game begins. Even though I know nothing about football it doesn't take me long to realize that Hafiz is really good. He streaks up the pitch like a bullet, constantly chasing after the ball. He's so fast he makes the other players look as if they're playing in slow motion. Just a couple of minutes into the game he kicks the ball at the goal. The other team's goalkeeper only just manages to save it.

"Unlucky!" Mr Kavanagh calls.

I smile as a couple of Hafiz's teammates run over to slap him on the back. Who knew that football could be such a feel-good experience? The goalkeeper kicks the ball out and it arcs high in the air, coming down halfway up the pitch. A player from the other team gets it and starts running towards the goal. In a flash of red, Hafiz is on his tail. My heart starts pounding as I watch him race up beside the player and kick the ball out from under his feet.

"Yes!" Mr Kavanagh yells. "Lovely play."

Hafiz passes the ball to another player, then starts racing up the pitch again, calling back over his shoulder. The player passes back to Hafiz. He's still quite a way from the goal but he brings his leg back and strikes the ball hard. It goes soaring into the air, then curves round and zooms into the corner of the net.

Hafiz's team erupt in cheers. Even the players standing on the sidelines, the substitutes, join in the cheering. Except one. A boy from our class called David Price. For some reason, he's looking really angry. Hafiz disappears in a bundle of his teammates. I'm so happy for him I want to jump up and down yelling too – something I never thought I'd feel watching football!

Things continue like this for the rest of the first half – Hafiz chasing the ball all over the field, running as if his life depended on it, and being involved in every attempt at a goal. When the whistle blows for half-time the score is three–nil to Lewes High and it would have been much higher if the other team's goalkeeper hadn't been so good. I watch as Mr Kavanagh calls the team over into a huddle. I see Hafiz looking around for me and he waves and grins. I feel so proud of him. But then, as the boys break away from the huddle and grab their water bottles, David Price goes over to Hafiz and says something in his ear. Hafiz turns round and shoves him on the shoulder. Price stumbles backwards and falls onto his back. But something doesn't feel right about the way he falls. It looks too theatrical.

"Sir, Hafiz attacked me!" Price calls out to Mr Kavanagh, who has his back turned.

Mr Kavanagh goes running over. Price is still lying sprawled on the floor. But Hafiz didn't push him that hard. He's faking it. He has to be. Mr Kavanagh says something to Hafiz. Hafiz shakes his head. Then David Price says something, clutching his shoulder like he's in agony. Mr Kavanagh turns to Hafiz and looks really cross. Hafiz pulls off his football shirt and throws it down. As he marches back towards the changing rooms David Price gets to his feet, his face twisted into a sly grin.

# HAFIZ

*Do you remember the story I told you about the boy who couldn't control his temper?* Dad's voice echoes as I make my way back to the changing room. But I push the memory from my head. I don't want to think about that story.

I can't believe I just did that. I let Price win. But when he said that all Syrians were terrorists and rapists, I had to get him out of my face. I didn't even push him that hard. There's no way he should have fallen over like he did. I bet he's used to diving to try and get a free kick. I slam into the changing room and go over to my bag. Every time I blink I see the look of disappointment on Mr Kavanagh's face.

"Why did you push him, son?" he asked me.

What could I say? I'll never tell tales. So Price got what he wanted and I'm off the pitch. I should have known it was too good to be true – that I'd never fit in here. My teammates are all going to hate me and … Stevie! What about Stevie? She will have seen what happened and is going to think I'm some kind of thug. I quickly pull on my jumper and shoes and stuff my boots in my bag. Uncle Samir spent a fortune on those boots and now it'll all be for nothing. I consider climbing out of the window, trying to slip away unseen but then the door bursts open and Stevie marches in. Her face is flushed. She looks really angry. I take a deep breath, prepare myself for whatever she's about to yell at me.

"What happened?" she says. "What did he say to you?"

I pause before replying. Does this mean that she understands what happened, that she knows I was provoked?

"I saw David Price talking to you," she answers, coming over to me, "and I could tell that whatever he said wasn't nice. What was it?"

"It doesn't matter." I don't want to repeat those words, don't want to say them out loud, especially not to Stevie.

"He was totally faking that fall too," she continues, her green eyes sparking with indignation. "There's no way you pushed him hard enough. And he started grinning as soon as you left."

My anger builds again.

Stevie starts pacing up and down the middle of the changing room. "You should tell Mr Kavanagh. I can tell him what I saw too. There's no way you should be in here. You should still be out there – playing."

"No, I shouldn't. I lost my temper. I pushed a teammate."

"But he did say something horrible to you, right?"

I nod. "Can we just get out of here?"

Stevie sighs.

I head for the door and hold it open for her.

"You played brilliantly," she says, with one of her shy smiles. "I really enjoyed watching you and, trust me, that means loads, because I'm not normally the greatest fan of football, as you know. But you were easily the best player on the pitch."

My cheeks flush. "Thank you."

But as I trudge out of the changing room, my heart deflates like a burst balloon. I played brilliantly – but I threw it all away.

## *Stevie*

I get home feeling weary and drained. Hafiz barely said a word after leaving school. It was horrible to see him so dejected. And then, just when I think things can't get any worse, I walk into the cottage to find Mum sitting at the bottom of the stairs, fully dressed and in her coat, hunched over and sobbing.

"Mum! What is it? What's wrong?"

"Th–the assessment," she stammers. "The benefits assessment."

My heart sinks. I should have insisted on going with her. I shouldn't have gone in to school. I crouch down on the floor in front of her.

"Did you have a panic attack?"

She nods. Now I can see that she's trembling. I take hold of her hands. They're icy cold.

"Don't worry. I'm sure we can arrange another date. I can call tomorrow – tell them you missed the meeting because you were ill."

"I didn't miss the meeting." She pulls her hands from mine

and clasps her head. "I had a panic attack after the meeting —
on the way home."

"Oh." I lean back on my heels, trying to make sense of
things. Maybe the stress of it all caught up with her. "Well,
at least you went to the meeting. At least it's all done now."

"They're going to stop my benefits," she mutters through
her hands.

"What?"

"They're going to stop my benefits. They're going to stop
my benefits. They're going to stop my benefits." Her voice is
getting shriller and higher and she starts rocking back and
forth.

"But why?" I look at Mum's hollow face and haunted stare.
Surely anyone can see she's ill just from looking at her. "What
did they say?"

Mum keeps rocking.

"Mum! What did they say? Why are they stopping them?"

She stops rocking and hugs her knees. "They don't believe
I'm ill. I could tell. The questions they were asking. It was
like they were trying to catch me out."

"But what did they actually say about your payments?"

"They said they'd be sending a written report about our
meeting to the Department for Work and Pensions and
they'll write to me with their decision."

"Wait, so you don't actually know what their decision is
yet?"

Mum's eyes fill with tears. "Not officially, but I know what it's going to be. I know they're going to stop my payments."

*How do you know?* I want to say. But I don't want to risk upsetting her any more.

"They tricked me," she whispers.

"How?"

"They started asking about you."

"What? Why?"

"They wanted to know how I could be a good parent to you if I wasn't able to work."

"Oh, Mum." I feel sick.

"I didn't want…" Mum starts crying again. "I didn't want them to think that … I didn't want them to take you away from me, so I pretended … I pretended that I'm not as bad as I am."

For a horrible moment I don't have a clue what to say or do. I sit back, lean against the hall wall to try and ground myself. *Anne Frank. Malala. Stevie Nicks. Hafiz. You need to be strong just like them,* I tell myself. But then I think of Hafiz on the football pitch – the way he pushed David Price, how upset he was afterwards. People aren't superheroes. We all have a breaking point. I look at Mum, still rocking backwards and forwards. I take a deep breath. This is *not* my breaking point.

"It's all going to be OK," I say to her firmly. "Tomorrow I'll go online at the library and find out what to do if they do stop your payments. There must be someone who can help us and I'm going to find out who."

173

Mum looks at me through red-rimmed eyes.

"Do you want a camomile tea?" I say, getting to my feet.

She nods.

"And then shall I brush your hair?" Mum loves having her hair brushed. It always calms her down. She nods again.

"Right." I go into the kitchen and switch on the kettle. This is *not* my breaking point.

## HAFIZ

Even though I'm deliberately late for school Stevie isn't in the form room when I get there. Neither is the teacher. David Price is, though. He smirks at me as soon as I walk through the door, but I manage to stay calm. Last night, when I was lying in bed, I allowed myself to remember the story my dad told me about the boy who couldn't control his temper. He told it to me after I got a red card in a match for losing my temper with the ref. In the story the boy's father gives him a bag of nails and tells him that every time he gets angry, he has to hammer a nail into their fence. On the first day, the boy hammered over thirty nails into the fence, and it was really hard work. So, over the next few weeks, the number of nails dwindled, as the boy realized that it was easier to control his temper than spend hours hammering in the nails. His father praised him for his good work but then he made him take the nails out and look at how the fence was now covered with holes. "These are the scars your anger leaves," the father told his son. "No matter how many times you say sorry, those wounds will never properly heal."

After he told me that story I never got a red card again. I don't care what Price says, I'm not going to let him get to me.

Stevie comes rushing into the room. Her long hair is messy and she looks really flustered.

"Hey," she says, crashing down into the seat next to me.

"Hey," I reply.

"I wouldn't sit there if I was you!" Price calls out.

Stevie turns and glares at him. "Why not?"

"Haven't you seen the stories in the papers about people like him?"

I feel anger prickling beneath my skin. *Remember the story, Hafiz,* I imagine my dad saying. *Don't stoop to his level.*

I expect Stevie to turn back round but she doesn't. Instead she gets to her feet.

"What do you mean, 'people like him'?"

"Asylum seekers."

The rest of the class, who'd been chattering away, fall silent. It's a terrible silence. The kind that expects the worst.

"I'm proud to sit next to him," Stevie says. "It's way better than sitting next to a cheat."

"What did you say?" I hear the scrape of a chair and turn to see Price get to his feet. His pale face and neck are stained with angry red streaks. In a split second I'm standing too.

"I said, it's better than sitting next to a cheat," Stevie repeats clearly.

"Ooh!" Priya says from the table behind us. "Stevie's losing her temper over a boy."

"And I don't know what your problem is," Stevie hisses to her. "You of all people should understand how Hafiz feels."

"What's that supposed to mean?" Priya asks.

"I've seen people picking on you before. How can you do the same thing to someone else?"

Priya slumps back in her chair, silent for once.

"Are you calling me a cheat?" Price says, coming over to Stevie.

My fists automatically clench.

"Yes, I am," Stevie says. "I saw what you did in the football match yesterday."

"It's OK," I say. I stare straight into Price's beady little eyes. "I guess when you do not have the talent, cheating's all you've got." *Perfect strike! One–nil to Hafiz!* my inner commentator cheers.

"What?" Price takes a step towards me. I don't break my stare.

"Why did you do it?" I ask calmly. "Why did you roll around on the floor like a big baby? Scared you weren't good enough to win your place on the team?" *And it's two–nil!*

"Shut up!" Price shouts. But before he can do or say anything more the door opens and the teacher walks in.

"What's going on?" she says, taking in the silent classroom and all eyes on Price and me.

"Nothing, miss," I say, sitting back down, my heart pounding with the joy of victory.

"Hmm." She looks at us both suspiciously. "Sit down,

Stevie. Go back to your seat, David." Then she turns back to me. "I've just been talking to Mr Kavanagh in the staffroom, Hafiz. He'd like to see you in his office after school."

Great.

At lunch break Hafiz and I go to the library. I've told him I need to look up some videos on guitar technique – and this is what I usually do when I come here – but really I need to try and get some info for Mum. As I log on to a PC I think back to what happened in registration with David Price. I can't believe I said those things to him. David Price is the kind of kid you never mess with. He's always getting into fights and rumour has it his dad is some kind of small-time gangster who's currently in prison for drug dealing. But I was so tired and fed up after everything that's happened with Mum I just didn't care any more. Hafiz was great too. I glance at him, sitting at a PC a couple of desks down from me, staring at something on his screen, his face deadly serious. I wish he hadn't got off to such a bad start here. It seems so unfair, and now he has to deal with Priya and Price. But maybe after everything he's been through, they seem trivial in comparison. I hope so.

I type "benefits and mental health" into the search engine. It brings up loads of articles and blog posts about people just like Mum. Story after story about benefits being cut after the recent change from the Disability Living Allowance to the Personal Independence Payment and the stress and pain it's causing. I start feeling sick. Surely there's something we can do. I know Mum doesn't want anyone in our family to know but surely there must be someone official we could ask for help. Most of the mental health charities' websites recommend getting a letter from your doctor to support a claim, so I look up our GP's surgery. Their website says that they don't have any appointments available for over a week, so I jot down their phone number and go into the corridor to call. The receptionist sounds as if she's suffering from the same permanently frowning condition as Mrs Barber and at first I think she's never going to give me an appointment. I end up getting so stressed she eventually takes pity on me and I manage to get an emergency appointment for Mum for tomorrow morning. I go back into the library, stare blankly at the screen and breathe a huge sigh of relief. Panic over, for now at least.

"You wanted to see me, sir," I say, poking my head round Mr Kavanagh's door. He's sitting at his desk fiddling with the strings on a tennis racket. Outside the air is full of the sound of chatter and laughter as the rest of the students make their way home.

"Ah, yes," he says. "Come in. Sit down." He nods to the chair opposite him, puts the racket down and looks me straight in the eyes. "So, you going to tell me what that was all about yesterday?"

I look away. "I'm sorry, sir. I should not have lost my temper."

Mr Kavanagh leans back and sighs. The awkward silence is broken only by the ticking of the clock on the wall, which seems to get louder with every second. "You must have been through a lot to get here to the UK."

"Oh." I'm surprised by this sudden turn in the conversation, not sure what to say. "Yeah, I guess."

"And there are a lot of very ignorant things being said about the refugee crisis and Syria in certain quarters."

I nod. This really isn't how I imagined this conversation going at all. I thought he was going to tell me off but he's acting as if he knows what Price said, like he might even be on my side.

"A lot of eejits crawling out of the woodwork to spew their hate," Mr Kavanagh continues.

I'm not sure what *eejit* means but I like the sound of it and I'm guessing that Price is one of them.

Mr Kavanagh goes over to a kettle in the corner of the room and switches it on. "Cuppa?"

"Er – OK."

"I was your age back in the eighties," he says as he pops a couple of teabags into mugs. "And if you haven't already guessed from my Celtic accent, not to mention charm, I'm from Ireland originally. My parents came here when I was eight years old, right at the height of the Troubles. Are you familiar with the Troubles, son?"

I shake my head. He takes some milk from a tiny fridge on top of the counter.

"It was a time of great conflict in Northern Ireland and some of that conflict spilled over into terrorism."

At the sound of the word *terrorism*, my skin prickles. Where is he going with this?

The kettle stops boiling and Mr Kavanagh pours some water into the mugs. "Milk? Sugar?" he asks.

"Just sugar. Two, please."

He adds the sugar and gives it a stir. "There were terrorists on both sides of the conflict but the Irish Republicans carried out several attacks over here. They once almost killed the Prime Minister with a bomb in Brighton." He hands me the drink. "So by the time I was your age a hell of a lot of people in England hated the Irish. And with my name and accent I was a prime target for their hate. Seriously if I'd had a pound for every time I was called a terrorist or mocked for being as thick as … well, I wouldn't be sitting here. I'd be on a yacht somewhere, drinking a pina colada." He looks straight at me. "I know what it's like to be wrongly accused of something, son. I know what it's like to be on the receiving end of a racist's ignorance and it's feckin' crap. Am I right?" He's grinning now.

The tension in me dissolves and I find myself grinning back. He understands. He gets it. He knows something of what it's like to be me.

"Yes, yes it is."

"So, you have a choice." He sits back in his chair and takes a swig of tea. "Either you let it get you down – and you let them win – or you do whatever it takes to prove them wrong."

"Like what?"

"Like standing your ground. Like speaking the truth. Like not letting the eejits get you down – or make you lose your temper."

"I'm sorry, sir. I really wish I hadn't."

He puts his mug down and leans forward. "Do you want to report him for what he said?"

I shake my head. "I can't. I don't tell tales."

He sighs. "OK. Hafiz, you are a really gifted footballer. Seriously. I've never seen someone your age with so much skill. Your passing is excellent and when you make a run…" He whistles through his teeth. "I want you on our team. We *need* you on our team. And I'm thinking that maybe – maybe you need us too."

I nod.

"The thing you have to remember is that the true idiots in this world are few and far between. Most of the kids here, in this school, are good kids. How do you think I know what happened last night? One of your teammates came to see me after the game. He was really angry about what Price said to you. I am too…" He breaks off and looks away. "So much of this kind of thing is born out of ignorance. I understand that you don't want to report him but I really think you need to do something." He scratches his head and looks thoughtful for a moment. "Have you thought about telling the other kids what you've been through?"

"How do you mean?"

"Well, Ms Potts and I agree that there's no place in this school for hatred or racism of any kind. We feel it would be great if you could share your story – or some of it at least – with the other kids. Help them to understand what's really happening in Syria and to refugees, so that they don't fall for the lies."

"But how – how would I share it?"

"We were wondering if maybe you could do some kind of talk, or presentation, for an assembly." He looks at me and smiles. "It would be your chance to set the record straight, to get your voice heard."

"Oh, I don't know, sir."

"Think about it – think about being able to tell everyone the truth. You can do it, son, I know you can."

It's like he's giving me a pep talk before a big game. And it's working. I think of finally being able to have my say; of telling people what it's really like back home and on the refugee trail, and my pulse quickens like it does before a match.

"What do you say, son?" Mr Kavanagh looks at me. "Are you up for it?"

My head nods automatically. "Yes, sir."

## Stevie

I take the long route home from school, past the super-cheap supermarket, where I manage to find some real bargains in the reduced goods aisle. It's only when I step back outside into the sunshine that it dawns on me that maybe getting stupidly excited over a seventy-seven-p chicken breast isn't exactly rock and roll. I somehow doubt it's something Lauren LaPorte would ever do. I feel a wistful pang as I think back to that night in the record store. Back then it had seemed possible that I might make it as a musician one day, lead the same kind of life as her, but now I'm not so sure. How will I ever be able to leave Mum? Who would take care of her? The sunshine suddenly seems over-bright, burning at my eyes, burning away my dreams.

When I get back home I find Mum curled up fast asleep in her armchair. I go into the kitchen and start making dinner. Finding such cheap chicken breasts means we can actually have something resembling a proper meal tonight. I chop the meat into small pieces and start frying them. The smell triggers a memory in me. I'm back in our old kitchen in London,

Mum is cooking and Dad is perched on the counter, reading his latest article to her before he sends it off to his editor. I'm sitting on the floor, playing "Justine Bieber" with my Barbie doll. Justine Bieber was a game I invented where my Barbie was basically the female equivalent of my then-hero. She got to tour the world – or our kitchen at least – playing sell-out gigs to a crowd of cutlery and cooking utensils. I was a pretty eccentric kid.

I loved our kitchen in London. It was the opposite of our Lewes kitchen in every way. It was huge and light and bright and always full of music and fun. Often, my parents had what they called "kitchen discos", where we'd each take it in turns to be the DJ and pick the next track. It was when I kept picking songs by Justin Bieber that Dad decided to make *Stevie's Book of Big Song Wisdom* for me. He said he wanted to teach me about "proper music" before it was too late. When he first gave me the book, along with his teenage record collection, I didn't pay much attention, to be honest. It was only after his death that they became so important to me. The words in the book and the songs were the closest I could get to hearing Dad talk to me. It's like I'm still able to turn to him for support and advice. Sometimes it makes me shiver to think that he gave them to me just six months before he died. It's almost as if he knew he wouldn't be there for me for much longer.

I give the chicken a quick stir and I think of the kitchen in the refugee centre and the women who were cooking there and how happy they seemed, in spite of what they'd been through. It's weird to think that cooking once made Mum happy too. It's how she met Dad. She used to run a catering company called *Eats and Beats* that specialized in cooking for musicians while they were on tour. She met Dad while they were both touring with the band Oasis. She was making the food and he was writing a series for *NME* called "On the Road and Mad fer It". (Apparently "mad fer it" was the favourite saying of the Oasis singer.) Mum sold her business after I was born so she could be at home to take care of me, but she still loved to cook and carried on catering for small parties. It was only when Dad died that her love of cooking died too – along with most of the rest of her. I hear a sound and turn to see Mum standing in the doorway. She's got that drowsy, slightly confused look she always has after she's been asleep.

"Hi, Mum. I'm just making some dinner," I say, undoing the jar of sweet and sour sauce – down from £1.50 to 99p.

She comes over to the sink and pours herself a glass of water. Then she looks at the pan. "Chicken? How much did that cost?"

"Don't worry, it was really cheap. I got it reduced. The whole dinner only cost two pounds, fifty-three," I say proudly.

Mum sighs. "You should have just got beans on toast."

*And you should have just got out of bed and made dinner yourself!* I suddenly want to yell. I turn back to the saucepan, angry tears stinging my eyes. I take a deep breath, try and compose myself, remind myself I have some news. "I made you an appointment at the doctor's for tomorrow morning."

"What? Why?" The chair scrapes as Mum sits down at the table.

"Well, I looked into your benefits online and loads of websites said that you should go to your GP and get a letter saying you're not able to work."

"But I did that earlier in the year. And my medication isn't due to be reviewed for another couple of months. Surely that proves I'm still ill."

I leave the chicken and come over to her. "Yes, but maybe you need a new letter – for the new benefits system or something. You know, just to confirm that you're still sick."

Mum sighs. "Why does it have to be so difficult? It's like they're trying to make me worse, not better."

"I know, but I'm sure it'll all be sorted once you've got that letter. I can come with you, if you like."

Mum looks at me hopefully. "Would you? It's just that I get so stressed having to do all of this stuff on my own."

"Of course." I give her a hug. She feels thinner than ever; the sharp angles of her shoulder blades dig into me as the chicken begins to burn.

# HAFIZ

When I get into school this morning there's no sign of Stevie. At first I think she might be late but there's still no sign of her when the bell rings for first period, which is history. It turns out that neither Price or Priya do history. I make a mental note to always look forward to this lesson. I actually enjoy the subject matter too. It's nothing like the history lessons we used to do back in Syria but it's interesting to see the past from the UK point of view. Just like it was interesting to learn about the Irish Troubles from Mr Kavanagh yesterday.

As I jot down some important dates from the Second World War, I think back to my conversation wth the PE teacher. I can't believe that I agreed to share my story in assembly. When I was chatting to him it felt like the right thing to do but now the thought of getting up onstage in front of the rest of the school fills me with dread. I wonder where Stevie is. I hope she's OK. She seemed worried yesterday, distracted. I wish I had her number so I could send her a text. I'll have to ask her for it.

At break I hang out in the library. I log on to a computer

and look up the refugee camp in Athens where my mum and dad are staying. It feels so weird to think of them in Greece and me in the UK. For so many years I took it for granted we'd always be together, in Syria – until I grew up and moved out. But the war picked up families and scattered them like pieces of shrapnel. I sit back in my chair and stare at the white huts and tents. I picture Mum and Dad walking through the scene. Mum laughing as Dad gesticulates wildly, telling her some story or other. Or is he? I think back to the conversation I overheard between Uncle Samir and Aunt Maria. What were they trying to hide? What didn't they want to tell me? This is the thing I hate most about the war – this endless feeling of uncertainty.

## Stevie

"Good morning, Mrs Flynn," Dr Ennis says as we walk into her room. Her long grey hair is swept up on top of her head in a bun. She has a stethoscope round her neck and a pen behind her ear. "Oh, hello," she says when she sees me coming in behind Mum.

"Hi," I say, hovering by the door as Mum takes a seat. "I – er – I said I'd come with my mum, as she was feeling a little anxious."

"Ah, I see." Dr Ennis taps something into her computer and looks at the screen. "OK, well, take a seat."

I sit down next to Mum. I feel awkward and embarrassed. Inside the cottage Mum's illness doesn't seem so bad but when she's out it's suddenly magnified. I guess it's because I'm seeing her through everyone else's eyes. Suddenly she seems way too thin, way too grey, like a character sketched in pencil trapped inside a colour movie.

Dr Ennis puts her elbows on her desk, brings her hands together like she's about to pray and gazes at Mum over the top of her glasses. "So how can I help you today?"

"It's my benefits," Mum says. It isn't just her body that's shrunk since she got ill, her voice has too, and now it's barely more than a whisper. "They're going to stop my benefits."

"Mum had to go for a meeting about her disability allowance," I explain. "She thinks they're going to stop her payments."

"I know they are," Mum says quickly. "They tried to catch me out with their questions. I didn't want them thinking that I was a bad parent. But I'm not well enough to work. I'm not. I can't." Her voice is ragged now as she gasps for breath. "I just don't know how much more of this I can take."

Her words strike fear into me. What does she mean by that? I push the question away. I have to help her. I have to get us more money.

"But if you wrote her another letter," I say to Dr Ennis, "saying that she's still really ill, that would help, wouldn't it? That would make them change their mind?"

Dr Ennis keeps looking at Mum. "I see that you didn't go to your appointment with the counsellor."

I frown. What appointment with what counsellor?

Mum shakes her head. "I'm finding it really hard to leave the house. I've been feeling really anxious lately…"

Dr Ennis looks back at her computer screen. Who was this counsellor she was talking about? Why didn't Mum tell me?

"Is this anxiety a recent development?" Dr Ennis asks.

Mum nods. "It's been getting worse all year."

"Hmm. I think we might need to try you on a different

medication." She taps something into her computer. "I'm going to prescribe you a different antidepressant which is also very effective at dealing with anxiety ... and insomnia."

"That sounds perfect, doesn't it, Mum?" I say cheerily, like I'm naïve enough to believe that the answer to all of her problems can be contained in one little pill. This will be the third medication Mum's tried since she first went to Dr Ennis. She needs more than pills but I have no idea what.

Mum nods glumly.

"I know it's frustrating but it is perfectly normal for people to have to try several different medications before they find the right match," Dr Ennis says. She looks from Mum to me and back again. "But once we've found the right one you should start to see improvements within weeks. And it really would help if you saw a counsellor too."

Mum's eyes fill with tears. "I know. I'm sorry I missed the appointment. It's just been so hard lately..."

Dr Ennis nods sympathetically. "Is there anything that's happened to trigger the anxiety you've been feeling?"

Mum nods. "The anniversary – the second anniversary – of Danny's death."

Dr Ennis takes off her glasses. "It must be very hard – for both of you."

I feel a lump growing in my throat. I nod, not trusting myself to speak.

"I feel so lonely – so afraid without him," Mum says.

I stare at her. She never talks about Dad like this. She

never talks about Dad at all. I hardly dare breathe in case she stops.

"He was my – he was my best friend, my partner in crime," she continues. "We did everything together. Everything. I know it's stupid. I know there was a time before I met him when I was able to cope with life on my own but it was so long ago I can barely remember it. Now it's like I'm too scared to do anything."

"What are you scared of?" Dr Ennis asks gently.

Mum starts to break down in tears. "I'm scared of it happening again."

"Of what happening again?"

"Of everything ending," Mum sobs. "Of everything being destroyed in an instant."

"So it's safer to stay inside and not do anything?" Dr Ennis says.

Mum nods.

For the first time since she became depressed I feel like I can really understand what's going on in her head.

"The trauma of losing someone in the way you both did cannot be overestimated," Dr Ennis says. She puts her glasses back on and looks at her screen again. "Especially the manner in which he died…"

I shift uncomfortably in my seat, wondering how the details of Dad's death are worded on her screen. Maybe it's like the tabloid newspaper headlines: MURDERED BY MUGGER. Or the coroner's report: FATAL FRACTURE

TO SKULL. Or the judge's verdict: INVOLUNTARY MAN-SLAUGHTER. I start feeling really dizzy.

"You need to process what happened. Talk about how you are feeling," Dr Ennis continues.

Mum nods. "I know. And I will. I promise. But what about my benefits?" She starts crying again. "We have no money. Please…"

I put my hand on her arm. "We have my paper-round money, Mum."

Dr Ennis looks at me. "How old are you, Stevie?"

"Fourteen."

"Shouldn't you be at school today?"

"Yes but – Mum needed me."

Dr Ennis nods. "How are you finding things – since your dad's death?"

"OK." I bite down on my bottom lip. How can I tell her I'm finding it really hard too? It'll just make Mum feel even worse.

"Are you sure?" Dr Ennis peers at me over her glasses. I wish she had the ability to mind-read. I wish she could see behind my mask to the fear and sadness. I force myself to smile and nod.

Dr Ennis prints something out and hands it to Mum. "Here's a new prescription. You need to take one at night, half an hour before you go to sleep. It will really help with your anxiety. And I'm going to refer you again for some counselling." She takes a leaflet from a pile on her desk and hands it to Mum. "In the meantime, here's some information about a mental-health drop-in in Lewes. You can call in any weekday and they run some free therapy workshops at the weekend."

Mum nods. "But what about my benefits?"

"I can certainly write a letter supporting your claim, but you have to understand that my job is to try and help you to get better, Mrs Flynn. And I'm sure that's what your daughter wants too, isn't it, Stevie?"

I nod. It's what I want more than anything, only it's so hard to imagine it ever happening.

"It's just so hard to get better when I'm worried about money all the time," Mum says.

I take hold of her hand. "I told you, Mum, we've got my extra paper-round money."

Dr Ennis types something into her computer and the printer on her desk whirs back into life. She takes the print-out and hands it to Mum. "This might help make things a little easier. It's a voucher for a food bank." She reaches into her desk drawer and brings out a leaflet, which she also hands to Mum. "Here's a list of local food banks. All you have to do is take the voucher along and you'll be given a few days' food."

Mum stares blankly at the voucher.

"Thank you," I mutter, but inside I feel sick. We're now so poor we have to beg for food.

## HAFIZ

I don't know if what I'm about to do is really stupid but, if I don't do it, I'm going to spend the entire evening wondering, *What if?* And – unlike all the *what ifs* I have about my family and friends – this is one I can actually answer. *What if I just went round to Stevie's house to see how she is?* The truth is, it was crap having to spend a whole day at school without her. Especially as I had to dodge Price and Priya. Not that I had any real problems with them. Priya now seems to be acting like I don't exist and, in the couple of lessons I had with Price, he didn't say a thing. I guess he thinks he's won, after what happened in football. It'll be interesting to see his face when I come back to training.

I start walking up the steep hill that leads to Stevie's house. When Uncle Samir and I walked her home the night she magically appeared beneath the street light it was dark and hard to see anything much. But in the late afternoon sun the street looks really pretty. It's narrow and cobbled and, unlike the tall, thin houses on Uncle Samir's street, these houses are all short and tiny. Stevie's especially. I stop outside and take a deep breath. The paint on the door is faded red and peeling. The curtains in the downstairs window are tightly closed. Maybe it was a mistake to come. She's probably sick. Why else would she not be in school? But now that I'm here…

I knock on the door and take a step back. I won't knock again. If she doesn't answer I'll just go. If she's ill she probably won't appreciate being dragged out of her sickbed. I'm about to turn and head down the hill when I hear the door creaking open.

"Hafiz!"

Stevie's wearing a black T-shirt with Dark Side of the Moon printed on it and her torn black jeans. Her long hair is down and she isn't wearing any eye make-up. She looks a bit tired but not ill.

"What are you doing here?" she asks.

"I – uh – I was worried. When you weren't at school. I just wanted to make sure you're all right." I scuff the toe of my trainer against one of the cobblestones in the road. This is so embarrassing.

"Oh. That's really nice of you. Thank you."

I glance at her. She seems genuinely grateful to see me. "I don't want to disturb you though – if you're not feeling well – or if you're busy."

"I'm fine!" she exclaims, then immediately looks guilty. She steps out onto the pavement, pulls the door shut behind her. "Well, actually, I was feeling ill this morning, but I'm much better now."

"Great. That's great."

She glances back over her shoulder at the front door, like she's worried at what might be about to come out of it. "Do you want to do something?"

"Sure. Like what?"

"I don't know." She looks up and down the narrow street. "We could go to the Grange."

"The Grange?"

"Yes. It's just at the end of my road. The gardens there are beautiful."

"OK."

"Right. Stay there," she commands, before disappearing back into the house.

A couple of minutes later, she reappears. She's tied her hair back and put on a pair of flip-flops.

"OK, let the tour of the jewel in Lewes' crown begin," she says dramatically. I know she's being sarcastic but I don't care. Going anywhere with Stevie makes life more fun.

## Stevie

When I first saw Hafiz standing outside the cottage I was really shocked. But then, when he said that he'd been worried about me, well, it was exactly the kind of killer twist my lousy day needed. Now I lead him past the stone wall of the Grange, round to the narrow gate on the corner.

"Are you ready?" I love watching people's faces when they first see the garden. Sometimes I sit on the bench just inside the gate so I can watch the dazzled expressions of the first-time visitors again and again and again. It's one of the few things left that makes me feel warm inside. It reminds me that wonder is still possible.

Hafiz nods and I lead him through the gate. Even though it's the start of autumn, the garden is still a riot of colour. The flower beds are bursting with poppies and roses, and tall sunflowers stoop and bob in the breeze.

"Wow!" Hafiz exclaims. "You weren't being sarcastic."

"What?"

"When you said the thing about the jewel in the crown. I thought you were being sarcastic but you weren't." He gestures at the garden. "This is – amazing."

He automatically assumed I was being sarcastic and I decide to take it as one of the highest compliments I've ever been paid. "Thank you. I think it might be my favourite place in all of Lewes – apart from the record shops, of course."

He nods. "Mine too, now."

We walk over to a corner of the garden, away from the parents and toddlers that have congregated in the middle, and sit on the dry grass. It feels so good to be outside in the sunshine, especially as Mum went on a major downer after we saw Dr Ennis and I've spent all day trying – and failing – to cheer her up.

"I was wondering…" Hafiz says, then breaks off.

"Yes?"

"Could I ask you to help me with something?"

"Of course."

He rolls onto his stomach and picks a strand of grass. "You know how I had to see Mr Kavanagh yesterday?"

"Oh, yes! Sorry, I forgot. How did it go?"

"It was good. He was really nice. One of the other players told him what Price said to me."

"That's great! Is Price being kicked off the team? He should be."

Hafiz shakes his head. "Mr Kavanagh asked if I wanted to report him but I said no. I don't tell tales, you know. Mr Kavanagh was OK with it, but he's asked me to do something else instead."

"What?"

"He wants me to do a talk in assembly – about what it is like in Syria and what it's like to be a refugee."

"That sounds like a great idea."

"Does it?" He looks at me anxiously. "I wanted to do it when he asked me but now I'm not so sure. I don't know if…" He breaks off and looks at a nearby flower bed.

"What?"

"If I want to stand up and talk in front of everybody."

"Yeah, I get that." The thought of standing up and giving a talk in front of the entire year makes me feel sick. Like, even if they asked me to talk about the joys of listening to music on vinyl I don't think I'd be able to do it. But the idea of Hafiz telling his story seems such a good one. Then I have an idea. "Maybe there's a way you could do it without actually having to get up in front of everybody."

Hafiz frowns. "How?"

"Maybe you could make a video and they could play it in assembly."

Hafiz sits up again. "What kind of video?"

"Just you talking about what you've been through. Like an interview. I could help you if you want, ask the questions."

He looks thoughtful for a moment, then slowly nods his head.

"And that way you could edit it too – and only say what you want to say."

He nods again, this time more enthusiastically. "Are you

sure you don't mind though – helping me?"

"Of course not." The truth is, I'd love to do it – and not just for selfless reasons. It would finally give me the chance to find out what happened to Hafiz before he came here, without seeming insensitive or nosy.

"Thank you. Shall we – are you free tomorrow?"

"Tomorrow?" I don't know why I'm double-checking. Tomorrow is Saturday. I have the social life of a cloistered nun, especially on a Saturday.

Hafiz nods. "Maybe we could make a start then. But don't worry if you're busy."

"Er, no. I just have to do my paper round in the morning. Oh, and get some food." I cringe as I think of having to visit the food bank. "But after that I'm totally free."

"What is a paper round?" Hafiz asks, looking really puzzled.

"It's when you deliver newspapers to people's houses. I do it every morning. To earn some cash."

"Every morning?"

I nod. "Yeah. I used to just do weekends but now I'm doing weekdays as well. I need the extra money ... for my guitar fund."

"Ah, I see." Hafiz looks over to the queue of people at the ice-cream kiosk by the Grange. "Would you like an ice cream?"

"Oh – I – I don't have any cash on me."

"That's OK. I'll buy them. I want to – to say thank you."

"What for?"

"Helping me with the video for the assembly – and…" He looks away, like he's suddenly embarrassed.

"What?"

"Being my friend?" He says it like he's asking a question.

"Who says I'm your friend?" It pops out before I realize that maybe occasionally sarcasm is the lowest form of humour. He immediately looks crushed and I feel like crap. "Sorry, I was only joking. Of course you're my friend." Now we're both blushing. He has the advantage of being able to flop his curtain of hair forward. I really wish I hadn't tied mine back.

"OK. Good." He scrambles to his feet. "Let's – let's go get those ice creams."

# HAFIZ

This morning, when I come down for breakfast, the kitchen door is closed and I can hear Uncle Samir and Aunt Maria talking. I press my ear to the door and try to make out what they're saying, but I can only catch the odd word. "Recover" and "journey" from Uncle Samir, and "phone" and "terrible" from Aunt Maria. "Terrible" echoes menacingly around my head long after she's said it. What's terrible? Are they talking about the same thing they were talking about the other night? The thing they decided not to tell me? I need answers so I march into the room.

Uncle Samir is sitting at the kitchen table looking at something on his laptop and Aunt Maria is standing at the sink by the window, washing some dishes.

"Good morning, Hafiz." Uncle Samir greets me with a smile. Aunt Maria turns and also smiles. It's as if they haven't just been discussing something "terrible" at all.

"Morning," I say, sitting down opposite Uncle Samir. "Have you heard anything from Dad?"

Uncle Samir shakes his head. "No, but I have been

emailing one of the workers at the camp in Athens and I've transferred some money to your dad's account for the next leg of the journey."

"When will that be?" I pour myself a glass of orange juice and Aunt Maria brings me a plate of scrambled eggs.

"In a week or so, maybe."

"A week? Why so long?"

Uncle Samir looks at Aunt Maria very quickly but I notice it. "His papers need to be processed."

"Oh, right." I relax a little, thinking back to when I landed on the Greek island of Lesbos and how long I had to wait for my papers to be processed.

"Don't worry," Uncle Samir says, smiling at me. "At least he is out of Syria. At least he is on his way."

"Yeah," I mutter and start eating my breakfast.

It's only when Uncle Samir and Aunt Maria have gone out shopping and I'm getting ready to meet Stevie that I realize he didn't once mention Mum.

## Stevie

As soon as I finish my paper round I come home, have a shower and get changed into the closest thing I've got to a superhero's outfit – in that it gives me special powers of confidence. The outfit consists of a vintage Sex Pistols T-shirt that once belonged to my dad, my trusty ripped black jeans, my buckled black boots and an armful of silver bangles. Then I flick through my *Little Book of Big Song Wisdom* until I get to the page: *SONGS TO HELP YOU TAKE ON THE WORLD*. I know I'm not exactly taking on the world by going to a food bank but it definitely feels like a huge challenge. I scan the list of songs my dad wrote down for me. I wonder if he ever imagined that I'd one day be needing them because Mum and I would officially be paupers. Somehow I doubt it. I decide upon "Sunday Bloody Sunday" by U2. The minute the opening drumbeat begins thudding from the record player I feel better – stronger – ready to take on anything.

"Thanks, Dad," I whisper as I start strumming my air guitar in time to it.

Outside, the sun is shining and Lewes is bustling. Everyone's loving the late summer that's finally arrived – and now I'm not in my school uniform I'm able to appreciate it too. I make my way along the high street, past the old Norman castle and the grand courthouse and the delis and the coffee shops. The food bank is in a church down on Cliffe High Street, at the other end of town, in the shadow of the huge chalk cliff. It's got a totally different vibe to my end of the high street. The pedestrian precinct and quirky stores make it a haven for buskers and street performers. As I get closer I hear "Somewhere Over the Rainbow" being played on a trumpet. There's a farmers' market on Cliffe today. The stalls were being set up when I was on my way to my paper round earlier, now they're in full flow as people crowd around, eager to fill their shopping bags and baskets with fresh bread and cakes and meat and cheese. The sight of all the delicious food makes my stomach rumble and my heart sink. I wonder what kind of food you get at a food bank. How does it even work? Is it set up like a supermarket, where you just help yourself? Or does your voucher entitle you to only certain things? The voucher Dr Ennis gave us doesn't specify what it's for. I'm starting to feel so nervous I'm not sure I can go through with it. But I have to. The threat of having our benefits cut means that Mum needs to save what little money she's got for the bills.

I make my way over the bridge and down the cobbled street that leads to the church. It's a lovely old building.

Sometimes I wish I was religious, just so I could get to hang out in a church. They look so peaceful and soothing. At least, old ones like this do. I take a deep breath and turn the handle on the old wooden door. It opens with a loud creak. I step inside, where it's cool and dark and smells of incense. The floor is stone and there's a brightly coloured stained-glass window straight ahead of me. It's beautiful. Well, it would be beautiful if it didn't show Jesus nailed to a cross. As soon as I see it I feel sad.

I look around. There's no one in sight. *Just go*, my inner voice tells me. *Use your paper-round money to buy some food.* But I'll need my paper-round money for the bills too if Mum does lose her payments. I hear a noise from the far end of the church, by the altar, and see an old man with white hair moving some chairs about. I walk over to him nervously. He's wearing a vicar's white collar.

"Hello," I mutter.

"Oh, hello." He looks surprised to see me. "Can I help you?"

"Er, yes, I hope so. I'm – er – looking for the…" I'm too embarrassed to say any more so I hand him the food voucher.

The vicar looks at it. "Ah, the food bank is in the hall. Come with me."

I follow him out of the church and round to the side, where there's a much newer building. He holds the door open for me. We walk into a large airy room. Long trestle tables have been set up along one side, containing rows of cardboard boxes. There's a man standing by the tables, looking at the boxes. He's got long, dirty blond hair and he's wearing dark baggy clothes. He's one of the homeless men who sits in the doorway by Boots. The one who writes *HELP* in chalk on the pavement in front of him.

"Is this the first time you've used a food bank?" the vicar says to me.

I nod. I don't feel able to speak. It's as if all of the sadness I've been pressing down inside me has risen up and filled my throat.

"All you need to do is take your voucher to one of the volunteers over there." He points to a corner of the room but I can't look. I can't move. "They'll give you a box of food. Is it just for you or...?"

"It's for me and my mum," I somehow manage to stammer.

"OK. Well, they'll make sure you have enough for you and your mum for the next few days."

"Thank you."

He hands back my voucher. I turn and head in the direction he pointed me, to a table in the far corner, housing a kettle and some mugs. There's a couple of women behind the table, with their backs to me.

I walk over and cough to get their attention.

One of the women turns and both our mouths drop open in shock.

"Stevie!" she exclaims.

I want to run. I want to hide. I want the ground to open up and swallow me whole. Instead I open my mouth and force some words out. "Hello, Miss Kepinski."

Uncle Samir and Aunt Maria are still out and I've spent the past couple of hours going over our recent conversations for any mention of Mum. But there wasn't any. I asked Dad how Mum was and he said OK. But he didn't ask me if I wanted to speak to her. Why not? And why didn't she want to speak to me? These are the questions that are filling my head when Stevie arrives.

"Hey," she says as I open the door. She looks really fed up. She isn't smiling and her eyes aren't as sparkly as usual. She's probably regretting that she offered to help me. She probably has a million other, better things she'd rather be doing. Like her homework. She'd probably rather be doing her home-work than talking to me about what it means to be a refugee.

"I've had a really rubbish day," she says, walking straight past me into the hall. "And it isn't even eleven o'clock yet!" She looks at me imploringly, like she needs me to say something or do something to make her feel better. I'm relieved. At least it isn't the thought of helping me that's making her look so sad.

"Why? What's happened?" I gesture at her to go into the

kitchen, where she goes over to the table and plonks down heavily into a chair.

"I don't think I can tell you," she says, resting her head in her hands. "I have a horrible feeling that would only make it worse."

"Oh. I see." But really I don't see at all. "Would you like a coffee?"

"Sure." Her expression brightens a tiny bit. "What kind?"

I go over to the cupboard where Aunt Maria and Uncle Samir keep the coffee and tea. "Instant? Filter? Decaf?"

Stevie frowns. "Decaf is a swear word to me. Ditto instant."

I laugh. "Sorry."

"Could you make Syrian coffee? You know, like you were telling me about the other day?"

"Oh. OK. Yes, sure." I look in another cupboard and bring out the silver coffee pot and matching small, silver cups.

"Wow. It looks so ornate," Stevie sighs.

"Yes. We take our coffee seriously."

Stevie watches as I put some coffee and cardamom in the pot and add boiling water. It's so long since I've made coffee this way. It makes me feel happy and sad at the same time. I put some dates on a plate to serve with it. *Did I ever tell you the tale about the date merchant and his donkey?* Dad's voice echoes in my head.

I pour some coffee into one of the tiny cups and pass it to Stevie and she takes a sip. "This is delicious!"

"Thank you." Her happiness is infectious.

I offer her a date. She takes it eagerly and nods her head in appreciation. "Mmm, this is lovely."

"Have another. Please." I pass her the plate.

She eats another. There's something about the way she eats so eagerly, so *hungrily*, that reminds me of the camp in Calais, and the way we all ate when we received our one meal of the day. I go and get some of Maria's baklava and put it on the table. "Help yourself."

Three cups of coffee and a plate of dates and baklava later and we are both buzzing from caffeine and sugar.

"OK then," Stevie says. "Are you ready to be interrogated?"

"Interrogated?"

"For your video. Are you ready to be interviewed?" She puts her bag on the table and pulls out a notebook. "I jotted down some questions last night. I hope they're OK. If they're not, just say, and I can ask you some others."

The happiness I was feeling fades slightly. I wonder what she's going to ask me.

"Do you want to see them first?"

I shake my head. Probably best not to know in advance or I might not want to answer them.

"I also thought we could talk about Sanctuary by the Sea in the video. Ask people if they'd like to donate books for the library."

I nod.

Stevie looks around the kitchen. "Where do you want to film it?"

"I don't know. Shall we try in here?"

"OK."

I take my phone from my pocket. I feel nervous all of a sudden but I'm not sure why. It's just me and Stevie, I remind myself. If I don't like how it goes I don't have to show it at school.

"How are we going to film it?" Stevie asks. "Should I hold the phone? Or do you think we should rest it on something?"

"It's OK. My uncle gave me this. He uses it when he's FaceTiming with overseas students." I fetch a small tripod from the kitchen counter and attach my phone to it. Then I switch the phone camera to video and try different positions until I've got my chair in shot. "Right. It's ready."

"OK." Stevie clears her throat. "Hi, I'm here with Hafiz Ali, who has just started at Lewes High and is a Syrian refugee. I was wondering if you could tell us, Hafiz, how and when you became a refugee?"

## *Stevie*

Hafiz looks so uncomfortable. Maybe this was a dumb idea. Maybe being filmed is making him feel even more self-conscious. He leans back in his chair, then forward. He coughs and pushes his long hair from his face. "I – I became a refugee two years ago," he says, looking at me, then the camera, then down into his lap. "The war in Syria was getting worse and worse. So many people were getting killed or injured. My best friend, Aahil…" He breaks off and looks back at me. "Aahil lost both of his legs in a rocket attack. So my parents decided to pay for me to go to Europe. To come here to the UK, to stay with my uncle and aunt. They thought it would be safer for me."

I nod. I decide to ignore the next question on my list and ask one of the new ones that has instantly sprung into my mind. "When you say your parents paid for you to go to Europe, what do you mean?"

"They paid the smugglers."

"Smugglers?"

"Human smugglers. The people who help Syrians cross

the border into Europe." He gives a little laugh. But something tells me that whatever he's thinking about isn't at all funny.

"How much did they have to pay them?"

"Thousands of dollars. Most of their life savings." Hafiz sighs.

"Wow. So, why didn't your parents come with you?"

"They didn't want to leave my grandma. She's very old and frail. She wouldn't have been able to make the journey." He looks really stressed now. I decide to change course.

"Which countries did you travel through to get here?"

"We went by land into Turkey and then by boat to an island off the coast of Greece."

"When you say 'we', who do you mean? Who were you travelling with?"

"A friend of my dad's, our next-door neighbour, Adnan." Hafiz sighs again. He's looking even more uncomfortable now.

"Are you OK?" I whisper. "Do you want to stop?"

He shakes his head.

"Could you tell us a bit about the boat journey? What was it like?"

He swallows. "It was hell."

Crap. I shouldn't have asked. "I'm sorry. Let me just…" I look back at my notebook for another question.

"The smugglers don't care if you live or die. All they care about is your money," Hafiz continues. "When we told them that the boat was getting too crowded they beat us with sticks to get us to sit back down. They wouldn't let us get off again. They just kept forcing more and more people onto the boat and then…" He looks down at the floor. "Then, when the boat capsized, there was no one to help us."

"The boat capsized?" A shiver runs up my spine.

Hafiz nods. "Yes, midway through our journey. There was a storm. The sea got really rough. We had been given these orange what-do-you-call-them – life jackets – before we got on but they were so flimsy, they didn't do a thing. They didn't help the people who couldn't swim. I lost all of my belongings that night, apart from the clothes I was wearing and what I had in my pockets. But I was one of the lucky ones. The woman next to me…" He tails off into silence.

"Did she drown?" My voice is barely more than a whisper. I'm dreading his answer.

Hafiz shakes his head. "No."

I breathe a sigh of relief.

"Her baby did."

# HAFIZ

Something weird has happened. Something I really wasn't expecting. Now I'm finally talking about my memories from that night, I don't seem to want to stop.

"Her baby drowned," I say again. And now I'm not just speaking to Stevie or the camera on my phone, I'm talking to the whole school. And most of all, I'm talking to Price and Priya. I want them to know exactly what refugees have been through. I want them to see that it isn't about greed or wanting to steal things from others, it's about being so desperate you'd risk your own life, or the life of your baby. "When the waves crashed into the boat they swept her baby away. Other people too. Adnan, the man I'd been travelling with. He drowned as well." I glance across the table at Stevie. Her eyes are shiny with tears. It snaps me back to reality. "I'm sorry. I didn't mean to upset you." I stand up and switch off the camera.

She shakes her head. "No, *I'm* sorry. I'm so sorry."

We both sit there for a moment in silence. The only sound is the faint drip-dripping of the tap. I feel weird. Light-headed. I don't know if it's all the coffee or the relief of finally having spoken about the nightmare that's been haunting me for months. But should I have spoken about it to Stevie? I look at her, try to work out what she's feeling. She's staring at the coffee pot, deep in thought.

"I'm sorry if that was — if it was too much just then," I say.

She shakes her head. "Is that why you don't like the sea?"

I nod. Then I sigh. "It's weird because I used to love it. It's where I'd always go when I wanted to feel happy. When I wanted to feel free. We live — *lived* — right on the coast, in a town called Latakia. I loved swimming — when I wasn't playing football. My mum said I was part human, part fish. But now…"

"It must have been so scary. I can't even imagine. And that day we went to Brighton, I made you go onto the pier!" She looks mortified. "I'm so sorry."

"No. It was good. You made me confront my fear. Well, kind of. Inside the arcade it was easy to forget about the sea. The claw is a great distraction." I grin at her, trying to lighten the mood.

"Before I came here today I was feeling really sorry for myself," she says quietly. "But now … now I feel so lucky." She puts her notebook back in her bag. "Do you fancy getting out of here for a while?"

"Sure."

"Good, because I have an idea." She stands up, causing all the bangles on her wrists to jingle. "And I think … I *hope* it might be a good one."

# Stevie

I think my idea might be a good one for precisely fifteen minutes – the time it takes for me and Hafiz to leave his uncle and aunt's house and get on the bus. As soon as the bus begins winding its way along the road out of Lewes I start worrying that my idea is awful. But I had to do something. It was so heartbreaking to hear about what happened on the boat and see how it's affected Hafiz. I don't want him to be afraid of the sea for ever. I want him to love it again. And if anywhere is going to make him love the sea again it's Cuckmere Haven.

I first came to Cuckmere Haven when I was a little girl. I can't remember exactly how old I was but I know I was heavily into the Mr Men at the time and I was inseparable from my cuddly Mr Tickle toy, so I'm guessing I was about five or six. My parents and I had come to Eastbourne on holiday and one morning, Dad announced that we were going on an adventure. Dad was so good at creating excitement out of nothing. He could make even a trip to the post office seem like the most thrilling thing ever. But Cuckmere is so magical he didn't really have to work that hard.

By the time Hafiz and I get to Cuckmere the weather has changed dramatically. The sun is still shining but a strong wind is blowing huge iron-grey clouds across the sky. I lead Hafiz into the valley and onto the footpath that winds beside the river – the river that will eventually lead us down to the sea. I wonder if I ought to warn him now or let the valley work its magic first.

"This place is awesome," Hafiz says as he drinks it all in. The shadows cast by the clouds are scudding over the hills to our left. The river is sparkling. "Thank you for bringing me here."

"You're welcome!" I'm starting to feel nervous now. What if my plan backfires? What if he sees the sea and starts freaking out? "There's something I need to—"

"Look at that sheep!" Hafiz points to a sheep grazing on the grass to our right. Unlike the others, its wool is pure black.

"A black sheep. My spirit animal," I quip. Maybe I shouldn't warn him. Maybe it's better to say nothing. We walk on in silence. The wind grows stronger. It's the kind that blows right through you. My hair becomes alive, whipping in long thin strands around my face. I think back to this morning at the food bank, to the horror of seeing Miss Kepinski there. And I picture the wind blowing all of the shame out of me. I turn and look at Hafiz.

"This river – it is leading to the sea?" He looks at me questioningly.

"Yes," I say, preparing to turn around and leave. But he nods and keeps on walking.

"I don't want you to hate it any more," I say quickly. "If any place can make you love the sea again it's here. Trust me."

"I do," he says quietly.

"Oh. Thanks." I feel almost giddy with relief. The footpath twists round to the left and in the distance I can hear the sea. The *whoosh* of the water perfectly harmonizes with the rush of the wind.

> *A*
>
>     *river*
>
>         *runs*
>
>             *through*
>
>                 *the*
>
>                     *island*
>
>                         *of*
>
>                           *you.*

I let the words drift away on the wind like autumn leaves. This is definitely not the time or place for me to start writing a song. There's a little tree up the slope from us, its branches bent over at a right angle away from the sea. The weather gets so wild here the tree has become permanently fixed in this position.

"What's that?" Hafiz asks, referring to a square-shaped,

concrete construction on the side of the hill.

"It's a bunker from the Second World War. The Germans were planning to invade Britain along this part of the coast, so the British army built them as lookout posts. Do you want to go inside?"

Hafiz nods and we head off the path and up the hill. As we get close to the bunker I have a sudden flashback from out of nowhere. My dad, carrying me on his shoulders, my Mr Tickle toy dangling from my hand. "We're going to see the house where I lived when I was a little boy," he's saying. I hear Mum giggling. "Danny, please!" I stand still and watch Hafiz go down the stone steps to the entrance of the bunker. I see my dad picking up a stone, carving something into a wall. I blink hard. Am I imagining this? I don't know where these thoughts are coming from. I can't tell if they're actual memories. I follow Hafiz down the steps and into the bunker. The floor is covered in cigarette butts and empty beer bottles. The cool, dark air smells acrid. Hafiz goes over to the window – a small rectangular slit in the concrete. The hairs on the back of my neck stand up. I know that it looks out over the sea.

"Are you OK?" I ask, going to stand next to him.

He nods. "It actually doesn't feel so bad, looking at it from in here."

"Good."

He turns to face me. "It's strange, isn't it, thinking of the soldiers who would have been in here all those years ago?"

I nod. "Yeah. I wonder how it must have felt, waiting and watching for the Germans to arrive."

"Really creepy I reckon – especially at night."

I look around the small, concrete bunker. I picture Second World War soldiers, nervously smoking cigarettes, staring out into the endless darkness for any sign of the enemy.

"But the Germans never did arrive," Hafiz says.

"No."

"The soldiers were lucky."

Sunshine is pouring through the slit in the wall, onto Hafiz's face, which looks so beautiful it makes me want to take a picture but obviously I can't for all kinds of stalker-related reasons. So I look at the wall instead. Someone has scrawled *KILL THE POLICE* on it in dark blue ink. Then I see the outline of a heart carved into the concrete. I move closer and I can barely breathe as I trace my finger over the faint grooves of the letters that have been carved inside: *STEVIE + SADIE*. Me and Mum.

# HAFIZ

I stare out at the rectangle of dark grey sea through the slit in the cold stone wall. For some reason I feel OK looking at the sea like this. It's like looking at a picture. A picture framed in solid concrete. But how will I feel when we leave this place and walk down to the bay? I don't have to go, I remind myself. But if I don't, I'll look weak and pathetic in front of Stevie and I don't want that, especially as she's trying so hard to help. I've never seen a place as wild and beautiful as this. She was right: if anywhere is going to help me overcome my fear of the sea it's here. The wind, which has been whistling around the bunker, dies down for a moment and I hear something else. A sniffing, gasping that sounds like crying. I turn and see Stevie leaning against the wall, her face in her hands.

"Stevie? Are you OK?" I take a step towards her.

She nods but she doesn't take her hands away from her face. "I'm sorry," she mumbles. "I just – I saw something…"

I look around the bunker. It's hard to see anything in the gloom. All I can make out are a couple of empty beer bottles and the ends of cigarettes. Maybe she doesn't like litter. Maybe it really upsets her to see a historical place like this all messed up. Although bursting into tears would be a bit of an overreaction. "What was it?" I ask, unsure if I should step closer, put a hand on her shoulder or even give her a hug.

She turns and points to the wall beside her. Someone has written *KILL THE POLICE* in big dark letters. Ah, so maybe she hates graffiti – or loves the police. But enough to cry over it…?

"It was so weird." Stevie's face is shiny with tears. "When we were coming down the steps into the bunker I had this flashback. Only it didn't feel like a flashback because I couldn't remember it happening in the first place, but I saw my dad writing something and then … there it is." She points to the wall again.

I stare at her in disbelief. "You saw your dad writing that?"

She nods. "We came here on holiday once – when I was little. I remember coming into the bunker with him and my mum. He told me this was where he lived when he was little. He was kidding – obviously. But I'd totally forgotten what he put on the wall until just now – and it's still there!" She smiles dreamily. "It's so weird to think that my dad did this."

"Yeah." I'm really confused now. "So, your dad, he didn't like the police then?"

"What?" She frowns, then looks back at the wall. "Oh – oh no! He didn't write that! He made the heart. Look." She grabs my hand, places my fingers on the wall. "Can you feel it?"

Now I'm up close I can see a heart carved into the wall. There are some words inside, beneath the graffiti about the police. I start tracing the letters with my finger – S – T – E – V – I – E.

"He carved my and my mum's names inside," Stevie says quietly.

"Wow."

"Sorry for getting all emotional." She wipes her eyes. "It's just that I haven't… My dad … he died."

A sudden thin beam of sunlight pours through the slit in the wall. It catches the side of her face, making her pale skin glow. She looks so beautiful. Like a china doll.

"I'm so sorry," I say. And I am. My worst nightmare is Stevie's reality. She has actually lost a parent.

"It's OK," she replies. "Even though I'm crying I'm not really sad. Well, I am, but I'm happy too. Do you ever get that – where you feel happy and sad at the same time?"

I nod.

"I mean, it's really horrible that my dad's gone, but finding this – it's like getting a message from him."

I think of how my dad's voice keeps popping into my head, how reassuring it feels. "It *is* a message from him."

Stevie stares at me and for a moment it's like everything stops – the wind stops blowing, the waves stop crashing, the sunshine fades – and we're suspended in the middle of it all, in this bunker, held together by our gaze. And then she looks away, back to the wall. "We don't have to go down to the sea if you don't want to," she says quietly. "When we were in your kitchen I felt so strongly that we had to come here, and at the time I thought it was so I could get you to face your fear, but maybe…" She breaks off and starts tracing the heart with her finger again. "Maybe it was so I could discover this."

"Maybe it was both," I say, looking back through the slit in the wall to the dark rectangle of sea.

I follow Hafiz out of the bunker. The sun has disappeared and the sky is covered in thick grey cloud. I can't believe I cried in front of him. But most of all, I can't believe it didn't feel embarrassing. Maybe it's because he's cried in front of me – the night he spoke to his dad. It's weird because Hafiz and I are from such different backgrounds, such different worlds, and yet it feels like we have so much in common. We keep walking on in silence until we reach the point where the footpath blends into the beach and the river flows into the sea. The cliffs loom to our left, jagged and chalky white, topped with green. It's as if the Downs have been sliced down the middle like a giant cake.

"Wow!" Hafiz exclaims, staring up at them.

"They're called the Seven Sisters," I tell him. "They're meant to be one of the most beautiful sights in all of the UK."

"I can see why." Hafiz takes a deep breath, then looks at the sea. The waves are wild and frothy and the air smells fresh and salty. The sight and smell of the sea always make me feel happy, but how is it for Hafiz? His hair is being blown all about, so it's hard to see his expression. "This place reminds me of a story my father once told me," he says. "About a sailor called Sinbad."

I wait, unsure whether this is a good or bad thing.

Hafiz turns to me. "Do you know the story?"

I shake my head.

"One day, a very poor man who works as a porter stops to rest on a bench outside a beautiful palace in Baghdad." Hafiz stuffs his hands in his jeans pockets and turns to face me. "As he's resting he hears lots of music and laughter coming from inside the palace. The happy sounds make him really envious, and so do the delicious smells of food cooking, so he asks one of the servants standing outside who it is that owns the magnificent house. The servant tells him that it belongs to a famous traveller named Sinbad, who has sailed every sea. The poor man, who has barely enough money to feed his family, is angry that he should have nothing while people like this Sinbad live in such splendour. So he starts ranting to God about the injustice of it all – and Sinbad overhears him."

"What does Sinbad do?" I ask. And I really want to know, because I can so relate to the poor man and his feelings of envy. "Does he punish him?"

Hafiz shakes his head. "No, he invites him into his palace and gives him some food and drink and then he tells him about all the hardships he endured during his adventures at sea." He breaks off and looks back at the cliffs. "On his first voyage he and his shipmates landed on what they thought was a small island but it turned out to be the back of a huge whale."

I start to laugh. "No way!"

Hafiz grins. "Yep. Then the whale wakes up and Sinbad is flung off into the sea. He manages to spot some proper land, and he climbs up some cliffs to safety." He points to the Seven Sisters. "When my dad used to tell me the story I always pictured them looking just like this." He falls silent again and stares out to sea.

I move closer to him. "Are you OK?"

He nods, then looks back at me. "I suppose I might be a bit like Sinbad."

"Really? How do you mean?"

"He experienced so many hardships at sea. He almost died so many times, but so many good things happened to him too."

"And that can be the same for you," I say.

Hafiz nods. "I hope so."

I remember what Hafiz told me about his dad telling him he needed to find his story. "Do you think maybe the Sinbad story is your story?"

Hafiz looks back at the crashing waves, then shakes his head. "No. I mean, it's a good story but I don't ... I don't feel it – you know, in here." He puts his hand on his chest and sighs. "Maybe I'll never feel that way about any story."

# HAFIZ

I gaze at the frothy tips of the waves as they crash and break on the beach. High overhead a seagull gives a piercing shriek. It reminds me of the night in the boat and the woman's scream. I'll never forget that scream. I'll never forget that night. I can't do this. I can't go near the water. My throat tightens. I can barely breathe. I need to get away. My legs tense, ready to break into a sprint.

"We can go if you like?" I feel Stevie's hand on my arm.

More than anything I want to turn and run away. But if I do that now, will I spend my whole life running from my fears? I think back to the first time I ever played in a cup final and the game went to a penalty shoot-out. I was the fifth player up for Hutteen and if I scored it meant we won. I'd never felt pressure like it. The entire stadium fell silent. Or maybe it was fear that deafened me. I hadn't let that fear stop me though. I ran at the ball with everything I'd got and smashed it into the top corner of the goal. I take a deep breath. Clench my fists. And I start to run. I start to run towards the sea. My legs move faster and faster. I lose my footing on the wet stones but I scramble back up and keep going. Fear is not going to beat me.

"Aaaaaaaaaaaarrrrrrrrghhhhhhh!" I roar as I charge down the beach.

And now my fear is replaced by rage. Rage that the sea should have taken Adnan and that woman's baby and so many other lives.

"Aaaaaaaaaaaarrrrrrrrrghhhhhhh!" I roar again. *Why did the sea have to take them? Why did they have to die?* I keep on running and I don't stop, not even when I reach the water's edge. *Why? Why? Why? Why? Why?* A huge wave rolls in and crashes against my legs. *Why?* I look out at the huge, grey expanse of water. *Why did you take them?* Another wave crashes over me, this time reaching my waist. The spray lands on my face, salt water from the sea mingling with my tears. And then a thought pops into my head with the urgency of a newsflash: *The sea didn't kill them – other people did.* The people responsible for the war, the smugglers. The violence, the greed. That was what killed Adnan and the baby. The sea was … just being the sea. I bend over and catch my breath. Another wave breaks and I remember how, when I was a little kid, my dad taught me that you shouldn't fight against the waves when you were swimming in the ocean. "You need to let them carry you," he told me. "You need to let go. Don't fight." It was those words that had saved me that night and now I feel them saving me again. I inhale a lungful of salty air. I need to let go. The tide pulls away from me and I imagine it sucking my fear with it.

Far behind me, I hear Stevie whooping and cheering, then calling out, "Hafiz, are you OK?"

I turn and look back at her on the beach. And right at that moment, a finger of pale sunshine breaks from behind a cloud, forming a pool of light on the water around me. It's like God is sending me a message. Telling me that even on the darkest days, a ray of hope is still there. A huge wave crashes from behind, soaking me from head to foot, and I feel my fear being washed from me.

## Stevie

"You're soaked!" *And the prize for stating the obvious goes to . . . Stevie Flynn!* my inner voice of sarcasm jeers as I pick my way over the wet pebbles to Hafiz. He looks down at his sodden jeans and shrugs. "Are you – I mean, was it – OK?" I gesture at the sea. A wave crashes in, its foamy tip licking at our feet.

Now he's up close I can see that his face is wet too.

"Do you – would you like to talk about it?"

"Yes. In a minute." He turns and looks back at the sea. "Did you ever feel afraid of something and then realize that there was no need to be afraid of it at all?"

I nod.

"What was it?"

My face flushes at the memory. "It's going to sound really stupid."

"That's OK."

"When I was little I was sure there was a monster who liked eating children's books living under my parents' bed."

Hafiz stares at me. "A monster who liked eating children's books?"

237

"Yes. I was a real bookworm when I was a kid. That was, like, my worst fear ever." I stare at him defiantly.

He bites his bottom lip, trying not to grin.

"Do you find my fear of the children's book-eating monster funny?" I say, mock indignantly.

"No! Not at all. It's just – surprising."

"Yep, that's me. Little Miss Surprising."

"Little Miss…?"

"They was a series of children's books, the female equivalent of the Mr Men. Never mind. The point is, yes, I have been afraid of something I shouldn't have, because, guess what! It turned out that the children's book-eating monster didn't exist!"

Hafiz gives one of his dimply grins and I'm so pleased to see it I don't care if it meant making a fool of myself in the process.

"Shocking, huh?"

He nods. "How did you discover that it didn't exist?"

Now I'm grinning too. "My dad shone a torch under the bed and showed me that the only thing under there was a bunch of old magazines. He also put a sign on the door saying, BOOK-EATING MONSTERS, KEEP AWAY!"

Hafiz starts cracking up. "Your dad – he sounds like a great guy."

"He was." I feel a lump growing in my throat.

"My dad – he helped me to face my fears too. Here…" Hafiz holds out his hand.

I take it and he pulls me closer to him. The tide rolls out.

"Turn this way," he says, pointing back up the beach. Then he takes a step back, closer to the sea. I take a step back too. "Have you ever played chase with the ocean?"

I shake my head.

"You're not allowed to look behind you," he says. "You have to guess when the wave is going to break and then … run!"

I can't help glancing over my shoulder. A huge wave is swelling behind us.

"Oh no!" I yell and we both start to run.

Hafiz slips on the stones and pulls me down with him. The wave crashes over us. And now I start laughing so hard I can't stop. So does Hafiz.

"I didn't need to be afraid!" he gasps, wiping the water from his eyes.

# HAFIZ

I don't get home from Cuckmere until early evening. I hurry up to my room and change into some dry clothes, then head down to the kitchen, where Uncle Samir and Aunt Maria are cooking together.

"Hey," I say, sitting down at the table.

"Hey," Uncle Samir replies, coming over to join me. "How was your day?"

"It was good. We went to a place called Cuckmere Haven."

"Oh, I love Cuckmere," Aunt Maria says, opening the oven door and checking something inside. The smell of roast chicken fills the room. My mouth starts to water. But I mustn't think about food. I mustn't think anything until I find out the truth.

"Is my mum OK?" I ask.

"What?" Uncle Samir asks. I look at Aunt Maria. She's standing, frozen, with her back to me.

"My mum. Is she OK?"

"Of course. Why do you ask?" Uncle Samir picks up the coasters on the table, starts arranging them into a neat pile.

"I was just wondering why she didn't speak to me the other night, when I spoke to Dad."

"Oh." Uncle Samir looks relieved. "That was just because your dad no longer has a phone. He had to borrow someone else's to call here. He didn't want to talk for too long."

"So she's all right?"

"Of course." Uncle Samir nods.

"And what about my Grandma Amira? She's not well enough to travel. How were they able to leave her?"

"She's safe." Uncle Samir replies. "She's with friends up in the mountains. Your mum and dad left her so that they could be with you."

Aunt Maria comes over to the table and places her hand on my shoulder. "And hopefully they will be soon."

"Yes, God willing," Uncle Samir says.

I take a deep breath. Lean back in my chair. Maybe I imagined it. Maybe I misheard, or misunderstood. Maybe everything *is* OK and I can relax a little. As Uncle Samir gets up to help Aunt Maria serve the dinner I think of today at Cuckmere. I think of Stevie and how she cried in front of me. And how she whooped and cheered when I faced my fear and ran into the sea. And I think of how I managed to let go of my fear, and how the sun broke out from behind the clouds like a sign. Maybe I will be just like Sinbad, and the hardships I've endured will bring huge rewards. Maybe … God willing.

## Stevie

When I get back home Mum's sitting in the living room writing in a notebook. She's dressed in a pair of jeans and her favourite Glastonbury T-shirt. This is a good sign. I feel a prickle of hope.

"Hi, Mum."

"Hi, love." She puts the notebook down on the arm of the sofa. "Did you have a nice time with your friend?"

Wow. I'm so unused to her asking about me it takes me a second to answer. "Yes. We went to Cuckmere and…" I break off, not sure whether I should tell her about what I found in the bunker. She's clearly having a good day – or a better day – so I mustn't do anything to upset her.

"Cuckmere." Mum smiles. It's such a rare sight these days that I want to grab my phone and take a picture of it. It's a real smile too. One that shines through her eyes like sunlight. I wonder if she's thinking about our holiday there.

"Do you remember…? Do you remember the bunkers there, from the Second World War?"

Mum nods.

"I – uh – I found something, when I was in one of them today."

"Really? What?" She sits up cross-legged on the sofa. As she's still smiling I decide to risk it.

"I found a heart carved into the wall with both our names in it."

Mum's smile freezes. "Our names?"

"Yes. Stevie and Sadie, inside a heart."

I watch her, motionless, and pray she doesn't get upset. But to my surprise, she actually starts to laugh.

"Oh my God, that was your dad. I remember him doing it. He found a sharp stone on the floor and he…" Her eyes fill with tears. "I can't believe you found it."

"I can't either." I sit down next to her. "It was so weird because I'd totally forgotten that he'd done it, until we got to the bunker and then I had this weird flashback of all three of us. You know, like déjà vu? I knew we'd been there before. I could see all three of us in there. I could see you laughing at Dad."

Mum nods. "He always made me laugh."

I feel a wistful pang. I wish I could make Mum laugh like Dad did. "Do you think…?" I want to ask if she thinks we'll ever be that happy again but I stop myself. I have a feeling I won't like the answer.

"Do I think what?" Mum says.

"Do you think I should make some dinner? I got a load of stuff from the food bank today." It's weird. After my amazing day with Hafiz I don't feel nearly as mortified about having to go there, or even seeing Miss Kepinski.

"Yes, I saw." Mum pats the sofa next to her. I move up so that we're so close our legs are touching. "Thank you for doing that, Stevie."

"That's OK."

"Hopefully we won't need to go there again. Once the Department for Work and Pensions get my letter from Dr Ennis."

"Yes. Hopefully."

She puts her thin arm round my shoulders and hugs me. Her hair smells of coconut shampoo. "I love you, Stevie."

I lean closer to her, breathe in her smell. Breathe in this moment. "I love you too."

# HAFIZ

It's Monday morning and the weather is damp and grey. I trudge along the rain-soaked pavement, trying to convince myself that this video presentation for assembly is a good idea. But I still feel sick with nerves. Stevie and I spent most of yesterday filming, then editing the footage. Last night, when we played it back, I felt truly happy with it. But that was just me and Stevie watching. It's totally different imagining the entire year watching it in assembly. Especially when I think of Price and Priya. *But that's why you made it in the first place*, a wise inner voice that sounds just like my dad reminds me. That's why I made it — to try and shut idiots like them up. To make them see that I'm not a terrorist or a rapist or out to steal their country.

I start walking faster. The rain is thin and misty. The kind that gets right in your face. I think of Latakia. The dry heat and the sand and the sun. I long to be there. But I'm here now. Like Sinbad on one of his adventures, this is where the sea has cast me. Now I have to try and turn my adversity into triumph.

"Hafiz!"

I turn and see Stevie hurrying along the road. Her hair is tied into a long plait and as usual her eyes are lined with black.

"Are you ready for the assembly?" she asks breathlessly.

"Sure."

She smiles at me and suddenly I feel ready for anything.


Assembly isn't until after lunch. At first break I go and see Mr Kavanagh and explain that I've made a video to show instead of giving a talk. He watches the video on my phone in total silence and remains silent for what feels like ages afterwards too. I look at Stevie and raise my eyebrows, not sure what to make of this. She shrugs. But then, finally, he speaks.

"Bloody hell, son," he says, shaking his head.

My heart sinks. He doesn't like it. He thinks it's no good. I feel sick. What if he makes me give a talk instead?

"That was…" He clears his throat. "That was very powerful." After a pause he says, "Can you send me a link to the video?" He writes down his email address and gives it to me. "I'll show it on the big screen in the hall." He looks at me and Stevie. "Well done, both of you. It's a great video."

"Thank you, sir." I stand up, my heart racing. I only hope everyone else feels the same way.

# Stevie

As we all file into the hall I feel my stress levels cranking up to the max. So far, it's been a really crappy day. All through registration I worried that Miss Kepinski might say something about the food bank. She didn't but she kept smiling at me really sympathetically, and she asked if I'd go and see her after school, so I know the most-awkward-conversation-in-the-world is coming. Now I'm really nervous for Hafiz. I so badly want everyone to like the video – to like *him*. The hall is even hotter and stuffier than the humid air outside. At least I'm able to take my jumper off now, thanks to my new Lost Property shirt. I stuff my jumper into my bag and sit down. Hafiz sits next to me, his leg bouncing up and down like it always does when he's nervous or excited. And the fact that I know this about him instantly makes me feel a tiny bit better. It's so nice knowing someone well enough to know their little tics and traits.

Lucy Giles and her friends sashay up the aisle of the hall as if it's a catwalk. I catch a waft of her perfume – clean and crisp and expensive – as they file into the row in front of us.

Priya and her friend Gemma sit down in the row in front of Lucy. Across the aisle, David Price and his friends are sprawled in their seats, their faces in their default setting of totally vacant. The chatter in the hall lessens a little as Ms Potts goes up onto the stage.

"All right, Year Ten," she says. "Quieten down, please."

The hall falls quiet – but my heart is pounding so hard I swear the others must be able to hear it.

"Before I get on to the usual notices I have something a little different I'd like to share with you." Ms Potts takes a step towards the front of the stage. "Now, I'm sure you're all aware of the war that's going on in Syria. We've all seen the stories on the news. But most of us – and I include myself in this – don't actually know anyone who's been directly affected by the conflict. Until now." She pauses and looks out into the crowd until she spots Hafiz and smiles. "This year we've been lucky enough to welcome Hafiz Ali to our school. Hafiz is from Syria and he's come to the UK to seek a safe haven from the war."

I hear David Price mutter something across the aisle. Hafiz's leg stops bouncing up and down and his whole body stiffens.

"Hafiz has very kindly made a short video about his experiences, helped by Stevie Flynn, and we're going to play it for you now. I'm sure you'll agree that it's worth watching. OK, Mr Kavanagh." Ms Potts gestures to Mr Kavanagh. He taps something into his laptop and an image of Hafiz flickers onto the large screen suspended above the stage. I close my eyes. *Please, please, please let people like it.*

My voice suddenly booms out around the hall. *"Hi, I'm here with Hafiz Ali, who has just started at Lewes High and is a Syrian refugee. I was wondering if you could tell us, Hafiz, how and when you became a refugee?"*

Normally, in assembly, there's a low-level background buzz of people shifting in their seats or whispering to one another. But total silence falls as Hafiz answers my question. When he talks about his friend losing his legs a few people gasp out loud. And when he gets to the bit about the woman's baby drowning, the silence thickens. I see Lucy Giles turn to her friend with a look of genuine horror. Priya is completely motionless, staring up at the screen. Then the video cuts to the footage from Cuckmere and another close-up of Hafiz's face.

*"After the incident on the boat, how did you feel about the sea?"* I ask, the wind whistling in the background.

*"It made me hate it,"* Hafiz replies. The camera pans out to a shot of the waves, frothy and wild. *"But one thing I'm learning is that you can't let your fears beat you. You can't let hate win."*

The video cuts to a shot of Hafiz walking along the beach, beside the sea, his dark hair billowing in the wind.

*"I used to love the sea,"* Hafiz says in voice-over. *"My home town of Latakia is on the Syrian coast. I don't want to look at the sea and think of death any more. I want to look at it and think of fun and hope."*

The video cuts to a clip of Hafiz running into the water. The camera zooms in as he stands motionless and a wave washes over him. We edited out the sound of me whooping and cheering at this point and added some music instead. Seeing it on the big screen and hearing the music through the hall speakers makes it even more moving. Especially when Hafiz turns back to the camera and the sun breaks out from behind the cloud, shining down like a spotlight on him. Seriously, it's as if Mother Nature had decided to go all Steven Spielberg on us.

"*What do you hate most about being a refugee?*" I ask as the video cuts to a shot of Hafiz sitting on the grass by the bunker.

"*Being so far from my parents and friends,*" he replies. "*And not knowing if they are safe ... not knowing anything.*"

"*What do you mean, not knowing anything?*"

"*Like, will I ever get back home again? Will I even have a home to go back to? What will happen to Syria?*" Hafiz looks directly into the camera. His turquoise eyes are even more vivid in the pale sunlight. "*I love my country. Just like you love your country. But imagine if a bunch of crazy people started killing each other and dropping bombs here. Imagine if it was no longer safe to even travel somewhere as close as Brighton. Imagine if half the buildings in your home town had been blown up and all the schools had to shut down... OK, maybe that wouldn't be such a bad thing...*" Hafiz looks to me behind the camera and grins.

A ripple of laughter echoes around the hall. It fills me with hope.

"*Imagine if everyone around you knew someone who had died in the war and loads of people who'd been injured. Think of your best friend.*" He looks straight into the camera and his gaze is so intense it gives me shivers. "*Think of your best friend and imagine them losing their legs. Imagine them no longer able to play football or swim or run or dance. How would that make you feel? And then imagine you had to leave the UK – leave your parents, your friends, your home, and try to make it on your own to safety – somewhere far, far away.*"

I glance around the hall. Everyone is mesmerized. "*And imagine. . .*" He breaks off and looks away. "*Imagine if the only people who could help you were human smugglers – gangsters who didn't care if you lived or died, who only wanted your money. Imagine arriving in a foreign country, where you don't speak the language, imagine being shoved into a camp where it's dirty and cold and the local people and the guards hate you. Imagine getting to a point where you are so lonely and scared you don't care any more if you live or you die. . .*"

"*What do you wish other people would understand about refugees?*" I ask.

"*I wish they would understand that we do not want to take anything from you,*" Hafiz replies. "*I wish they would understand that for a person to leave everything and everyone they love they have to be truly desperate.*" He sighs. "*All I want is to be with my family and play football and have fun with my mates. I don't want to hurt anyone or do anything wrong. I wish people wouldn't act as if we were invisible . . . or worse.*"

"What do you mean by 'worse'?"

Hafiz looks away from the camera. "Did you know that some people, they wait outside – what are those places called, where people go to wash their clothes?"

"Launderettes?"

"Yes. Some people, they go and they wait outside launderettes to attack refugees because they know that we will need to go there to wash our clothes because most refugees do not own washing machines."

"What?" My shocked voice echoes round the hall.

"Why do people want to hurt us?" Hafiz asks. "Why don't they want to help?"

"Maybe some people do want to help but they don't know how," I suggest. "What could these people do?"

Hafiz looks back at the camera. "There is a place in Brighton – Sanctuary by the Sea, it is a centre for refugees – they are setting up a library there and they need books."

"OK, cool, so if people want to make a donation they can come and see you?"

Hafiz nods.

"Thanks so much, Hafiz. And finally, after going through so much, please could you tell us your wish for the world?"

"For all of us to live in peace." Hafiz starts to grin. "And for Syria to win the World Cup."

The video ends and there's a second of pin-drop silence. Then applause starts echoing around the hall.

They're cheering. They're cheering so loud it's as if they just saw me score a goal from the centre circle. And now Mr Kavanagh is standing up and clapping and all the students around him are starting to stand up too. It's like a wave building in the ocean, as row after row, they all get to their feet. I look at Stevie and raise my eyebrows. She grins at me and shakes her head in disbelief. And now I'm grinning too.

Ms Potts goes back onto the stage. "Come here, Hafiz," she says, beckoning to me.

Feeling numb, I stand up and make my way to the front of the hall. Ms Potts comes down to greet me and shakes my hand.

"You are very welcome here," she says, above the applause. "And I can tell you now that the school would be delighted to coordinate the appeal for the Sanctuary by the Sea library."

Another cheer goes up.

"Thank you," I mutter. Then I feel a tap on my shoulder. I turn and see a girl who'd been sitting in the front row. She smiles and she puts her arms around my shoulders and gives me a hug. I feel weird and embarrassed and surprised but most of all I feel grateful. The girl sits back down in her seat but now her friend is standing in front of me and she's hugging me too. And as she sits down another girl comes up to hug me, and another and another. And now there's a boy and he's shaking my hand. And another boy I recognize from the football team is patting me on the back.

"I'm sorry," he mutters gruffly in my ear.

Now there's a line of students snaking down the aisle, queuing up in front of me. Ms Potts smiles and nods, blinking hard, like she's trying not to cry.

One after another after another, the students hug me or shake my hand or high-five me. Most of them don't say anything but they all look so serious and genuine. With each one I feel a little bit stronger, as if they're lining up to pour hope into me. Finally there's only one student left in the queue. Stevie. Her eyes are full of tears.

"Nice work, movie star," she says with a grin.

I put my arms round her thin shoulders and hold her close.

Everything has changed. Since the assembly Hafiz has become an instant celebrity. During English loads of people came up to talk to him and now, as we walk out into the quad for break, all eyes are on him. Now the stares aren't nosy or cold, they're friendly and supportive. The only person who doesn't look happy is David Price. He and his friends were the only ones not to get up and greet Hafiz in assembly. The three of them are huddled in a corner, looking sullen.

"Hey."

I turn to see Lucy Giles and a group of her friends standing right behind us. She's smiling her perfect smile at Hafiz.

"Hey," he mutters back. I notice the tips of his cheeks flush pink and for some reason this sight makes me feel slightly queasy.

"I just wanted to say I thought you were amazing in that video," Lucy says. Her voice is low and husky.

"Th–thank you," Hafiz stammers. Why is he stammering? My queasy feeling grows.

"I'm so sorry you've been through what you have," Lucy

continues, flicking her thick, honey-blonde hair over her shoulder.

I notice other students watching, including Priya, who looks totally confused. It's not hard to guess why. Her hero is talking to her nemesis. This must be causing some major short-circuiting in her brain.

"Thank you," Hafiz says again. This really annoys me. *Stop saying thank you to her!* I want to yell. *She's not that special.* I'm starting to feel really hot. I undo the top button on my shirt and roll up the sleeves.

"We were wondering..." Lucy says to Hafiz, her gaze still fixed on him. "We were wondering if you'd like to hang out with us today after school." She nods to her friends, who smile at Hafiz. "We were going to watch a movie."

"Sure." Hafiz looks from Lucy to me and back again. "And Stevie too?"

"Oh." Lucy looks at me, surprised. It's like she hadn't even realized I was there this whole time. "Yes. OK." She's still smiling but I notice that the warmth has gone from her eyes as she looks me up and down. "Wait a minute." She stares at me. "Where did you get that shirt?"

My heart starts thudding. "What?"

She steps closer. "The shirt you're wearing. Where did you get it?"

"I – uh – a shop."

"What shop?"

"I can't remember. It was a long time ago," I answer lamely.

I see Hafiz staring at me and all of Lucy's friends too. I notice Priya and Gemma moving in closer, like sharks circling their prey.

Lucy stretches out one of her thin golden arms and takes hold of one of the buttons. "This is my shirt," she says loudly.

"No, it's not," I mutter. I pick up my bag, pull out my jumper, as if that's going to help.

"It is. I recognize the buttons. Let me see the label." Before I can get my jumper on Lucy has grabbed the back of my shirt collar.

"Hey!" Hafiz cries.

"No!" I wriggle out from her grasp.

"Why not?" She stares at me defiantly. "If you've got nothing to hide?"

"Yeah, why won't you show her, Stevie?" Priya says slyly.

"We must have got it at the same shop," I say.

"Oh, really?" Lucy's eyes spark defiantly. "My mum bought that shirt for me when we were in France. In a shop called Amelie. Go on, show us the label."

*Crap! Crap! Crap!*

"Are you telling me you just happened to go to that exact same shop in the south of France too?"

"Oh my God!" Priya exclaims, giving me a wide-eyed stare. "Did you steal Lucy's shirt?"

"No!" My entire body is burning from a horrible mixture of heat and shame.

"You must have done," Lucy says. "How else would you have it?"

I take a deep breath and try to compose myself. "I got it from Lost Property," I mumble.

"You stole my shirt from Lost Property?" Lucy looks horrified.

"Yes. No. I didn't steal it. I thought it was mine." Oh God, I sound so stupid.

"Yeah, right," Priya says, making me want to punch her.

I glance at Hafiz. He's looking shocked. I think of how he just managed to win the entire year over and make them like him. And now I've gone and ruined it.

"I want my shirt back," Lucy says.

There's something about the way she says it that turns my shame to anger. The fact is, she hadn't even realized the stupid shirt was missing. Why else would it have been in Lost Property? She probably has two shirts for every day of the week, one for the morning and one for the afternoon. She doesn't have a clue what it's like to have hardly anything. To be so poor you have to go begging for food.

"OK," I say. "I'll give it back tomorrow." I'm filled with panic as I realize that I threw my old shirt out, and I don't have any others.

"I think she should give it back right now," Priya says.

And now I can barely breathe. I have to get out of here, away from them. Even Hafiz. I should never have tried to make a friend. I pick up my bag and I run.

# HAFIZ

Stevie has disappeared and I don't know what to do. Yesterday she left school at afternoon break and she hasn't been back since. Some of the girls in our class are calling her a thief but I know there has to be more to it than that. She would never knowingly steal another person's shirt. There must be some misunderstanding. I've tried calling her but her phone is switched off and when I went round to her house this afternoon after school there was no one in – or no one who wanted to answer the door anyway. I don't know what to do. Downstairs I hear the murmur of Uncle Samir and Aunt Maria chatting while they get the dinner ready. There's been no word from Athens. I don't know if my parents are still there or if their papers have been processed and they're on the move again. And I still haven't heard anything from Aahil. I hate all this not knowing. It's like being cut adrift at sea. I lie on my bed and stare up at the ceiling. Sinbad didn't give up when he was cut adrift. He kept swimming until he found hope and safety. That's what I must do too. I need to keep swimming.

## Stevie

My life can now be summed up in the grimmest of maths equations:

*Miss Kepinski seeing me at the food bank + stealing Lucy's shirt = never being able to set foot in school again.*

I've been off sick since I ran out of school yesterday. Although I'm sure everyone will know that I'm not really ill. The news of my shirt theft will have spread through the school like wildfire, especially as the shirt belongs to school royalty. There's no way Queen Bee Lucy is going to let this drop quietly. The only thing that is keeping me vaguely happy is the thought that at least now everyone likes Hafiz. Including Lucy. A picture of Hafiz and Lucy pops into my mind. They're sitting in the back row at the cinema. And now my stupid imagination zooms in on a close-up of their hands, which are entwined. I walk up and down my bedroom, which takes precisely three seconds. This has got to be the worst room ever for pacing. I wonder if Hafiz went to the cinema with Lucy and her friends. I picture them all huddled together, discussing how terrible I am. The thought of Hafiz thinking of me as a thief makes me so ashamed.

I pick up my *Little Book of Big Song Wisdom* and start flicking through. What would Dad think if he knew what I'd done? There's no page in the book titled *SONGS FOR THIEVES TO STEAL SHIRTS TO*. Clearly he expected greater things from me. I stop on the page titled *SONGS FOR WALLOWING IN MISERY TO* instead, and search my record collection for anything by The Smiths.

# HAFIZ

Number of months since I've seen Mum and Dad: twenty-five. Number of days since I've seen Stevie: three. For some weird reason I feel almost as sad about not seeing Stevie as I do about not seeing my parents. But I can't think about that now. I have to push these thoughts aside. I have a game of football to play. Our match is away this time – at a school on the outskirts of Brighton. I can tell as soon as our mini-bus pulls up that we're in a very different neighbourhood to Lewes. The houses near the school are tatty and rundown. Most of the front gardens are full of junk. The school isn't much better either. The walls are crumbling and the paint-work is chipped. We drive past a sign saying WELCOME TO PRESTON HIGH. Someone has sprayed a red line through the word HIGH and replaced it with HELL. The minibus drives round to the back of the school and parks alongside the play-ing field. The grass is patchy and worn.

The whole way to the game I've avoided eye contact with Price. It hasn't been that difficult, to be honest. Since the assembly, my other teammates are being really friendly. It's only now, as we get off the bus, that I look at him.

"You'd better not mess up," he mutters as he walks past me.

"Don't worry, I won't," I reply. Price doesn't realize that he's doing me a favour saying stuff like this. It doesn't intimidate me, it does the opposite. It helps me to raise my game, to prove him wrong.

After a quick warm-up we take our positions on the pitch. Mr Kavanagh has put me on the left wing and moved Price to centre midfield – something which definitely won't help things between us. Not that I care. The ref blows the whistle and we're off. Within seconds, all of my stress about my family and Aahil and Stevie has gone. My vision narrows until it's just me and the ball and the desire to win. Price quickly gets possession and I race into a wide space in front of the goal.

"Over here!" I call. But he ignores me and tries to get past one of their defenders instead. The defender wins the ball and runs off down the wing.

So this is how petty Price is going to be. He'd rather we lose than help me to score.

"Price, next time pass to Hafiz!" Mr Kavanagh yells from the sideline.

Price scowls. I run after the ball and win it from one of the other team's midfielders. I turn and make a break down the wing. Out of the corner of my eye I see Preston's players closing in. I activate the Hafiz rocket, and go flying through them. I'm running so fast it feels as if I'm flying. Price is running up from the midfield, his hand raised.

"Pass it to me!" he yells.

I look up. I could strike from here. I have a clear shot on goal and I've scored from further back than this before but Price is now closer and he's free. I pass the ball over to him. It lands right at his feet. He shoots. The ball goes flying over the crossbar. The Preston fans jeer. Price's face flushes red as our teammates all groan in disappointment.

"That was a crap pass," he mutters as he runs past me.

What?! "It landed right at your feet!" I call back. "What do you want me to do next time, hand-deliver it with a bow on top?"

"All right, lads, cool it down," Mr Kavanagh calls over to us.

But he doesn't have to worry. Price isn't winding me up, he's proving to be all the motivation I need.

Five minutes later I score the first goal. By half-time, I've scored a hat-trick.

## Stevie

I put the needle on the vinyl and the haunting opening chords of "Heaven Knows I'm Miserable Now" by The Smiths fills my room. It's Friday. Traditionally the happiest day of the week ... for people who have a social life. But not for me. Especially now. It's official. After months of fighting it off, I've finally caught Mum's depression. I've given in to the darkness, let it swallow me whole, and here's the weirdest thing: in some ways it's a relief. Not to have to bother trying any more, to just give up and let go. I used to think there was nothing positive about having a mum with a mental illness but now I know I was wrong. There's a massive positive – she's so wrapped up in her own crap she hasn't even noticed me slip under. And that's exactly how it feels, like slipping under. I once read somewhere that drowning is the nicest way to die – once you stop fighting it and just let it happen. But then I think of the woman on the boat with Hafiz and how awful it must have been to watch her baby torn from her arms by the sea. To watch her baby slip under. I bet she screamed and wailed. Because parents are supposed to care about their kids.

*"WHY DON'T YOU CARE ABOUT ME,"* I feel like yelling down the stairs to Mum, *"LIKE YOU USED TO WHEN DAD WAS HERE?"*

When I told her I needed to stay home from school because I wasn't feeling well she didn't even bat an eyelid. She didn't even ask what was wrong. She didn't even ask how I was well enough to do my paper round but not go into school. All she can think about and talk about and stress about are the stupid benefit payments. I pick up my guitar to try and distract myself.

> *Selfish*
> > *selfish*
> > > *selfish. . .*

I strum angrily at the strings. One of them breaks with a sickening thwang. Great. I hurl the guitar and it hits the corner of my dresser and ricochets onto the floor. There's now a massive dent by the sound hole. I slump down on my bed, tears burning my eyes. I've broken my guitar. The last guitar that Dad gave me. Not that it matters. I'll never be able to live a life like Lauren LaPorte. I'm going to be stuck here, in this stupid room, in this stupid house, taking care of Mum for ever.

"Heaven knows I'm miserable now," Morrissey sings, as if he's right there, inside my head, wailing my thoughts into life.

What if I just gave up totally?

I mustn't give up totally. *Anne Frank. Malala, Stevie Nicks, Hafiz.*

Hafiz. I miss Hafiz. I wonder what he's doing. Who he's with. He's had an entire week at school now without me to mess things up for him. He's probably friends with everyone. He's probably dating Lucy. I hate Lucy. I sigh. I lie down. I put a cushion over my head. I'm so horrible. I'm the one who's done something wrong, not her. She's the one who should hate me. I stole her shirt. Even if I didn't know it was hers, I knew it wasn't mine when I took it from Lost Property.

I roll onto my side and I see the letter from Miss Kepinski that arrived in the post this morning. She said that she's worried about me, that she'd really like to talk to me. I crumple the letter up and throw it on the floor. The record comes to an end. I hear Mum's footsteps creaking on the landing and it gives me the tiniest pinprick of hope. Maybe she heard me throwing the guitar. Maybe she's come to check that I'm OK…

"Stevie," she calls. "Could you pop to the shop and get some painkillers for me?"

## HAFIZ

One thing I've learned these last few years is that nothing is permanent. Even the things you think will definitely last for ever, the things that can't be broken, like your family, your school, your entire country, can all crumble away in no time at all. But something else I'm learning is that sometimes this can work in your favour. When I started at Lewes High I never thought I'd make any friends, that I'd be on my own – an outsider – for ever. But now here I am, on a Friday night, out in town with a whole group of people. OK, so I can't really call them my friends, they're actually friends of Lucy, but they're talking to me and they want to be with me.

We've come down to Cliffe High Street. The sun is setting, painting the tips of the cobblestones gold, and the restaurants and pubs are bustling. A busker is singing and playing guitar on the bridge. I don't recognize the song but it's happy and uplifting – the perfect soundtrack to the summery scene. Then I remember Stevie and how she played in the guitar shop. If only she were here too, then it would be perfect. She hasn't been back to school all week. Miss Kepinski told me that she phoned in sick but I can tell that she's worried about her. She keeps asking me if I've heard from her but I haven't.

Lucy smiles at me. There's no denying she's incredibly beautiful, especially now she's not in her school uniform. She's wearing a short skirt made of faded denim and a tight, white vest top that ends halfway down her tanned and toned stomach. She looks perfect. But that's the problem. Perfect is dull to me. I turn away. The two other boys in our group – James and Will – are also on the school football team and they're talking about one of my goals.

"Where'd you learn to curve the ball like that?" Will asks me.

"Yeah, it was sick, bruv," James slaps me on the back.

"I'll have to come and watch you play," Lucy says, linking her arm in mine. *Why is she doing this?* "If you want me to, that is?" She looks at me. Up this close I see that her brown eyes are flecked with amber.

"Oh – yeah – sure," I stammer. *Get a grip, Hafiz!* my inner commentator yells. *This is a terrible display!* I'm not sure why I feel so unsettled by Lucy's suggestion. She's been so nice to me this week and she looks amazing. But … but she isn't Stevie.

## Stevie

Hafiz is with Lucy. I take a step back into the shop doorway and try to remember how to breathe. I blink hard, then look back out into the precinct. I wasn't seeing things. They're still there. Hafiz is with Lucy. My worst nightmare has come true. OK, so they might not be holding hands in the cinema but they're standing in the middle of Cliffe High Street and *her arm is linked with his!* How has this happened? How have things changed so quickly? Now I'll never be able to be friends with him again. As this realization sinks in I feel sick. My life is officially over. School was bad enough last year when I had no friends but at least back then I didn't know what I was missing. This past couple of weeks with Hafiz gave me a taster of what life could be like but now it's been snatched away. I can't go back to being a social outcast again. I can't watch him being friends with everyone else and going out with Lucy. I can't.

A woman barges out of the shop, tutting at me for blocking her way. I pretend to look in my bag for something and glance back at Hafiz. He's wearing skinny black jeans and a bright white T-shirt. His hair is tied back in a ponytail, making his cheekbones even more pronounced. He says something to Lucy. I picture a speech bubble coming from his mouth with the words, *I love you!* I need to get a grip. I need to get away. I need to leave and never come back.

I watch as Hafiz and Lucy and the rest of her golden gang head into the coffee shop. I turn and start marching away from town. I turn and start marching towards the cliff.

# HAFIZ

We all sit down at a round silver table inside the coffee shop. Lucy takes a sip of her drink, some kind of iced coffee, topped with butterscotch syrup and a mountain of whipped cream. I think of the coffee shop in Brighton where I went with Stevie. I can never imagine Stevie ordering a drink like Lucy's – and that only makes me miss her more. I tune back into the others' conversation. Lucy's friend Imogen is asking her where she got her lipstick.

"New York," Lucy replies. "It's called Sex Bomb." She purses her bright red lips and Imogen giggles. Lucy's wearing a lot more make-up than she does at school. Her eyelashes are long and black like spiders' legs and her face is covered in something beige and powdery. It makes her look like a doll. I prefer the way Stevie does her make-up. It's more like a work of art. Lucy's is more like a mask.

The girls start talking about perfume. I turn to Will and James. They're talking about music, arguing good-naturedly about who's the greatest hip-hop star. There's something about the way they banter with each other that sends a pang of loss through me. I miss Aahil and the way we used to laugh and joke like this. I take my phone from my pocket and check it for messages. Nothing. I try and focus back on the café and Lucy and her friends. But now it feels as if I'm watching them through a screen. I don't belong here. I don't fit in with these people. I'm used to this feeling. For the past two years I've had to slip into new worlds like I'm putting on new outfits – but none of them have fitted. Until I met Stevie.

"Are you expecting a message?" Lucy asks, nodding at my phone. She must have noticed the disappointment on my face.

"What? Oh no, not really."

"Have you heard anything from that Stevie girl?" Lucy's other friend, Lily, asks.

I shake my head.

"I still can't believe she stole your shirt," Imogen says, shaking her head in disgust.

Lucy sighs. "I know. And she still hasn't given it back. She's such a coward, running out of school like that, not having the guts to apologize." She places her hand on my arm. Her fingers are long and thin and golden like the rest of her and her nails are painted pale pink. "Oh well, at least you don't have to hang out with her any more."

I frown. "What do you mean?"

"Now you've got us."

"Oh."

The others all smile like I've just won some kind of prize. But all I feel, yet again, is the hollow pain of loss.

## Stevie

The path up to the clifftop is so steep it tears at the backs of my legs and makes my lungs burn. But I keep walking faster. I like the pain. I *need* the pain. It distracts me from all the hurt I'm feeling inside. As I get close to the top I see a sign on the edge of the path warning of the steep drop below. It shows a black stick figure tumbling to his doom. I stop and peer over the wire fence; the drop is so sheer it makes me dizzy. I look out over Lewes. I'm so high above the town now it's like looking at a map. I think of tiny versions of Hafiz and Lucy somewhere down there, laughing and joking and linking arms. I turn and carry on up to the top.

I let myself through the gate behind the golf club and onto the Downs. The view is stunning and – even though I feel horrendous – it still takes my breath away. The velvety green hills are dotted white with sheep. I stop for a moment and look around. Now what do I do? I'd been so desperate to get away I hadn't really given any thought to what I'd do when I got up here. The sun has set and the sky is a deepening blue, streaked with gold and pink. Why does it have to look so beautiful? Mother Nature, why can't you give me a break? I don't need Instagram-able sunsets, I need dark storm clouds and howling winds and driving rain. I turn slowly, scanning the horizon for inspiration. One thing's for sure – I can't go back into town and I can't go home. I spot the outline of Mount Caburn in the distance. Apparently, Mount Caburn was once an Iron Age fort. I'm not entirely sure when the Iron Age was but I know it was long, long time ago, like way before Jesus. I turn and start marching towards it.

## HAFIZ

"What shall we do now?" Lucy asks, finishing her drink.

"We could go down to the river," Imogen suggests.

"Or the Priory," Will says, taking her hand. Ah, so they're together. Then I look at Lily and James. What if they're a couple too? That just leaves me and Lucy. Lucy, who linked arms with me and keeps staring up at me through her long, spider-leg eyelashes.

I think of the day Stevie and I followed our hearts to Brighton and how right it felt. The feeling that I don't belong here, with these people, at this café, grows stronger and stronger.

"Where would you like to go, Hafiz?" Lucy asks.

"I'm really sorry but I have to go home," I say, finishing my coffee.

"What?" Lucy's eyes widen. "But it's still early."

"I know. I'm sorry. But I – I need to help my uncle with something." *Ooh, lame attempt at an excuse from Hafiz*, my inner commentator mocks. But I don't care. I can't do this any more. I need to find the one person in this town who makes me feel like I fit.

Lucy's red lips start to pout. I get the feeling she doesn't end up on the receiving end of "no" very often.

"I'm sorry," I say again, getting to my feet.

"Message me," she says, and there's something about the way she says it, like it's a command, that instantly makes me want to do anything but message her.

"Sure," I mutter before saying goodbye to the others and walking away.

I don't go back to Uncle Samir and Aunt Maria's. Instead I walk straight up the high street and keep walking till I get to Stevie's turning, then continue down the narrow cobbled street, mentally rehearsing what I'm going to say. *Hi, I was just wondering how you are... Hello, why haven't you been in school...? Hey, I miss you...* No, that last one is way too corny.

I get to Stevie's door and knock loudly. I see a movement out of the corner of my eye and notice the curtain in the downstairs window twitching. She's in! I take a deep breath and prepare to deliver my opening line. The door opens and I take a step back. It's not Stevie, but a thin woman with long brown hair, wearing a dressing gown and slippers. She has a faded kind of beauty. There are dark shadows under her eyes as if she hasn't slept in a very long time.

"Yes?" she says.

"I – uh – is Stevie in?"

"Do you know where she is?" the woman says. She looks scared.

"No, I – I thought she'd be here."

The woman, who I assume is Stevie's mum, starts chewing nervously on the corner of her thumbnail.

"I don't know where she is," she says. "I sent her out to get some painkillers over an hour ago and she still isn't back."

"Oh." I don't know what to make of this. "Maybe – maybe she's gone to the record shop."

The woman stares at me. "Who are you?"

"I'm Hafiz." I hold out my hand. She just looks at it. OK, this is getting seriously awkward, so I run my hand through my hair, like that's what I was meaning to do all along. *Another lame attempt from Hafiz,* my inner commentator jeers. "I'm Stevie's – her friend from school."

"Oh. I see." She frowns. Maybe Stevie hasn't mentioned me. I don't quite know why but this makes me feel really disappointed. "The one from Afghanistan?" she says eventually.

"No, Syria."

"Oh." She glances anxiously up the street. "Where do you think she is?"

"The record shop, maybe," I say, louder this time, so it might actually sink in.

The woman shakes her head. "We – she's got no money to spend on records."

"Oh." I glance around, unsure what to do. "Is she OK?"

"What do you mean?"

"She hasn't been at school since Monday. Is everything all right?"

The woman looks at me blankly. A seagull squawks on

a rooftop behind me, making me jump.

"I should go," I say. I don't want to go. I want to stay and make sure Stevie gets home safely but the woman is so jittery I don't think I'd be helping.

"Do you think she's OK?" she asks, tightening the belt on her dressing gown.

This is fast becoming one of the weirdest conversations I've ever had.

"I'm sure she is," I reply. "Could you tell her I came round? Ask her to give me a call?"

"She's got no credit on her phone."

"Oh. OK. Well, if you could tell her I came round?"

"Mmm." The woman looks up and down the road again. I'm not sure she's heard a word I was saying.

As I start walking down the street I hear the door closing behind me. When I get to the bottom of the hill I stop and sit on a wall. I need to know that Stevie gets home safely.

# *Stevie*

By the time I get to the top of Mount Caburn it's almost completely dark. Apart from the sheep, there's no one to be seen for miles. The rolling hills, which looked so beautiful in the dying sunlight, have now turned to black mounds on the horizon. The tightness in my chest loosens. I can breathe again.

The walk here was tiring but refreshing. It feels good to be so far away from everybody and everything. I sit down on the grass and look up at the sky. The first of the stars are starting to appear. I lean back on my elbows and gaze up at them. I think of the universe stretching on and on to infinity. I think of all the time that's gone before and all the time that's yet to come. Really, my Lost Property shirt drama is like a tiny speck of dust – the split-est of split seconds in the grand scheme of things. And yet it feels as if the pain I'm in is going to last for ever. One of the stars is winking brightly. It reminds me of a song in my dad's record collection called "When You Wish Upon a Star", from a Walt Disney soundtrack he had as a little kid. I hear the lyrics echoing around my head. I keep my eyes fixed on the star. According to the song, when you wish upon a star your dreams come true. I'm pretty certain there's no scientific evidence to back this up. But one star-related fact I do know is that everything in the universe is made from the dust of exploded stars. Everything, including us. I look at the way the star's shining so brightly. We might be made of the same thing but I feel zero in common with it. But then our minds aren't made from stardust. Our minds aren't made from anything apart from thoughts – and stories.

I think of Hafiz and what his dad told him about everyone having a story inside them. The truth is, we all have a million stories inside us. There are the stories we get from books and films and there are the stories we get from other people. And what about the stories we tell ourselves? I think of the story I've been telling myself about my life being over and my dreams being pointless and there being no hope of ever escaping my destiny of inheriting Mum's depression. It feels like a horror story. But is it true? And then I have one of those realizations that, if my life were a cartoon, it would be shown by a zany light bulb flashing above my head: *We're all creating our own stories every single day.*

I sit up, and let this notion sink in. We should be able to create the kind of life stories we want but sometimes it's so hard. I think of Hafiz— *Don't think of Hafiz!* But I can't help it. The pathways in my brain crack and fizz with thoughts of him. He would never have created a life story which saw him torn from his family and friends, just as I would never have created a life story in which my dad died. I look back at the stars. I would never have chosen the way he died, either. I would never have had him fall down those steps after the mugger pushed him, leaving me and Mum so plagued by *if only's...* And I would never have created a mum who gave up. I'd have created a mum who was strong and feisty and fearless, a mum who was there for me. Then a thought occurs to me, like a shooting star blazing through my brain: *I can create me.* I might not be able to control the other characters in my life story but I can become the kind of hero I aspire to be. *Anne Frank. Malala. Stevie Nicks. Hafiz.*

I hug my knees as more thoughts start leading me out of the gloom. I can't control what happens with Mum or with our benefits, either, or even that stupid school shirt, but I can control how I react. I can choose to be happy and strong in spite of it all. I just have to figure out how. Suddenly I hear a noise behind me. I turn slowly – and see a pair of eyes glinting at me through the darkness.

It's now pitch black. I'm still on the wall and Stevie still isn't back. I must have been here for almost two hours, watching and waiting. It's getting cold and I'm starving but I can't go, not now, because I'm really worried. She can't have gone to the record shop – it must have shut ages ago – so where is she? Part of me wants to go looking for her but if I do that I might miss her coming home a different way. So I'm stuck here. Waiting.

A car goes by at the bottom of the hill. I hear laughter and chatter drifting down from the high street. I check my phone for messages. None. I count the bricks in the wall. Two hundred and sixty-seven. An uneasiness builds inside me, churning in my stomach, prickling at my skin. What if something's happened to her? Something bad? What if she needs my help but I'm not there?

I look up into the dark sky. The stars are shining brightly but there's no sign of the moon. Maybe that's gone missing too. I sigh and keep looking. *OK, God, I'm going to give you one more chance. Please watch over Stevie. Please let her be OK. Please bring her home safely*. It feels weird to pray again after so long. A bit like an awkward conversation with a long-lost friend. *And please let Aahil be OK too, God. Please let him be safe. And my parents too. And please let peace come to Syria soon.* I sigh. Close my eyes. A feeling of calm washes over me. *Thank you.*

# *Stevie*

The eyes belonged to a sheep. But, trust me, that did not make it any less scary. I once read an article about death by farm animals – seriously, it's an actual thing. Most of the victims were trampled by cows but one was listed as "death by sheep". At the time I couldn't figure out how a sheep could possibly kill a human but now I know – it probably crept up on them in the dead of night and gave them a heart attack!

I run all the way back across the Downs, then down the steep path. I don't stop until I reach South Street at the edge of town … and crash straight into someone.

"I'm sorry!" I gasp, bending over to catch my breath.

"Whoa!" a man cries. "Stevie?"

Crap! It's Simon from the record shop. I stand up straight. My sides ache.

"Are you OK?" he asks.

I nod. "I'm sorry. I just – I was just out for a jog."

He glances at my definitely non-jogging attire of skinny jeans and boots. "Jog? That was more like a sprint!" Thankfully he laughs. "Are you sure you're OK?"

"Yeah." I can't help sighing though. I'm back for literally one second and I'm already looking like a total idiot.

"Are you heading into town?" Simon asks, nodding towards the high street.

"Yeah."

"Cool. I'll walk with you."

We cross the road and start walking back along Cliffe High Street. I wonder if Hafiz and Lucy are still around. At least I won't feel so pitiful if they see me with Simon. There's a certain amount of street cred to be had being seen in the company of the local record store owner.

"I loved meeting Lauren LaPorte the other night," I say, trying to make conversation.

"Yeah, she's awesome, isn't she? Have you used the slide she gave you?"

I shake my head. "My guitar broke."

"Oh no." Simon seems genuinely horrified, as only a true muso would. "Well, if you're looking for a new one, I just got some new classical acoustic guitars in. They're going really cheap."

"How cheap?"

"Ninety-nine quid."

"Oh." I sigh. "That's a little out of my price range."

"How much is your price range?"

Now I feel really embarrassed. I wish I'd never mentioned Lauren. I wish I'd never bumped into him. I wish I'd stayed up on the Downs being haunted by psycho sheep. "About

286

fifty," I say. Although even this is a lie. Fifty pounds is practically all of the paper-round money I'm getting tomorrow.

"Right." We walk on in silence for a bit, then Simon says, "What if I let you have it for fifty and you could pay the rest in instalments – say, a fiver a week?"

"Seriously? But that would be – that would be…" Maths was never my strong point. "That would be a lot of weeks."

"Not really. And every artist needs a break. Just remember me in your first album credits."

"That is so never going to happen."

Simon shakes his head. "I've heard you play, Stevie."

My skin starts tingling with something dangerously close to excitement. "Are you – are you sure?"

He stops walking and grins at me. "Yep. One hundred per cent. Come down the shop in the morning and we'll sort it. Right, I've got to meet a mate." He gestures to a nearby pub. The door opens and a man stumbles out, bringing with him a waft of beer and the sound of chatter. "I'll see you tomorrow."

"OK. Yes. Thank you." I can barely get the words out.

I carry on walking along Cliffe High Street. The old-fashioned street lamps are spilling pools of orange light onto the cobbles. This part of town always makes me feel like I'm walking through the pages of a Dickens novel – especially at night. But I can't get all literary now.

I don't know what to do. If I give Simon most of my paper-round money there'll be nothing left for Mum and me. And yet, will I ever get a chance like it again?

I hear the opening chords to "Wish You Were Here" by Pink Floyd being strummed. A bearded busker is sitting on the bridge, cross-legged, hunched over his guitar. As I walk past I see a cap on the pavement beside him, glimmering with money. And suddenly I get another shooting star of an idea. What if I used my paper-round money to buy the guitar and then I used the guitar to busk? It could be a way of making more money. OK, so it would be a big outlay at first but I could look at it as an investment. It's the kind of thing entrepreneurs and business owners do all the time. It's called "speculate to accumulate". I know this because one night when I was super bored I ended up watching a YouTube video on business skills called "How to Get Rich, Biatch" by an American business coach. Back then it had seemed like a total waste of ten minutes of my life but now I'm not so sure. I picture myself busking on the bridge in Cliffe High Street and I break out into a cold sweat. But even though the thought terrifies me, it would be a way of making money and also help me hone my guitar skills. And more than that, it would be a way of taking back control of my life story.

# HAFIZ

I've now counted all of the bricks in the wall, all of the stars in the sky and all of the cobbles on my stretch of pavement. I'm about to start counting the leaves on a nearby tree when I hear footsteps coming down the hill. I step back into the shadows and watch and wait. I see a figure walking along the pavement. As she passes beneath a street light I see that it's Stevie. I suddenly relax. She reaches her house and I'm about to go over when the door opens and the thin woman with the tired eyes comes flying out.

"Stevie! Where have you been?" she cries, before grabbing Stevie in a hug.

Stevie stands motionless for a moment, then returns her hug. "For a walk," she replies.

"A walk?" The woman steps back a little and stares at her. In the glow of the street light I see that her face is shiny with tears. "I've been so worried about you."

"Have you?" Stevie sounds genuinely surprised.

"Of course. I thought something had happened to you."

"I'm fine, Mum. I just needed to get out."

"I'm so sorry," Stevie's mum says. "I'm so sorry."

I frown. Why is she sorry?

"That's OK," Stevie says.

"Your friend was here."

"My friend?" Now Stevie sounds surprised. "What friend?" There's something about the way she says this that makes me feel horrible. Like she doesn't believe she has any friends.

"The boy from Syria. I'm sorry, he did tell me his name but I was so worried about you I forgot it."

"Hafiz?" Again Stevie sounds really surprised and again I feel horrible. Why would she be so shocked at the thought of me coming to see her?

Stevie's mum nods and grabs her arm. "Come on. Let's go inside and get a cup of tea."

"Hafiz came here, tonight?"

"Uh-huh. A couple of hours ago." Stevie's mum steps back into the house.

"A couple of hours ago, but…" Stevie follows her. As she turns to close the door I see a huge smile on her face, so bright it seems to light the entire street.

## Stevie

I follow Mum into the kitchen and watch as she puts the kettle on. Why was Hafiz here? He was out with Lucy. He was *linking arms* with Lucy.

"Was he on his own – my friend – when he came round?"

"Yes." Mum opens the cupboard and takes out the tea. "Camomile OK?"

"Sure." Camomile is perfect. I need something to calm my racing mind.

"Where did you walk to?" Mum asks.

"Mount Caburn."

"Mount Caburn?" Mum looks horrified. "You were up on the Downs on your own in the dark?"

"Yes. Well, it wasn't dark when I first went up there."

"Oh, Stevie." Mum sits down at the kitchen table. "I was so worried. I don't know what I would have done if anything…" Her voice fades away to a whisper. "I don't know what I'd have done if I'd lost you too."

"I'm sorry." I sit down opposite her.

Mum looks around the room and sighs. "Why have you been off school?"

"What?"

"This week. Why have you been off school?"

I look down at the table, start picking at a peeling piece of the Formica. "I've had the flu."

Mum shakes her head. "You're just like your dad. He could never lie convincingly."

I look at her confused. "What do you mean?"

"You haven't been ill, have you?"

I shake my head.

"So what's been going on? Your friend who came round here. Harry—"

"Hafiz."

"He seemed really worried."

"Did he?" This news fills me with a stupid amount of joy and surprise.

"Has something happened?"

I get up and walk over to the sink. "If I tell you, do you promise you won't let it make you sad?"

"Of course."

I tell Mum the saga of the school shirt, then I stare out into the darkness of the backyard. "I'm sorry I took the shirt, Mum. I just didn't know what else to do. I was desperate." I turn and look at her, waiting for her to tell me off, but instead she gestures at me to come back to the table.

"Oh, Stevie." She shakes her head.

"I'm sorry."

"No!" Her voice is stronger now, louder. "No, I'm the one who should be sorry." She reaches for my hand and squeezes it tightly. "I'm so, so sorry."

# HAFIZ

First thing Saturday morning Uncle Samir and I drive to Sanctuary by the Sea. He's going to help out with the new library while I play five-a-side with some of the other refugees. As he pulls up outside the centre I bend forward in the passenger seat to tighten the laces on my football boots.

"Oh no!" Uncle Samir exclaims as he brings the car to a standstill.

"What is it? What's wrong?" I sit up. "Oh…"

The front window of the centre has been smashed in. The pavement outside glimmers with broken glass and the bright and cheery shopfront has been sprayed with black graffiti:

*ASYLUM SEEKERS GO HOME!*

The words leap from the sign, every letter a poisoned bullet boring its way inside me. *Don't let it hurt you. Don't let it hurt you.* But it's no good. I look at Uncle Samir. He's still staring at the centre in shock. Then he leaps into action, undoing his seat belt and opening the door.

"Come on," he says.

Numb, I follow him out of the car. Shards of glass crunch beneath my feet. Then I have a terrible thought. Whoever did this must have broken into the centre. What if they've caused even more damage? What if they've hurt somebody? I follow Uncle Samir in through the front door.

"Hello!" he calls down the darkened corridor.

"Samir!" Rose comes running up to us, ashen-faced.

"When did this happen?" Uncle Samir says, gesturing to the debris outside.

"Last night," Rose replies. "We only just found out when we came to open the café for breakfast. The women are so upset."

"Is there any other damage?" Uncle Samir asks.

Rose nods; she looks close to tears. "They broke in round the back and they – they've trashed the place. I've called the police. They're sending someone as soon as possible."

Uncle Samir sighs and shakes his head. The sickness I'm feeling builds. I'm not even able to speak.

We file down the corridor behind Rose into the open-plan space at the back. The plates and cups and glass front of the café counter have been smashed and the tables and chairs flung all over. The green baize of the pool table has been slashed and covered in black spray paint.

"The library!" Uncle Samir exclaims. I follow his gaze over to the right of the room and have to lean on the wall to steady myself. The shelves, which had taken so long to build, are now covered in graffiti. And the books Uncle Samir had started to collect and which the school had donated have been ripped apart. The floor is littered with empty covers and torn pages.

As we walk through to the kitchen I have to bite down on my lip to stop myself from crying. There's destruction and debris everywhere. Bags of rice have been slashed and spilled all over the counters. The contents of the rubbish bins have been tipped onto the floor and the white walls are covered in graffiti. All of it abusive. Hate is literally dripping from the walls. Adiam is sitting on a chair in the corner, rocking backwards and forwards, crying quietly. Uncle Samir leans against the counter, his head in his hands. I think of Adiam and the other women and how much joy this kitchen has given them. How cooking and sharing their traditional dishes provided them with a little slice of home, a reason to feel happy again after so much fear and pain. And now suddenly it's gone.

I want to kick something. Smash something. Yell until I lose my voice. But I know that if I do, the people who did this really will have won. *Did I ever tell you the story about the boy who couldn't control his temper?* Dad's voice echoes in my mind. Yes, you did, and I learned the lesson.

"Well, don't just stand there," I say to Uncle Samir, my voice cracking. "We've got work to do."

## *Stevie*

As soon as I've finished my paper round and picked up my wages from Tony I head straight to the record store. If I don't buy the guitar now I never will. And if I never do it I'll never change the tragic story that is my life. As I walk along Lansdown Place I try not to think about Hafiz. I try, but I don't succeed. Firstly, it's really hard when he lives across the road from where I'm going and secondly, I still can't get over the fact that he came to my house last night – especially as he'd been out with Lucy. It doesn't make any sense. Unless... An awful thought occurs to me: what if Lucy sent him for her shirt? My heart sinks. I bet that's what it was. I'd been planning to buy a new school shirt with my paper round money, and now I feel doubtful about buying the guitar. What if I don't make any money from busking? I won't be able to go back to school.

As I get closer to the tiny coffee house opposite the art gallery I smell the rich aroma of coffee. The coffee house is on my weekend paper round. It's my favourite place to deliver to. Mainly because they always give me a free coffee to take away. If it's cold and raining I get a free cake too.

"Hey, Stevie!" Rick, the American hipster owner, calls out to me. He's wearing his usual uniform of rolled-up trousers, brogues and blazer. He crouches down and starts writing something on the chalkboard outside. "You stopping by for a coffee?"

I shake my head. "No, I'm on my way to buy a guitar actually." I nod across the street to the record store.

"No kidding?" Rick stands up and smiles.

"Yep, and then I'm going busking." I'm working on the theory that if I tell people what I'm planning, I'm going to have to do it.

"What's up? Paper round not paying enough?"

I shake my head. "'Fraid not."

Rick looks thoughtful for a moment. "Tell you what. Why don't you come by one afternoon and play me a tune. If I like what I hear maybe you could have a regular spot. I could pay you in coffee, cake and tips."

"Seriously?"

"Sure. Why not? We had musicians playing all the time at my old coffee house in Brooklyn."

"That would be amazing!" And terrifying, but I don't tell him that. "Thank you so much."

"No problem." He crouches back down and continues writing on the chalkboard: MAY YOUR COFFEE KICK IN BEFORE REALITY DOES.

I carry on walking along Lansdown Place with a spring in my step. This is a sign. It has to be. I need to keep the faith and buy the guitar.

# HAFIZ

I'm not sure what has happened to me. I know I should be angry, despairing, raging at humanity, but I've been taken over by the desire not to be beaten. Since seeing the attack on the refugee centre I've become a man on a mission. First, I went with Uncle Samir to buy some paint, then I went to the five-a-side pitch and told the guys what had happened and got them to come to Sanctuary by the Sea. Now half of them are repainting the sign at the front of the centre and the others are helping to clean up the mess inside. I've popped out to get some more paint. This evening, once the centre has closed, we're going to redecorate the kitchen.

I hurry along North Street. It's crowded with shoppers. I scan their faces – any of these people could have attacked the centre. Any of these people could want to send me home. I walk faster and faster. They're not going to win. They're not going to beat me. I'm tired and worn out but I can't quit now or I'll have nothing. It feels as if I'm deep into extra time in a gruelling football match, but I've got to keep going – keep running – keep chasing victory.

## Stevie

It feels so great to be holding a non-broken guitar again. To *own* a non-broken guitar again. Even if it isn't my beloved guitar from the shop in Brighton. And even if it's the first guitar I've ever owned that wasn't given to me by my dad. It's still a guitar and it's a start. As I tune the strings I smile at Simon and say thank you for about the thousandth time.

"You're very welcome," he replies from behind the counter. "So what are you going to call it?"

I look at him blankly. "Call it?"

"Yeah. You've got to give your guitar a name." Simon comes out into the shop and starts putting some new records on the shelves. "All the best guitarists give their instruments a name. Willie Nelson calls his guitar Trigger. Stevie Ray Vaughan has a Stratocaster called Lenny. And B.B. King had his beloved Lucille."

Hmm, I definitely won't be calling my guitar that – it sounds way too much like Lucy.

Simon puts some records into the bargain basket by the counter. I make a mental note to check them before I go.

"Maybe you could name it after your favourite musical inspiration."

I start to smile. Of course. I hold the guitar up in front of me and whisper, "Hello, Danny."

Naming my guitar after my dad proves to be a stroke of genius because now, as I prepare to busk for the very first time, I need all the moral support I can get. In the end I was way too nervous to busk in Lewes, afraid I'd be seen by Lucy or Priya or anyone from school, so I've come to Brighton instead. I walked for what felt like miles until I found a suitable pitch. A side road just off North Street. It's not too busy but not too quiet either. After all, I do need to make some money, especially as I spent the last of my cash on the train fare up here. I rest against the wall and start tuning up. I'm directly opposite a cosmetics shop, and the air is filled with the sweet scent of lavender bath bombs. The strings don't really need tuning but I have to buy a bit of time, ease myself into this. I feel so nervous and exposed, I might as well be standing here naked. This thought definitely does nothing to help. My fingers are trembling so much I'm not even sure I'll be able to play but I can't chicken out now. I can't go home penniless, especially when Mum is making such an effort. My disappearing yesterday seems to have shocked her out of her gloom. She even said she was going to go to the mental-health drop-in that Dr Ennis recommended.

I place my open guitar case in front of me, and strum.

I've decided to start with an acoustic version of "Don't Stop" by Fleetwood Mac, one of my favourite songs from my dad's collection. "You'd better not let me down, Danny," I whisper to the guitar and then I close my eyes and start to play. Closing my eyes is the only way I'm going to be able to do it. At least this way I can pretend I'm back in my bedroom. But it's hard to pretend you're in your bedroom when all you can hear is chatter and laughter and car horns and seagulls. It's not until I've finished the first verse that I'm able to tune out the background noise. It feels so good to be playing again – to sing the hopeful lyrics, to lose myself in the music. My voice gets stronger and louder as my confidence grows. I hear a clink and open my eyes a fraction to see two shiny coins in my guitar case. I close my eyes again and carry on singing. As I reach the final chorus I hear another clink and see that a handful of people have actually stopped and are standing watching me. This is so shocking I forget the next line. I close my eyes again and somehow get back on track. And finally I reach the last note. A small ripple of applause surrounds me. I open my eyes and prepare to say thank you. But no words come, because there, standing in front of me, is Hafiz.

# HAFIZ

The moment I heard the husky voice echoing out from the side street I knew it was Stevie but I didn't know *how* it was Stevie. Like, how she could be singing and playing the guitar here, in the middle of Brighton. It didn't make any sense. So I followed the sound off North Street and there she was, standing outside an ice-cream parlour, singing and playing with her eyes shut. A small crowd had gathered around her, nodding their heads or tapping their feet to the melody. There's something about the way Stevie plays and sings that's so mesmerizing. I'm struck with a mixture of awe at how good she is and amazement that such a powerful voice could come from such a thin body. And now, finally, she's opened her eyes and she's looking right at me.

"Hafiz!" Her pale cheeks flush pink. "What – why are you here?"

A man comes over and drops some money into Stevie's guitar case. "That was brilliant," he says. "One of my all-time favourite songs."

"Mine too," Stevie says. "Thank you." Her eyes look

greener than ever in the bright sunshine. "What are you doing here?" she says again.

"I need to get something from the shops, for Sanctuary by the Sea. What are *you* doing here?"

"I'm busking," Stevie says, like it's the most natural thing in the world. This is what I love about her – that she's always so full of surprises. "I – uh – I need to make some money." Her smile fades and she looks embarrassed.

I fumble in my pocket and pull out some change.

"No!" she says sternly as I'm about to drop it in her guitar case.

"What?"

She shakes her head. "I can't take your money."

"Why not?"

"Because."

I smell the unmistakable scent of victory. "Why do people put money in a busker's guitar case?"

"Because they like their music," Stevie mutters. "But…"

"Exactly." I drop the coins in the case. "And I *really* like your music."

"Do you?" She looks so earnest.

"Yes."

"Even though I…" She looks down at the floor.

"Even though you what?"

"Stole the shirt." Her voice is barely more than a whisper.

"You didn't steal the shirt. You got it from that lost place."

"Yes, but…"

"You thought nobody else wanted it."

"Yes, but…"

"You're not a thief," I tell her firmly.

"But…" She breaks off, starts fiddling with her guitar strings. "What about Lucy?"

"What about her?"

"Aren't you upset that I upset her?"

I frown. "Why would I be?"

"Because…" Stevie looks away. "I don't know. I just thought you might be."

"Well, I'm not." I think of Uncle Samir and the others back at the centre, waiting for me. I feel really torn. Then I have an idea. "What are you doing tonight?"

"Oh. I—" Her expression brightens then darkens again. "I said I'd hang out with my mum. We were going to watch a movie."

"Oh. OK." The disappointment I feel at this seems way out of proportion.

"Why?"

"It's OK. It was just that the refugee centre was attacked last night and—"

"What?" Stevie's black-lined eyes widen.

"It was attacked and broken into. They trashed the place – especially the kitchen – so some of us are going to repaint it tonight, after the café's closed."

"I can't believe someone would do that," Stevie says, shaking her head.

"Yeah, well…"

"I want to help," Stevie says determinedly. "Can I check with my mum and let you know later?"

"Are you sure?"

Stevie nods.

"Thank you. Uncle Samir and I will be coming back to Lewes this evening to pick up Aunt Maria. How about I call round then, on our way back to Brighton?"

"OK." Stevie starts tightening one of her guitar strings. "My mum said… Did you come round to my house last night?"

"I did."

"Why?"

I stuff my hands in my pockets, look up and down the street. "I was worried about you. I wanted to make sure that you were OK."

"Ah. Well, uh, thank you. I'm fine."

"Yes. I was very relieved when I saw you get home."

"What do you mean?"

*Spectacular own goal from Hafiz!* my inner commentator mocks. I can feel my face burning. I look away. "I waited at the end of your road," I explain. "On the wall under the tree."

"But why?"

*Ooh, he's never going to win this challenge,* my inner commentator sighs.

"Because your mum seemed so worried."

"Did she?"

"Yes. And that made me worry too." There, I've said it. I wait for Stevie to frown or burst out laughing but she just looks at me and grins.

And now I don't even feel embarrassed. I feel back-of-the-net happy.

## *Stevie*

As I walk up the hill from Lewes station I feel a weird mixture of heavy and light all at the same time. Heavy because I'm laden down with my new guitar and a bag full of shopping and pockets full of money. Light because I *have* a new guitar and a bag full of shopping and pockets full of money. My plan worked. I speculated and I accumulated. I now have a new school shirt, a couple of days' worth of food and pockets full of money. Admittedly I got the shirt from a charity shop and the food came from the cut-price supermarket and most of the money I have left is in small coins but still. My busking was a success. This whole day has been a success. I have a guitar again and a whole new way of making cash. Plus I saw Hafiz. I feel a pang of sorrow as I remember what he told me about the refugee centre. I think of Adiam, who made us dinner the night we went there, and how happy she'd been in spite of everything. How could people destroy something like that? How could they want to hurt the people who've been through so much and have so little?

As I let myself into the cottage I hear a sound that makes

me do an instant double take. Music. Music that isn't coming from me or my record player. I follow it into the kitchen. The window is wide open and a gentle breeze is causing the wind chimes hanging from the curtain rail to dance. Mum's standing on a chair reaching into one of the top cupboards, wearing her Rolling Stones T-shirt and faded jeans. The radio's on and a rock anthem from the nineties is blaring out. It's so weird to hear music in the kitchen. Even weirder is hearing Mum humming along.

"Hello?" I say, not sure I can trust what I'm seeing. Maybe the excitement of everything that's happened today is causing me to hallucinate. Maybe I'm experiencing some kind of post-busking high...

"Oh, hey, Stevie." Mum smiles over her shoulder before pulling an old food processor from the cupboard. "Do you remember this?"

"Of course." As she places the food processor on the table a montage of memories plays in my brain, most of them involving her incredible chocolate cake and the mouth-watering treat of licking the bowl.

"It's been so long since I baked," Mum says wistfully, before looking at me. "You've got a guitar!"

I nod. Take a deep breath. Prepare to deliver my case for the defence. "I bought it with my paper-round money. But don't worry, it was an investment. I've been busking – in Brighton – and it was amazing."

Mum frowns. "You've been busking?"

"Yes." I lower my head, pray she isn't going to get too angry.

"Oh my God."

"It was fine, Mum, honestly. People were so nice – about my playing and singing." I glance up at her.

"I can't believe you've been busking." She sits down at the table.

I feel terrible. She actually seemed close to happy when I first walked in and now I've probably gone and ruined it all. Now she'll get sad again. I can't let that happen. "I really enjoyed it. Well, after I got over my nerves. And look…" I plonk the shopping bag on the table. "Look at the food I got. And I bought a new school shirt. Well, a second-hand shirt from a charity shop but it's in really good condition."

Mum takes a deep breath. "You shouldn't have to do all of this."

"But I want to. I want to help."

"But I'm the parent. I should be taking care of you." She glances down into her lap and sighs. "I hate being like this, Stevie. I hate this depression. It's like being sucked into a long dark tunnel and no matter what anyone says or does, I just can't see any light at the end."

I want to tell her I know how this feels. That it's exactly how I was feeling last night. But I can't.

"I saw a really nice therapist today," Mum continues, "at that drop-in place that Dr Ennis recommended."

"Really?" I see a tiny glimmer of hope at the end of the tunnel.

Mum nods. "She showed me how certain thoughts I'm having aren't helping me. She gave me some worksheets to help me challenge my thoughts, see things differently."

"That's great, Mum."

"I want to get better, Stevie. Honestly." Her eyes fill with tears. "I want to go back to how I used to be." She looks at the food processor and I realize how much it must mean to her — a symbol of how her life used to be.

I sit down next to her. This is the first time she's ever said that she wants to get better. And although I'm not an expert, I have a feeling something really important is happening.

"You will get better. You will get back to how you used to be. You still *are* who you used to be."

"Am I?" Mum looks at me with the eagerness of a little kid who's just asked if Santa's coming.

"Of course. You've been ill, that's all."

She gives me a weak smile. "Since when did you get so wise?" Then she looks at the bag of shopping. "Let me make dinner tonight."

"Are you sure?" I know I shouldn't get excited by what's happening. Mum's had good days before and soon gone crashing back down. When I've got my hopes up in the past the disappointment's been crushing. I decide to allow myself to feel happy but with conditions, like the health warnings you get on cigarette packs: *DANGER — THIS HAPPINESS COULD BE SERIOUSLY SHORT-LIVED.* Today has been a good day for both of us and, as this event is as rare as a total eclipse of the sun, I'd be a fool not to enjoy it. I'm about to help unpack the shopping when there's a knock on the door.

Mum raises her eyebrows. "Are you expecting somebody?"

"Oh, I – I think it might be Hafiz."

I see a flicker of tension in Mum's face and I get that familiar sinking feeling. I won't be able to help at the centre tonight. I'll have to tell Hafiz to go without me. I can't risk doing anything to make her feel down again. I can't snuff out this glimmer of hope.

# HAFIZ

As soon as Stevie opens the door I can tell something's wrong.

"Hey," I say. "We're on our way back to Brighton – but don't worry if you don't want to come."

"It's not that I don't want to come." She steps so close to me she's practically standing on the pavement. "It's just that it's a little difficult at the moment – with my mum."

"Is she OK?" I think back to Stevie's mum last night and how anxious she seemed.

"She's just a bit…" Stevie sighs and steps out onto the street, pulling the front door behind her. "There's something I need to tell you about my mum," she whispers. "She's got depression. Like, so-bad-she's-not-able-to-work depression, and I don't think I'm going to be able to leave her tonight."

"Oh. I'm sorry."

"No, I'm sorry. I really wanted to come." Stevie looks genuinely gutted.

I hear a car door shut and see Uncle Samir heading up the street towards us.

"Hello, Stevie," he calls. "Thanks so much for offering to help."

I'm about to explain that she can't make it after all when the front door opens and Stevie's mum steps out.

"Hello," she says, smiling at me. Though she still looks really tired, she seems better than she did yesterday. Her hair is tied back in a ponytail, and she's wearing proper clothes instead of a dressing gown.

"Hello, Mrs ... Ms..." I look at Stevie for help, not sure how to address her.

"Sadie," Stevie's mum says. "Oh, hello," she adds as she spots Uncle Samir standing beside me.

"Hi. You must be Stevie's mum." Uncle Samir holds out a hand. Unlike last night with me, she actually shakes it.

"Yes. Are you Hafiz's dad?"

"No, he's my uncle," I tell her.

"Ah, I see."

There's a moment's awkward silence.

"You have a lovely daughter," Uncle Samir says. "It's very kind of her to give up her Saturday night to help us like this."

"Sorry?" Sadie asks, looking confused.

"Repairing the damage at Sanctuary by the Sea." Uncle Samir shakes his head. "It was such a terrible thing. But people like Stevie and their kindness restore my faith in humanity."

"Oh." Stevie's mum half smiles but she still looks really puzzled. Maybe Stevie hasn't told her what happened.

"Some people attacked the refugee centre in Brighton last night," Stevie explains. "Hafiz asked if I'd come and help repair the damage but—"

"There's room in the car for one more," Uncle Samir says, looking at Sadie. "Are you any good with a paintbrush?"

"I think they might have had other—" I begin to say, but Sadie interrupts me.

"I'm not sure," she says. Then she looks at Stevie. "But maybe – maybe I could come along anyway?"

## *Stevie*

I feel tense all the way to the refugee centre. I can't believe Mum wanted to come with us. On the one hand it's cool because it means I don't have to let Hafiz down, but on the other hand...

I keep glancing at her next to me on the back seat, checking for any signs of anxiety, but Samir and Maria are so friendly they seem to have put her at ease.

When we pull up outside the centre, dusk is falling.

"That whole window was smashed in," Hafiz says, pointing to the shopfront.

"But when I called a local window-fitter and told him what had happened he came and put in a new one for free," Samir says. "There are way more good-hearted people than bad-hearted in this world, Hafiz."

"I know." Hafiz looks at me and smiles and it's such a genuine smile it makes me feel warm inside.

We get out of the car and I look up at the sign. It's been painted over in yellow but it no longer says Sanctuary by the Sea.

"We need to get a proper artist to come and do the lettering," Maria says. Then she turns to Mum. "I don't suppose you have any background in art, do you?"

Mum shakes her head. "No, I'm a … I used to run a catering company."

"Really?" Maria looks at Samir. "Well, let me know if you ever fancy doing some voluntary work. We're always looking for people to help run the café."

Mum doesn't say anything but she does nod. It's so nice seeing her out of the house like this, interacting with other human beings again. I can't quite believe it's actually happening. What if this day is all some weird dream? Well, if it is, I definitely don't want to wake up.

"We've cleaned up the mess in the kitchen, but I need to warn you about the graffiti," Samir says as we walk round to the back of the centre. "It's pretty obscene."

I prepare myself for the worst as I follow him inside. Adiam is standing in the middle of the room, holding a broom. She's wearing a beautiful dress with a vivid peacock print. A thin white woman with pale blonde dreadlocks is standing beside her.

"We've recruited some more helpers," Samir says as Maria hugs the two women. "Stevie and her mum, Sadie. This is Adiam and Rose."

I look at Mum, to check again that she isn't feeling overwhelmed. But she's looking around at the walls, her mouth hanging open in shock.

As I read the hateful words scrawled on every wall I feel sick, especially when I think of Hafiz and Adiam and other refugees having to read it. I want to hug them, tell them that this isn't how most people in Britain feel. This isn't how *I* feel.

"I'm so sorry," Mum says. And for an awful moment I think that she's apologizing because she wants to leave. But she continues looking around and shaking her head in horror. "I'm so sorry this has happened to you."

Adiam walks over and gives her a hug. Mum is so small next to her she almost disappears in her embrace. "Thank you," Adiam says. "It is very kind of you to come and help."

Mum's face flushes. "Oh, no. It was… It's the least we could do." She looks at me and smiles. It seems as if something major is happening. Like the story of our life together might be turning the page onto a new chapter.

"Right, where's the paint?" Samir says.

Hafiz goes over to the corner of the kitchen and starts placing tins of paint on the counter.

"But this isn't white," Samir says, picking up one of the tins. "It's blue." He picks up another tin. "And this one's green. And this one's red. Why did you get red?"

"I got them for Adiam," Hafiz says, looking slightly embarrassed.

"For me?" Adiam looks at the paint.

"So that we have all the colours for the Eritrean flag."

Adiam looks at him. "My country's flag?"

"Yes, I thought it might help you to feel more at home

while you're cooking – and seeing as you are definitely the boss of this kitchen…" Hafiz grins, then he looks at Samir anxiously. "Is it OK?"

"You want to paint my flag in this kitchen?" Adiam's dark brown eyes widen.

Hafiz nods and points to the wall behind the large stove. "I thought we could paint it here. I bought white for the other walls. What do you think?" he asks, looking at Samir.

"I think it's a great idea," Samir replies with a smile.

Adiam marches over to Hafiz and flings her arms around him. "You make me so happy." She turns to Samir. "He makes me so happy."

I look at Mum. She's gazing at Hafiz and Adiam, her eyes shiny with tears.

We've been painting for a couple of hours now. Rose is taking care of the kitchen door, Aunt Maria and Sadie are painting one of the white walls, Adiam and Uncle Samir are working on another and Stevie and I are painting the Eritrean flag. Thankfully the background is a pretty simple design – three bold triangles. I'm not sure how I'm going to do the olive branch motif that goes on top but I can worry about that another day.

As I focus on filling in the red triangle I feel all the day's tension leaving me. It feels so good to paint over the vandals' hate with the bright red of the Syrian team. I thought my dream of playing for Syria was over but now I feel it sparking back to life. Football could be my way of beating the hate; of triumphing over adversity. After our game this week Mr Kavanagh said he was thinking of inviting scouts from Brighton and Hove Albion to come and watch me. He thinks I've got what it takes to play for a British premiership team. What if I made it big here in the UK, then went back to Syria once the war is over and played for the national team? What if I helped them achieve glory?

"Penny for your thoughts," Stevie says, standing on the counter to reach the top of the triangle she's painting green.

"Penny for what?" I zone back into the room. Aunt Maria is chatting away to Sadie about the work the women do in the café. Uncle Samir is coaching Adiam on the English alphabet.

"*A, b, c, d, e, f, g,*" she sings in her deep voice as she paints, "*h, i, j, k, m, l, p, o, z.*"

Uncle Samir laughs. "Almost."

"Penny for your thoughts," Stevie says. "It means, I'll give you a penny if you tell me what you are thinking."

"A penny?" I pull a mock frown. "My thoughts are worth way more than that."

"Oh, yeah?" She looks down at me and laughs. "OK, two p."

I dip my roller in the paint tray. Now my thoughts are full of Stevie and how happy I am that she's here. But I couldn't tell her that, not even if she paid me a thousand pounds. I see her glance at her mum anxiously, like she's checking she's all right. Getting to know Stevie has been like putting together the pieces of a jigsaw puzzle and it's only now that I'm starting to see the full picture – or a big chunk of the picture at least. Her dad is dead. Her mum is depressed – so depressed she doesn't work. That's why Stevie has to work so hard with her paper rounds and busking. That's why she took the shirt from Lost Property. All of these jigsaw pieces and the picture they build only make me like her more. Stevie's mum laughs at something Aunt Maria says and Stevie breathes a sigh of relief.

"Well?" she says, turning back to me. "What were you thinking?"

"I was thinking I'm starving," I say. It's only half a lie. I am starving. I just wasn't thinking about it.

"Me too." Stevie nods.

"Maybe we could—"

Uncle Samir's phone begins to ring. I see him exchange a look with Aunt Maria as he takes his phone from his back pocket. He looks at it, then looks back at Aunt Maria and nods. She looks straight at me. My stomach lurches. I have a sudden sense of foreboding. Like whatever it is that was too terrible to tell me is about to be revealed.

## Stevie

There's something up with Hafiz. The second his uncle's phone started ringing he looked as if he'd seen a ghost. I stop painting.

"Hello," Samir says into the phone and now he's looking at the screen, like he's taking a video call. "Hello."

There's a second's silence and then the sound of a voice speaking in Arabic.

"Dad!" Hafiz puts down his roller and hurries over to Samir. "Is it Dad?"

Samir nods, then looks back at the phone and starts speaking in Arabic.

"Dad, Dad, I'm here." Hafiz looks over Samir's shoulder into the phone. "Dad!"

I wonder how long it's been since Hafiz has seen him.

"Oh, Hafiz, my son! Oh, my son!" his dad says.

Hafiz leans right in close to the phone and says something in Arabic. It sounds like a question. An urgent question.

His dad replies and Hafiz's shoulders crumple and he starts to cry. I get a sick feeling in the pit of my stomach and

I look at Mum. She's standing, watching Hafiz, as still as stone. I go over and link arms with her.

"Where are his parents?" she whispers to me.

"In Athens," I whisper back. "In a refugee camp."

Adiam comes over to us. "So sad," she says quietly. "What this world is doing to families."

Hafiz gasps and I'm so scared for him I can hardly breathe. Something really bad must have happened, but what?

Then I hear a woman's voice coming from the phone. She's saying the same thing over and over again. Relief fills me as Hafiz turns slightly and I see that he's smiling through his tears. The woman says the words again. And although they're in Arabic, I'm pretty sure I know their meaning. I'm pretty sure she's saying, "I love you."

# HAFIZ

"Mum. I thought…"

"Hafiz, I love you. I love you, Hafiz," Mum says, over and over.

She's OK. Mum's OK. I take a deep breath, push my very worst fear from my mind. "How – how is Athens?"

"We're not in Athens," Mum says. She looks older. There are streaks of grey in the hair visible beneath her scarf and thin lines creasing the corners of her eyes.

"We have good news." Dad comes back into view as he puts his arm around Mum's shoulders. "They've processed our papers. We crossed the border into Macedonia earlier today."

"We didn't want to tell you until we knew for sure that their papers had been processed," Uncle Samir says to me. "We didn't want to raise your hopes."

So that's what he and Aunt Maria had been being secretive about. A bubble of joy fills me but almost immediately it bursts as I think of the journey ahead of them. Being herded like cattle on to countless buses and trains. The longing for a bath and a bed. And the walking, the endless walking, the hostile stares of strangers piercing your skin at every step. When I think of my parents in these circumstances it makes me feel sick. But at least they're not in Syria, I remind myself. At least they are safe from the war.

"Hafiz? Are you OK?" Dad asks.

I wipe the tears from my face. "Yes. Yes, I'm great. That's great."

"We are on our way to you," Dad says.

"Thanks to God." Mum moves closer to the screen. "Your hair is so long. Oh, my handsome son. It is so wonderful to see you."

I start to blush. Then I remember that Stevie and the others won't be able to understand what she's saying.

"'It is not in the stars to hold our destiny but in ourselves,'" Dad says. "Do you remember who said that, Hafiz?"

"William Shakespeare," I reply instantly.

Dad grins. "Indeed. Well, this is what we must hold on to now. We will make it our destiny to be together again. This is all I have been praying for for weeks. That we should see our Hafiz. Did you get my email?"

I shake my head. "What email?"

"I sent it to you this morning before we left the camp in Athens. We were allowed to use a computer there."

"No – I – I haven't had a chance to go online," I reply. "It's been kind of busy here."

"I've sent you a story," Dad says. "I think – I hope – it will help you."

"Thanks, Dad. I've really missed your stories."

He lets out a loud laugh. "Of course you have. I am one of the finest storytellers in the world. One of a long line of renowned Arabic storytellers."

Mum groans and Uncle Samir shakes his head.

"Yes, you are, Dad." I feel the sudden, overwhelming urge to read his story, so while Uncle Samir talks to Mum and Dad about the next leg of their journey, I say goodbye.

"We will phone you every day," Mum says.

"And we will see you soon, God willing," Dad adds.

"Yes, God willing." I reply, then I head to the door. "My dad's sent me an email," I say to Stevie. "I'm just going to go and read it."

She nods and smiles.

I slip out into the darkened café and check the emails on my phone. When I see Dad's email in my inbox happiness flutters in my ribcage like a bird. For so long I have prayed to see his name there. I click it open and begin to read..

My dear Hafiz,

I cannot tell you what a wonder it was to hear your voice the other night. Finally, after all this time. And when you told me that you'd been searching for your story it made me dance for joy. That awful night when we said goodbye, when I didn't know if I would ever see you again, I was trying so hard to think of something – to give you something – that would make your journey ahead a little easier. A little something that would hopefully help you feel that I was there with you, watching over you, as a father should. And so, now that I know you accepted my gift, I have to share one more story with you. It is a story that will hopefully solve the riddle once and for all…

## THE HAPPIEST MAN IN THE WORLD

*Once upon a time there was a young man named Hafiz. Hafiz was born into a fine family – his mother was as beautiful as an Arabian sunset and his father was one of the most gifted storytellers of all time, a handsome man and wonderful company. But, in spite of these blessings, Hafiz had one small problem – he didn't feel truly happy. He felt certain there had to be something more – something that his life was missing. So he tried everything he could think of to make himself feel better. He bought the finest Turkish delight at the souk; he went swimming in the sea; he watched his beloved football team play – but even though the Turkish delight was delightful and the sea was like liquid turquoise and his beloved team won, he still didn't feel happy. So he journeyed into the city to see if he could find happiness there. For days, he trudged along the alleyways and streets, seeking happiness in fine meals, good music, the smile of a beautiful girl. But still he felt that same emptiness inside. As he was about to give up and make his journey home, he bumped into a wise old man. Sensing Hafiz's sadness, the wise old man asked him what* was wrong. "I just can't seem to find true happiness," Hafiz replied. "I've searched everywhere but still I feel there is something missing."

"Aha," the wise old man said. "You need to find the happiest man in the world. And when you find him you must ask him to trade shirts with you. Then happiness shall be yours."

"Really?" Hafiz looked at the wise old man disbelievingly.

"You have my word," the old man replied.

So Hafiz set off on his quest. He travelled across deserts and through forests and into the heart of bustling cities. And he had many incredible adventures along the way. Everywhere he roamed he asked people to show him to the happiest man they knew. And every time, he asked these men one simple question: "If I were to give you a million pounds would it make you happier?" When each of them replied yes, Hafiz knew he hadn't yet met the happiest man in the world and continued on his journey. But then, he came across a man in a forest who was chopping some wood. The man was singing a song that was so happy and joyful it put even the birds to shame. Hafiz's mood lifted. This man sounded truly happy. He went over and introduced himself. "I'm looking for the happiest man in the world," he said.

*The man put down his axe and smiled. "Then look no further, you've found him."*

*"But if I were to give you a million pounds, would that make you happier?" Hafiz asked.*

*The man shook his head. "Of course not. I already have all I need to make me happy. Look..." He gestured at the bright blue sky and the wild flowers and the emerald-green leaves.*

*Hafiz clapped his hands together in glee. Finally, he'd found the man he'd been seeking. "Please, will you exchange shirts with me?" he said.*

*"But I do not own a shirt," the man replied, undoing his worn jacket to reveal his bare chest beneath.*

*"I don't understand!" Hafiz looked at him in confusion. "I've travelled for miles and miles over many years to find you. I was told that I had to exchange shirts with you to find true happiness."*

*"And have you experienced many adventures along your journey?" the woodcutter asked.*

*Hafiz nodded.*

331

"And met many interesting people?"

Hafiz thought of all the fascinating people he'd met along the way and all the wonderful stories he'd heard. "Yes."

"And you never gave up until you found me?"

"No."

"Then you now know that you have the strength you need to seek all that you think you need."

As the woodcutter's words sunk in, for the first time ever Hafiz felt truly happy.

Then the woodcutter slowly unwound the turban he'd been wearing and Hafiz realized that it was the wise old man who'd sent him on his journey.

"But why did you not tell me all this the day I first met you?" Hafiz asked. "You could have saved me the journey."

"Because there are some things you can only learn through experience," the wise man replied. "If I had told you that you already had all you needed to be happy, you would never have believed me. Now you know it to be true. And so you are free."

My dear Hafiz, have you worked it out yet? Have you understood the riddle of finding your own story? Do you see that it is within you, to be created and lived by you? I wasn't trying to trick you by making you seek your story in another. I'm hoping that the stories you've discovered on your journey have left you stronger and wiser. I hope that now, after all you've been through, you're able to see that you have everything you need inside you. Everything you need to create the masterpiece that will be your life story.

Your loving father,

Tariq

I sit in the darkness, letting the words of the story sink in. I had to learn that I already had all I needed. But I could only do that by looking outside of myself first. I think of all the people I met on my journey from Syria. All the stories I collected, some of them containing great wisdom, but none of them touching me deep inside, in my heart, until this one – this final story. Because now I know it to be true. I know that I have all that I need inside me. I know that I am the author of the story of me.

## *Stevie*

While Hafiz goes into the café to read his email from his dad, and Samir, Maria and Adiam start talking about making some food, Mum sits down at the table with me. Her hands are dotted with flecks of white and her hair is coming loose and tumbling in tendrils over her shoulders. She looks like a little kid who's just had the paints out at nursery. A *very tired* little kid who's had the paints out at nursery.

"Are you OK?" I ask instinctively.

She nods. "Hafiz and his dad – they seem very close," she says quietly so the others don't hear her.

I nod.

"You must really miss Dad."

I nod again.

"I wish he was still here for you."

I'm about to nod for the third time when realize I ought to say something. "At least I have the book he made me."

"What book?"

"*Stevie's Little Book of Big Song Wisdom.*"

Mum's face lights up. "Oh, we had so much fun making

that for you."

*"We?"* I stare at her. "You helped him make it?"

Mum nods. "Yes. We spent practically an entire weekend going through his records together, choosing the subjects for the book and picking out the tracks." She looks thoughtful for a moment. "I'm trying to remember which ones I chose for you. I know that one was 'Don't Stop' by Fleetwood Mac. I love that song so much."

An image sharpens into focus in my mind: Mum and Dad sitting on the living room floor, in the middle of a sea of records, laughing and singing and chatting as they always did as they made their amazing gift for me. All this time, I'd imagined Dad making it for me on his own. He was the one who'd given me the book; it was all in his handwriting; they were his records – I'd just assumed. But Mum had been there too. Mum *has* been there too, through the songs, these past few months, when I've depended on the book and its wisdom. I hug her and I don't want to let go. "I love you, Mum," I whisper in her ear.

"Oh, Stevie, sweetheart. I love you too," she whispers back.

I hear the strum of a guitar inside my head and for the first time in ages some fresh lyrics appear:

*When what you thought was the truth . . .*
        *turns out to be a lie . . .*
                *and you finally realize . . .*
                        *that love never dies.*

# HAFIZ

Stevie and I make our way onto the beach, the pebbles crunching beneath our feet. The faint sound of music and laughter drifts across the moonlit ocean from the new pier. We sit down in front of the skeletal remains of the old pier. It's quieter down here. There's more space to be alone, more space to think. And I need as much space as I can get for the huge thoughts inside my head. Mum is OK. There was no conspiracy. Uncle Samir and Aunt Maria just didn't want me to get my hopes up until Mum and Dad's papers had been processed. My parents are in Macedonia. Slowly but surely, they're making their way to me. And finally I understand the riddle of finding your story.

"A chip for your thoughts," Stevie says, offering me her bag of chips.

"Why would I want a chip when I have a bag of my own?" I say with a grin. "You have to offer me something I really want."

"OK, what do you really want?" Stevie pops a chip into her mouth and gazes out at the sea. There's barely any wind tonight and the water is mirror-still.

"What do I really want?" I look up into the sky and have a flashback to last night and how I counted the stars while I waited for Stevie to get home. "I really want you to be happy."

## Stevie

He really wants me to be happy. I sit for a moment, enjoying the salty taste on my tongue and the sound of his words in my head. *He wants me to be happy.*

"But what about Lucy?" The words blurt out before I have time to stop them.

"What about Lucy?" Hafiz bounces it back to me, like we're playing question tennis.

"Don't you…? Aren't you…?" I'm so glad it's too dark for him to see my flushed face.

"Aren't I what?"

I keep my eyes fixed firmly on the sea. Why did I suggest coming down here? Why didn't we just stay at the centre and eat with the adults? This is so awkward. It would have been way more fun watching Adiam teach my mum about Eritrean cooking. Actually it would have been way more fun watching the paint dry!

Hafiz nudges me. "Aren't I what?"

"Aren't you going out with her?"

"Lucy?" He sounds shocked.

"Yes."

"No!"

I dare to sneak a glance at him. "Really?"

"Yes. Why did you think I was going out with her?"

"I saw you – in town – yesterday. You were – she was – you'd linked arms with her."

"No." Hafiz sits upright and shifts closer to me. "*She'd* linked arms with me."

"And the difference is…?"

"There is a big difference."

"Oh."

We sit in silence, the quiet only broken by the gentle lap of the sea … and the thoughts in my head all switching themselves to happy.

# HAFIZ

She thought I was dating Lucy. Another piece of jigsaw-puzzle Stevie slots into place. She saw us together in town before she disappeared on her walk. I can't help wondering if the two things are connected. I lean back on my elbows and look down at the sea. Somewhere, on the other side of that water, in another part of Europe, my parents are making their way to me. I know that their journey will be long and arduous and I know that it could take months or even years to process their asylum applications in the UK but I have to keep faith that it will be our destiny. I glance at Stevie, who's staring out at the water too. I wonder what she's thinking.

"Ten games on the claw for your thoughts," I say with a grin.

"Ten?" She looks at me, eyes wide.

"Yep." No measly offer of a penny from me. I want to know what she's thinking, and I'm pretty certain I know her price.

Stevie leans back on the stones so she's level with me. "I was thinking, I'm so glad I didn't lose you as a friend," she says quietly.

"Why would you have lost me as a friend?" I ask.

"After everything that happened at school – with the shirt."

I shake my head and smile, move closer to her so our arms are touching. "Friends like us never lose each other." I think of the Shakespeare quote and Dad's email and I gaze up at the stars. It's true that we have to make our own destiny in life – write our own story – but I think it's also true that some things, some people, are meant to be. I smile at Stevie. "Friends like us … it is destiny."

# STEVIE'S LITTLE LIST OF BIG SONG WISDOM

SONG TO REASSURE YOU WHEN TIMES ARE TOUGH
"Don't Stop" by Fleetwood Mac

SONG TO MAKE YOU HAPPY TO BE ALIVE
"The Whole of the Moon" by The Waterboys

SONG FOR WHEN PEOPLE LET YOU DOWN
"Human" by Rag'n'Bone Man

SONG TO HELP YOU TAKE ON THE WORLD
"The Reckoning" by Nine Miles South

SONG TO GET READY TO GO OUT TO
"Heavy Dirty Soul" by Twenty One Pilots

SONG TO BE A FREE SPIRIT TO
"Undercover Agents" by Enter Shikari

SONG TO AIR-GUITAR TO
"Figure It Out" by Royal Blood

SONG TO REVISE FOR EXAMS TO
"Shake It Out" by Florence + the Machine

SONG TO HATE YOUR NEMESIS TO

"It's Not Me It's You" by Skillet

SONG TO HAVE A KITCHEN DISCO TO

"Born Slippy" by Underworld

SONG TO DREAM TO

"Cloudbusting" by Kate Bush

We've created a playlist with all the
songs mentioned in the book.

Search for **Stevie's Little Book of Big Song Wisdom**
on Spotify to tune in!

# ACKNOWLEDGEMENTS

Huge thanks as always to my amazing editor, Mara Bergman, for your guidance, eagle eye and, most of all, your care and support throughout the writing of this book. Ditto Emily McDonnell – thank you so much for your expert editorial insight. And thanks to all at Walker Books for publishing books about issues that really matter with such passion and flair. It's a real joy to be published by you. Huge thanks also to agent extraordinaire Jane Willis at United Agents.

I am massively grateful to Corrine Gotch and all at the Sharjah Children's Reading Festival for inviting me to come and speak there in 2015. It was while I was in Sharjah that I learned about the Berbers and their theory that we all are born with a story inside us. This planted the seed for Hafiz's story that would eventually grow into this novel. Thank you so much for the inspiration. My new(ish) home town of Lewes was also a huge inspiration for this book. Thanks in particular to the Union Music Store and Ground Coffee House.

This book is a celebration of friendship and I'm very grateful for the people in my life I'm lucky enough to call my friends. Tina McKenzie, Steve O'Toole, Sara Starbuck, Stuart Berry, Linda Lloyd, Jenny Davies, Sammie Venn, Sarah Walton, Sally Swithin, I'm talking to you. And to my Jedi brother/fellow Ripple Club founder, Steve Rockett.

Huge thanks also to my writing friends, especially the Snowdrop Writers – Tony Leonard, Adrian Bott, Michelle Porter, Liz Brooks, Paul Gallagher, Rachel Burge, Angus Walker, Frankie Stanton, Natalie Grahame, Miriam Thundercliffe, Natalie Heath, Jim and Katie Clammer – to name but a few! Thank you for making Tuesday nights so inspiring and such a chuckle-fest. Thanks also to Damian Keyes for teaching me so much about breaking all the rules when it comes to marketing! And to my fellow Facebookers – especially the Harrow and Uxbridge writers, the Nower Hill gang and K-Ci Williams – thank you for making our corner of social media such a fun and supportive place.

And a MASSIVE thank you and lots of love to my family: Jack, Mikey, Anne, Bea, Luke, Alice, Katie, Dan and John, and, of course, my multitude of American and Irish cousins.

Last, but definitely not least, thank you so much to all of the book bloggers who've been so supportive of my work and the readers who've taken the time to get in touch. Hearing from you means the world to me. Big hugs and thanks especially to Edi Xavier-Venn. I hope this book inspires you to create a wonderful story with your life.

**Siobhan Curham** is an award-winning author and life coach. Her books for young adults are: *The Moonlight Dreamers* and *Tell It to the Moon*, *Dear Dylan* (winner of the Young Minds Book Award), *Finding Cherokee Brown*, *Shipwrecked*, *Dark of the Moon* and *True Face*. She loves helping other people achieve their writing dreams through her writing consultancy, Dare to Dream, and she was editorial consultant on Zoe Sugg's international bestseller *Girl Online*. Find out more about Siobhan online: www.siobhancurham.com

🐦 @SiobhanCurham
@WalkerBooksUK
@WalkerBooksYA

📷 @WalkerBooksYA